Praise for the A-th

Status Single

'The private lives of Indian women are rarely seen as worthy of public discussion – the government censor board last year briefly banned a movie about four small-town women because of its 'lady-oriented content' – so the stories in Kundu's book read as bracingly frank.' *Los Angeles Times*

'…a wide-ranging and searing attack on the Indian patriarchy...' *TSG, The Sunday Guardian*

Sita's Curse

'A haunting treatise on female physicality, strength and self-discovery... ' *The Hindu*

You've Got the Wrong Girl

'Sreemoyee Piu Kundu's perspective is unconventional, her language is poetic and sensuous, the humour is highbrow and the narrative is replete with originality and philosophical ponderings on life, love and their mysteries…' *The Pioneer*

Books by the Author:

Faraway Music
Sita's Curse
You've Got the Wrong Girl
Status Single

CUT

The Death and Life of a Theatre Activist

Sreemoyee Piu Kundu

BLOOMSBURY
NEW DELHI • LONDON • OXFORD • NEW YORK • SYDNEY

BLOOMSBURY INDIA
Bloomsbury Publishing India Pvt. Ltd
Second Floor, LSC Building No. 4, DDA Complex, Pocket C - 6 & 7,
Vasant Kunj New Delhi 110070

BLOOMSBURY, BLOOMSBURY INDIA and the Diana logo are trademarks of Bloomsbury Publishing Plc

First published in India 2019
This edition published 2019

ISBN: 978-93-88271-58-5
E book: 978-93-88271-60-8

Typeset in Manipal Digital
Printed and bound in India by Thomson Press India Ltd.

Bloomsbury Publishing Plc makes every effort to ensure that the papers used in the manufacture of our books are natural, recyclable products made from wood grown in well-managed forests. Our manufacturing processes conform to the environmental regulations of the country of origin.]

To find out more about our authors and books visit www.bloomsbury.com and sign up for our newsletters

To

Basudev Kundu

November 18, 1948

Dear Baba

For your 70th birthday.

I'm sorry we took so long to become friends.

I know, like me, you wanted to own your own sky.

Paint it in your own colours.

Pick your own stars.

Describe the sunsets you longed for.

Thank you for this life.

I love you. I set you free.

ACT ONE

Mī Jivanta Ahē
(I Am Alive)

AMITABH KULASHESHTRA, 2002

The train pulls out of the station as I clamber on in a daze. My mind is abuzz, a million voices racing through it at the same time. Droplets of sweat trickle down my face as I push my way inside the cramped compartment.

Someone – *who are you, dammit?* – speaks in my head. Insistently. *Where are you going this time? Have you informed anyone of your leaving before setting out? What are you hoping to achieve? Here? In this crowded station thronging with the sweat of human traffic?*

The train pulls away. Everything grows distant; blurred. Far away, I see the dirty cement bench I had shared with a man and his monkey, buying bhajis for the three of us with a ten-rupee note, the last in my wallet.

The voice is back, growing louder, shriller, matching the commotion inside: *Haven't you burnt enough bridges? Does the murder of your colleague and the acquittal of that hateful man not haunt you enough? Can the professional, high moral ground you took justify your personal mistakes? The friends you walked away from? The women you let down? So, you want to make amends now? Can a man ever direct the course of his own life? Is it that simple, ever?*

I place my hands over my ears. The voice never stops; a monster that taunts me; revels in my follies.

I won't succumb to it. I have no one left to hurt now. I am a shadow. A story that has been told.

An end without a beginning.

A corpse in a casket.

A life exhausted of purpose.

An afterthought.

I grab the iron railing, jostling to my left, desperate to steady myself. The faded cloth bag I am carrying slides off my shoulder. My eye is caught by the intricate gold work on a lady's yellow sandal. My face is flushed from the unrelenting June heat.

'Ticket, *tickat!*' I hear the words from a distance, the din growing thicker as more passengers hurriedly scramble on to the bogey from other compartments. I am out of breath. A lady in a gaudy purple net sari elbows me viciously, making her way ahead.

I am sweating profusely. Clutching the cloth bag to my chest, I peer through the window at the man holding up a brass ring, running alongside the train, faster, faster. The *madari*, the monkey-man, widens his eyes and is saying something, gloating, as if at the challenge that suddenly poses itself.

Man vs. Animal.

'*Tick-at...!*'

A crippling pain pierces my chest. I lurch to the ground as the bag slips from my hands. I feel my body painfully slumping near the window. I try to remain focused; to not lose sight of the monkey; at the same time to not let go of the bag…

'*Tikīṭa kōṭhē āhē*? (Where is your ticket?)' I lip-read, as a pot-bellied man in a khaki cap thumps my chest roughly.

'My bag…the ba…' my throat is completely parched.

'Looks like he doesn't understand Marathi! And why is he lurking around the seats reserved for us?' A woman sniggers; poking me under my armpit.

'Hey, you, what's your name? Yes, you?' I swerve, as the ticket-collector grabs my collar, trying to haul me up, his sour breath engulfing my face. I cover my nose, my temples throbbing.

Where...where is the...where is the monkey? It's all happening too fast, jump, jump...you can...you can do it, c'mon, jump…it's simple…all you have do is raise your feet and…concentrate…can you hear me? There are always voices…so many of them…

I reach agitatedly for the iron rails: 'Where is my bag? That's my…it has everything…' I manage to hoist myself up, my hand accidentally touching the woman's heaving cleavage, the skin around it moist, tense.

Just then the monkey soars into the air as the station passes away at breakneck speed. '*Thāmbā!* (Stop!)' I scream, the veins on my neck protruding; pools of saliva collecting in the corners of my mouth. The sharp pain returns. I sink down on my haunches. My spectacles fall, shattering. I stretch out my hands, groping, grasping…

Someone kicks me hard in the pit of my stomach.

'Bastard, touching ladies in an indecent way? Is this why you boarded the train? Just who do you think you are? What bag, bag, huh? Bloody pickpocket…lecherous old man…'

'What's in that bag? Bomb?'

A motley crowd of women assembles, their eyes mean, each face more menacing than the next.

'What's your name? Yes, I am talking to you, mister!' A woman demands, her heavy, heaving bosom, rising and falling.

I cover my eyes, unable to bear the excruciating chest pain that has returned with redoubled intensity.

'*Madarcho*…'

'Amitabh, Amitabh, I think…I'm not sure…I can't be sure…' I falter, the air sucked out of my lungs.

'Tick-at....'

'What are you doing here? Don't you know these seats are specifically reserved for women? Can't you read, you *halkat!*'

◈

I blink a couple of times, my face dripping with sweat, trying to form a full sentence, wondering if someone has nicked my bag. My vision clouds...

There is Ammi, freshly bathed, her hair loosely knotted, her skin doused, dewy. Kneeling on a frayed prayer mat, reciting the Kalma. Her fine lips opening and closing as I study the movement of her slanted mouth through a transparent curtain...

'*Randechya!* (Son of a bitch!)'

'*Maar thyala!*(Hit him!)'

'Pickpocket!'

'Eve-teaser!'

My unmoving eyes dimly register the minuscule beads of perspiration trickling down the woman's ample cleavage. I clamp them shut, imagining her parted plump lips slowly settling over mine...

Sarla, as we made love, that night, minutes before I exploded inside her, lolling back her head, in languorous slow motion, her moans multiplying. The rains, unrelenting, outside our home in Pune... the sky a pensive purple. The scent of the fresh mogra flowers that she carefully entwined in her thick plait, permeating the stubborn stillness between us...

'Pervert.'

'Bastard.'

'Beggar.'

'Stupid.'

'Stupide, not stupid…' Marie burst out giggling when I asked her if I could kiss her. Calling me 'stupide' several times as we sipped on red wine straight out of a bottle, sitting cross-legged on a fancy, four-poster bed. Some of it splattering onto the clean white sheets as we leaned over, kissing clumsily, for the first time…Marie gently rubbing her pink, pointed nipples, her slender fingers etching porous patterns on her pale skin…

'Shall we pull the chain?'

'Think he's dead?'

'What if he's really carrying a bomb, or something? What if he is an *atankvadi*?'

'Terrorist?'

'Anti National?'

'Pakistani?'

'Same difference.'

I lay still, not responding. Sprawled out in the dirt.

Mrinalini, stubborn, sullen, way more arrogant than girls her age; didn't speak to me for days when I yelled at her for muffing her lines, calling her 'muka', dumb, in Marathi. Her dark, doe-like eyes had brimmed with tears but her back was held straight. Her face betrayed nothing. Standing tall, even as I flung the script at her. The look of scorn on her face…Like she wanted a fight…

◈

My body is inert; but my mind is everywhere, at once, scrabbling at memories, at the moments that defined my life.

That made and then unmade me…

'Put your hand on the Bhagwad Gita and swear you will speak the truth, the whole truth, and nothing but the truth…'.

The Sessions Court where my case was being tried was packed to the brim. At the back of the cramped hall stood a long line of press photographers and television camera crews; their flashlights pointing directly at my eyes, the intensity of the flickering red spots no different from the automatic rifles that the Rashtriya Dal goons had aimed at my troupe, in Malegaon. Prakash Lele, my leading man had stood between me and the mob, as Amol Rawat labelled me a Congress puppet. I think he used the word 'najais'. Prakash, who lost his life, defending me…

It was just after the Mumbai riots in 1992. Amol Rawat's words rang in my ears: 'Didn't I tell you to stop brainwashing these illiterate villagers? This play of yours is a bloody catalyst… politically motivated…what are you trying to tell them, huh? Teach this ignorant lot? That Muslims deserve equality…? That Hindus started the riots in Mumbai…? That we have blood on our hands? That the Koran is no different than the Gita? Ēka vēśyā mulagā (son of a whore) have you even read the Gita to know the difference?'

'Why the Gita?' I had asked in court, my forehead smarting from the stitches. 'Why the Gita? Why should I swear on the Gita that whatever I am saying, is the absolute truth?' I took a deep breath, adding slowly: 'Why not the Koran or the Guru Granth Sahib or the Holy Bible – why in a so-called secular country, must there exist this blatant form of subversive, identity politics? If I killed a man and touched the Gita and said I didn't – would that absolve me of my sins?'

The judge banged the table with his wooden hammer.

I grabbed the rails with my unbandaged hand and continued: 'I am a director of plays, your honour, a writer and a performing artist. I have no religion except my conscience. My atma is infinite. It belongs everywhere. I did nothing wrong in staging the play – I am as much the son of a Muslim trapeze artist, as I am of a staunch Maharashtrian woman, as I am of a cheap whore. All three were the same woman from whose womb I was birthed. I grew up in a travelling circus, slept beside the animals and shat in the same place where they defecated. The water I bathed in was the same that was used to quench their thirst on sultry, summer nights. The stage where my father, a blind clown, performed his legendary acts, was the same where young, underweight children hung precariously from coir ropes, and well-fed lions were tamed by starving men lashing thick whips, where everyone followed a mundane drill, where colourful clowns danced to the same songs every evening and where stuntmen in fake leather jackets astride noisy motorcycles balanced themselves precariously on one leg.

'What if that circus is *my country, my lord? What if my country* is *my conscience? What if the poor have no religion? Except to survive? To clothe their bare backs and feed their naked children? To just live out another day? What if our nationality, our religion, our gender, are all man-made concepts? A convenient construct to make people conform? Follow someone you can't see or fight? What if religion wasn't a loaded gun? A veiled threat? An election ticket?*

'What if you all killed him – killed my comrade, Prakash Lele? If everyone present here must shoulder the blame for his bloodied death? What if we all failed her? The Muslim girl who loved the Hindu boy, who wanted nothing more than an ounce of personal freedom and the dignity of choice? Whose prayer was penance…'

Amol Rawat's lawyer cut in harshly: 'Please, this is not a street play, here. You will be asked certain specific questions on the basis of the police case filed by the State in the light of the alleged murder of Prakash Lele, who was trying to save you, by the way.'

'Prakash saved my life and lost his own, yes, but we were trying to save something bigger, much bigger; we were not fighting a pitched battle, but a dangerous war. A war that is more than this…all this…that will not end with his unfortunate death…'

'You have levied a murder charge against Amol Rawat, but the court holds you guilty of inciting communal violence yourself. Sedition…do you even understand the meaning of that word, the severity of it…huh? There is a sedition charge against you,

Mr. Kulasheshtra. Conduct or speech, inciting people to rebel against the authority of a state or monarch...Why stage a political play in this hypersensitive environment...?'

'I am aware of the sedition law...incorporated into the Indian Penal Code in 1870 as fears of a possible uprising made the colonial authorities uneasy. Section 124-A...that is now being misused to browbeat anyone who protests, or put forward an alternate discourse, or speak in a separate vocabulary – into a mute compliance...a sign of a cowardly, spineless and oppressive state willing to use any methods to intimidate dissenters. How long can you do this? Criminalize dissent? Tribals resisting displacement... villagers who resist a nuclear project...student leaders in premier institutes...Muslims cheering for a rival nation in a cricket match...cartoonists...satirists...academicians...historians... anyone who advocates on behalf of the marginalized and displaced communities...how many more voices will you silence? For how long will you hide behind an archaic law that has lost its relevance, and in doing so, surrender the democratic legitimacy of our nation...forge a new and sinister ideological blueprint?'

Rawat's lawyer jumped up: 'I fail to understand what your *politics is, Mr. Kulasheshtra. Fighting for the starving farmers? Defending defunct trade unions? Flying off to Paris to sleep with some famous French starlet, not to forget your romantic fiasco in Mumbai...? My lord, this is a man of loose, wavering morals, who courts controversy to gain footage in the media...he is in no way the saint he portrays himself to be,' the counsel for the defence thundered.*

'What if sedition means taking a stand, my lord? What if there is another formula of freedom? What if there are no flags, my lord? Or kingdoms left to conquer...or swarthy, skin-and-bone slaves to take captive? Conquer? Colonize? Castigate? Castrate? What if we don't go to war, outside? If the war now flows in my veins, my lord? What if the revolution that we all fear so much, will be fought by artists? By ordinary commoners. By rank outsiders.

The have-nots. By an ugly, poor fellow, who stays hungry all night? Who writes stirring poems in the last light of the setting sun? And performs somersaults casting oblong shadows on the street pavement? The man who carries no weapons. Wears no uniform. Who doesn't need a passport. The man who has nowhere to go. The man who goes nowhere. The kalakaar. The kavi. The kissan. What if he is here, in this Sessions Court, today? Looking into the eyes of a fascist dictator?'

'Laal Salaam,' someone screamed.

'Order, order…' the judge hollered as the cameras clicked furiously.

'My lord, this man pretending to be a socialist, a mass leader, is actually a "desh-drohi"…a petty rabble-rouser, a rowdy street-fighter…he loves playing to the gallery, as you can well see,' the man defending Rawat accused in a high-pitched voice:'

'Tell us who you are, Amitabh Kulasheshtra? Patriot or pariah?'

◈

A dozen faces peer at me from above. A woman digs her heel into my right shoulder.

I meet her eyes. Like the monkey's. A sturdy, steely gaze.

Just then, I hear a harsh, screeching noise.

Has someone actually pulled the chain? Or is it the end of my journey?

I struggle to raise my head, my fingers trembling, saliva dribbles from my open mouth.

'Amitabh!' I whisper to my last audience.

'Amitabh?'

'Amitabh, *mī jivanta āhē…*'

It is the last time I hear my name.

The last time I try to answer all of them.

A darkness swallows me.

THE HINDUSTAN

PUNE, 10 JUNE, 2002

Well-known Indian playwright and theatre director Amitabh Kulasheshtra died today, collapsing suddenly in the midst of a heated argument with the women seated in the ladies' section of a Mumbai-bound train. No one knew his name at the time of his death or recognized him. His body lay unclaimed for several hours as the railway police tried to find some identification. Police finally located his whereabouts by phoning the address found in the wallet he was carrying, which was initially lost in the commotion following his death. His wife, Mrs Sarla Kulasheshtra, has now confirmed the news of his demise to local Marathi channels.

Kulasheshtra, who revolutionized cultural resistance to political authoritarianism for over three decades, was widely considered a messiah of the masses for his anti-establishment productions. The Robin Hood of the performing arts, he withstood many a police-lathi and flaunted Constitutional norms, taking theatre out of the proscenium to magically transform the street into his stage. Refusing a Padma Shri at the age of 42; combining perishing Indian folk-art traditions with lavish Parisian opera to stage the first ever Indo-French co-production of *La Legende de Sakuntalam*; fighting for the survival of defunct trade unions; adopting the cause of starving farmers in Vidarbha; protesting against the Rashtriya Dal for propagating anti-Muslim violence, beginning with the 1970 Bhiwandi riots that caused the death of 250 people; dissecting child abuse and incest in modern Indian homes – all Kulasheshtra's plays acted as a mirror to the atrocities and injustices that prevail in society. Kulasheshtra was also considered a leading proponent of the 'Third theatre' movement that stood ideologically against the state. Third theatre involved street plays, with actors being attired no differently than the audience. Performed in 'found' spaces, rather than rented theatre halls, sans elaborate lighting, costumes or make-up, where the audience was no longer passive, but participatory, this new form of theatre was responsible for adding a fresh realism to contemporary dramaturgy.

'Mī Jivanta Ahē,' (I Am Alive), was banned by the Rashtriya Dal in Maharashtra, as charges of sedition were slapped on Amitabh Kulasheshtra. Written as a reaction to the Bombay riots of December 1992 and January 1993 in which around 900 people died, it narrated the story of a Hindu clown who marries a Muslim acrobat, the play was a rousing, political satire; a musical drama set in a moving circus. The play demonstrated Kulasheshtra's deep study of group psychology and showed how a circus, viewed as a happy space, eventually also gets divided on narrow, communal lines, when a bloody riot erupts in a neighbouring town, incited by the ruling political party. It was during one of the shows of the play in Malegaon, that Rashtriya Dal backed candidate, Amol Rawat, assaulted the troupe and the audience with iron rods and firearms. Kulasheshtra sustained serious head injuries during the stampede and scuffle that followed. Lead actor, Prakash

Lele, succumbing to injuries on the spot. Kulasheshtra who levied a murder charge against Rawat went on to fight a prolonged legal battle against the Rashtriya Dal. Rawat, was ultimately let off, on bail, with hardly any witnesses against him. The case is still being dragged on in the courts.

According to sources in the theatre world, Kulasheshtra, who shied away from the limelight, may have also been battling advanced Alzheimer's. In the last decade of his life, Kulasheshtra mostly lived like a recluse, away from the public eye, and refused all public appearances and interviews.

In the early 90's, Kulasheshtra was also in the news for his involvement with Bollywood's reigning lead actress, Maya Shirale, who made her film debut in producer RK Chopra's, epic blockbuster Ishq. Over the years, she has however grabbed headlines for her drunken outbursts on set. She is currently in a live-in relationship with National-award-winning director, Avik Dasgupta.

Kulasheshtra was officially declared dead at 6.45 pm, this evening, at the Kamla Nehru Hospital, Pune, Maharashtra.

He is survived by his wife, Sarla Kulasheshtra.

MAYA SHIRALE

'Maya! Shot ready *hai.* Maya, we go live any minute. Face the camera. This way, please...Maya... *Maya*...Oh for...*Cut!*'

My head was reeling. The sun was burning my face. 'It's a bloody migraine attack!' I shouted, tired of repeating myself a million times, but they just wouldn't relent, refusing to change the location of the outdoor shoot.

I sat down in protest.

'My head fucking hurts; I told you guys I have been shooting in Filmistan Studios, nonstop, for the last two nights. I can't even think straight...I need a fag right now, so will somebody just get this damn microphone out of my face, please? And get me my mirror! Oh God, look at my eyes, I need a touch up...my base is all fucked up... *everything* is fucked up...' I put my hands on my head, pulling my waist-long tresses into a high bun. Deliberately leaving a few loose strands to gently brush my lips as I pouted, arching my neck sideways. *Always wanting to look the part.* I stood up in a huff.

'What the...?'

'Hey, where are you going?'

'Now what?'

'Maya? Let's get serious!'

I screamed: 'Okay! *Okay!* At least hold the spotlight correctly. He always said my left profile was better than my right.'

'Who?'

'We're running out of time! The studio is waiting for us to come on. It's a live telecast, Maya…'

'Maya?' The director beseeched.

I stared past him: 'My right eye always looks smaller, somehow. Like, I've been crying a lot. He hated tears; ironical, huh?' My lips quivered slightly.

'Who?'

'Maya what's going on? We will be live any minute now!'

'It's just a bloody, two-minute bite,' I snapped. 'So, shut the fuck up, will you? I'm Maya Shirale, not some two-bit Madhuri Desai type. I'll do as *I* wish, okay?'

'Okay, chill, please, we'll do the shot as you want.'

'Rosy…*Rosy!*…Cigarette!'

I flopped down again and pulled my oversized Gucci glares over my eyes. I felt so drained and exhausted! I just wanted to curl up in a dark corner and go to sleep. I couldn't believe that I was still being pushed around after working for twelve, non-stop years in this thankless industry. People were always taking advantage of me. This job made one so insecure. At thirty-five, my days of being a leading lady were already drying up. I was precipitously close to my expiry date. But today I just didn't care. Today, when I heard that Amitabh, that he…I shut my eyes, going back to the start, to another time…when my struggles had just begun…when I was not Maya. Not this Maya. Amitabh's creation. His construct.

◈

'Desire, desire, desire,' I'd giggled. My hair was tied in a high ponytail. It kept getting in the way as Sanju's fingers pushed my head, urging me to go down on him.

Mango stains marked the front of Sanju's imported polyester shirt, a gift from his rich father, who ran a successful export business, specializing in menswear. We were in the back seat of his father's Premier Padmini. I was in my first year of college, all of eighteen-and-a-half.

'You smell delicious, like a ripe *dussehri* mango juicy in the middle,' he moaned, ineptly trying to slip his hand inside my bra. I could tell he wasn't very comfortable or experienced. We were both perspiring a lot. It was just after the July showers.

I laughed coarsely. I was high on the cheap beer we had consumed together. I wiped the corners of my mouth, my eyes bloodshot. My mascara had bled in parts, making me feel wanton. Making me feel mean.

'*Uff!* Can't you just get on with it?' I scoffed, pointing at his crotch.

Sanju's stubby fingers fumbled at his zip. 'Damn you, *saali!*' He threw his trembling hands in the air. Suddenly feeling inadequate, he backed away: 'Can't we go a little slow, *jaan*? Maybe, talk some?'

'Weenie!' I teasingly said, pulling down his zip and planting my painted mouth on his stomach. Then looking up at him, I inserted my thumb in my mouth, sucking suggestively, lewdly.

Sanju was panting hard.

I grabbed his chest and lunged forward, sinking his swollen member into me. 'Talk? About what? *Tuh yahan baate karne ke liye laya tha mujhe*?' I grunted, picking up speed.

'I...I...' he lifted up my buttocks, his manhood clumsily sliding out of my dampness.

I laughed louder, biting him just under his chin, making him more nervous. '*Saare mard sex ko hamesha* over-intellectualize *kyun karte hain?* All men say the same thing, when they want the same damn thing from us. *Jaise, har aurat ko* over-emotional *hone ki bimari hai.* The same, *ghisse-pitte, filmi* dialogues…sex *toh akhir sirf* sex *hi hain, na? Toh jitna kum bolega, utna maza ayega, nahin toh kuch zyada hi* safe *ho jayega…samjha, chikna?'* I positioned myself expertly, my breathing rushed.

'No, no, please, there is something you should know,' he pulled me closer as my aroused nipples grazed his chest, pointing at his mouth.

'Know what?' I reached up and loosened my hair.

'I love you, I…am in love with you, madly…I want to marry you, but, but you know…my, my father…my family…everyone is into this caste business…everyone wants a woman of good character and…I mean…everyone knows your reputation…' Sanju blurted, as the rains came down.

There was a second or more of silence. 'You mean my reputation as a whore?' I asked point-bank.

Sanju stared, transfixed. Not really sure what to say next. 'No, no…who said that now? You are a fine actress, Mrinalini, but ours happens to be a business family…and…they are looking for a *gharelu bahu…'* he stuttered.

'Look, Sanju,' I cut him short, reaching below to cup his balls: 'I am not interested in becoming anyone's *dulhan* or whatever the hell you have been fantasizing about. I mean, let's be frank, I am just fucking you now because you promised me the part…and I want the role at any cost, only because you told me Amitabh Kulasheshtra is coming to judge our annual theatre competition and I will do anything – *anything* – for him to see me on stage once…'

Of course, Sanju had given me the role. The play was a success, especially the audacious kissing scene I had insisted on doing, even though Sanju was dead against it. But Kulasheshtra did not attend. Apparently, he had already flown out of the country, travelling with an entourage of over hundred artists to Paris. His first international project. Something Sanju had overlooked to mention.

Sanju had been ecstatic with the reception his play received: 'I'll wait in the car,' he'd winked after the performance. 'It is my uncle's imported vehicle, we can even push back the seats, if you wish…' he'd sidled closer.

I looked him up and down, and twirled on my heel.

'God, *jaan*, I desire you, so much, can't you even tell?' He planted wet kisses on my palms.

'Bhadwa, saala,' I tugged my hands away and strutted out into the dark, my cheap heels clacking on the street. Then, before Sanju could say anything, I turned on him: 'Why didn't he come? You swore Amitabh Kulasheshtra was going to judge this competition. That he was only leaving India by the end of this week. I kept searching for him all the while…'

Sanju dragged me into his arms. 'Can't *I* make up for it?' He said looking ardently into my eyes.

I spat my bubble-gum in his face.

Sanju sprang back. 'Slut! You just used me to land the role, huh? To get Kulasheshtra to see you? Bitch, you will stoop to any level, anything, to bag a lead role, to prove you are the best, to be where you want!' His eyes were on fire.

I shoved him away. 'Weenie…' I showed him my middle finger. 'I don't need you, *gandu saala.* I *am* going make it big in theatre. Take Mumbai by storm myself one day; go as far away as I can from this stifling, small town, where you think that you are a star just because you acted in some amateur play by some pretentious FTII fucks, who all think they're the next Amitabh Kulasheshtra…As if there can be another one, *ever!*'

Sanju was stung: '*Sanki kahin ki!* Just who do you think you are, talking to me this way? Everyone knows you're easy; I was never going to marry you, understand…everyone just lusts for you, Mrinalini Shirale, and you know why? Coz you can't survive without someone between your legs…that's all you are about, right? Your stiff eyelashes, your perfectly shaped buttocks, that jarring maroon lip-liner, that fake beauty spot between your breasts, the tight Lycra t-shirts…*Randi kahin ki…chali badi* heroine *banne*…Amitabh Kulasheshtra *ki* heroine!'

'*Heroine…*' I clenched my jaw, smiling wryly. It was my father's favourite name for me, too; that's what he called me every time he slid inside my bed, his organ throbbing as he massaged it back and forth over my crumpled cotton skirt.

I ran away from home a few days later.

Tired of Sanju's name-calling. And of being led on by men posing to either know Amitabh Kulasheshtra personally, or claiming they could introduce me to someone who did. I dropped out of college, I wasn't particularly bright anyway, no good at my studies, so honestly, there was no point continuing with the façade of graduating in English Honours.

Besides, the thought of returning every evening to my father repelled me. The sight of him shuffling cards for a game of *teen-patti*, sloshed silly all the time, the television blaring, my perennially sick, skin-and-bones mother confined to her modest single cot, the peeling, nondescript off-white paint flaking off the walls…

It's also probably why I gave in one last time on the night I left home. Letting my father grope me before he succumbed to sleep, snoring at the top of his voice.

'Where are you off to, at such an unearthly hour?' My neighbour's son, Vinod Bhaiyya, accosted me as I was creeping out. Though I had never confessed to anyone about my father's continued abuse, I sensed he knew everything about what went on inside my house. 'Where will you go from here?' He looked anxious when I told him.

'I have written a note to my mother, she won't look for me, they don't want me back, anyway...besides, I can't live this way, not anymore,' the colour rose in my cheeks.

'Best of luck,' Vinod Bhaiyya gave me a thumb's up, adding cautiously, 'but, what about money? Have enough to survive? And, and, what about your education? To give up, everything...?'

I was about to say something when he pulled out an envelope from his pocket: 'Father gave me this to deposit in the bank tomorrow,' he thrust a stash of notes in my hand. 'Here, keep this. This will help you...you can return it when you become famous. Rich...'

There was a second or two of silence.

'*Dhanyavad...*' I kissed him over his wiry moustache, knowing he had nursed a crush on me ever since I had turned thirteen.

I took the night bus to Yerawada where I got off at the bus-stand, making my way to Amitabh Kulasheshtra's modest, one-storied house in an auto-rickshaw. I had amassed all the necessary information on him. I stood outside his home all night, finally curling up on the kerb and trying to sleep.

Sanju's words echoed in my ears. *Would I always be seen as a whore? Another small-time, averagely-talented actress, desperate for work? Ready to do anything?* I wondered.

In the morning, my eyes smarted from high fever. I hadn't had a bite to eat. Neither was I carrying water or food. At noon, a woman walked out of the house.

'I've noticed you standing in front of the gate all through the night. Come inside, child, drink something. It's getting hot...' She was dusky, with thick hair rolled into a loose bun, clad in a cotton sari.

'What is your name, *mulgi* (daughter)?'

'M...Ma...Ma...' I fumbled, half fainting, the exhaustion of the wait and the exhilaration of escape completely overwhelming me.

'Maya? Did you say, your name was Maya?' The woman's eyes had filled with tears. 'Come in, here, take my hand…I am Amitabh Kulasheshtra's wife,' she had run her fingers gently through my tousled tresses soaked in sweat and shame, settling a few stray strands behind my ears. 'We live here…come on in, child, don't be nervous…'

She led me inside, not letting go of my hand, gesturing that I should leave my stilettoes outside on the threshold.

'You will have no need for such things, here, in my home,' she had smiled as she poured me a glass of water from a small copper urn.

That was how Aiyee and I had met. The first time.

◈

'Maya, why are you crying? Babe, we'll be on air any minute, now. We are linking live to the 9 pm news with Arunava Ghosh in the studio. There are other experts too, from the theatre world…everyone is waiting…'

'He's dead, right? Amitabh Kulasheshtra, I mean? Amitabh…?'

'Yes, it's all over the news. His wife has issued a statement. It's just come in. Mrs. Sarla Kulasheshtra…'

'So, is there any harm, then, if I *am* crying for a great man? A legend, like you people once called him? Doesn't that give me the right to also shed a real tear or two, like everyone else in the theatre world, who will inevitably appear on national television, all saying the same things…I mean, beginning with your very channel, mourning the way he died? The part that grabs headlines…all about him being mauled by an agitated mob of women, mistaken for a petty pickpocket, in the end? Suspected to be carrying a bomb, or, something…' I was breathing hard.

'Maya, *yaar*, not in front of the crew, please. Look, let's get back to deciding what you're going to say, when we roll…I promise to send Rosy and your Marlboro Lights too. Maya, please, look at me; you don't have to do this drama... Everyone knows what they have to, and those who don't, couldn't care a shit anyway, after all this time. Look, I know this must be bloody painful. This obituary thing, I mean… talking about Kulasheshtra…in hindsight…'

I ran my hand slowly over my face, dabbing some concealer under my eyes, puffy from lack of sleep. And just like that I was back in character:

'*Accha batao*, should I wear my hair loose? Won't it look more natural? Match perfectly with the cream, chikankari chiffon sari Manish Grover especially sent for me? It was his showstopper at the Lakmé India Fashion Week, grand finale…I am *always* his showstopper…'

AVIK DASGUPTA

I fidgeted listlessly with the television remote for a while, weighing it in my palm as I waited for my cell to ring. Looked like Maya had chosen to ignore me again tonight. Much in the way she had all of last week, and the month before, and the year before that. She was as cold as her plush, 28th floor Peddar Road high-rise felt after dusk, wrapped in anonymity and alienation. I tried to shut out thoughts of her and concentrate on the TV.

'*Kya aap ki aur koi khaas yaadein hain?*' A young television journalist was asking, pushing a hand mike into an old man's face. He shrugged his stooping shoulders, looking away from the camera.

I recognized him at once. Govind Deval, the revolutionary Marathi poet and a noted scriptwriter of his time; once an indispensable part of Sarat Chandra Joglekar's travelling theatre company, *Natya Mandali*, now ninety and wheelchair-bound. Perhaps, one of the last surviving men 'privileged' to work with Joglekar and Kulasheshtra, both.

'*Natya Samrat*' Joglekar was the only son of Vishwas Chandra Joglekar, considered the father-figure of Marathi regional theatre. Sarat Chandra Joglekar, popularly referred to as Dada Saheb, was attributed to having discarded the convention of having the *sutradhar* provide all of the singing. In his musical plays, known as *Sangeet Natak*, the characters themselves performed their own songs. Dada Saheb included some western-stage production techniques such as changeable scenery, and laid the foundation of commercial repertories in Marathi theatre that, subsequently, paved the way for the formation of *natak* companies and soon rose to become a towering figure in the region, overshadowing his father.

Amitabh Kulasheshtra, who had been initiated into the medium under his tutelage, was his son-in-law, by virtue of his marriage to his only daughter, Sarla, and had thereby inherited this formidable legacy. In his early plays, directed while Dada Saheb was still alive, Kulasheshtra was known to have incorporated the traditional forms of *tamasha* and *dashavatar* as both a narrative device and style.

I listened as Govind Deval began to speak:

◈

'I didn't much like Kulasheshtra at first; I was jealous of him, actually. The first time I was jealous of anyone. It was 1955. We were auditioning for a re-adaptation of *Sita Swayamvar*, first staged in 1843, in Sangli, an experimental piece based on the folk-theatre form of *Yakshagana*, from the neighbouring state of Karnataka. Dada Saheb, the great Sarat Chandra Joglekar, in whose travelling theatre troupe I happened to be the dialogue writer, had decided that we were going to tell the story beginning with Sita's *Agniparkisha*, mostly reconstructed as a flashback.

'The cast and screenplay was still being finalized. We had camped in Satara. Every day, for the past week, a young boy of about fifteen, unwashed, skinny, with an unruly mop of hair, took position by a solitary Banyan tree and watched us rehearse out in the open, where we had erected a makeshift stage. He seemed so absorbed in the goings-on that his gaze never moved off the action. He never left to eat, or even take a leak.

'One day – after a particularly intense rehearsal in which Dada Saheb had lost his temper with everyone – we had taken a short break for snacks and tea when his daughter Sarla, an impetuous 14-year-old, had turned to the stranger: "You! Why are you still here? How many times have you stood in the exact same place, over the past fortnight, huh? What do you want? Where are your parents?"

'"Go on, get lost...this is an audition for trained actors and musicians, this is not a small village play...not actors, Sarat Chandra Joglekar is on the lookout for real artists, understand?" I remember yelling at the lad.

'But the boy didn't seem at all fazed. "I am here to meet Joglekar, in person," he answered, walking towards Sarla with a self-important swagger. "I know he's staging *Sita Swayamvar.* I usually never miss any of his plays. In fact, I have been writing *natak* myself. Not happy ones, of course, not ones that revel mainly in *natya sangeet* and *tamasha.* My writing is rebellious - mostly against the system, for youngsters, for the poor. Did you know that Vishnudas Bhave who was the first one to stage this magnum opus would often base his dramas on particular episodes of the Ramayana and that he had also ventured into puppet shows, at some point? I am keen to add that element in this adaptation. I was raised in a circus. I know the way puppetry usually works...Heard of Ganesh Circus, have you? Our tents are put up on the outskirts of your town. This town."

'"My father already *has* a theatre group. Sadly, there is no place for rank outsiders, and, trust me, he doesn't meet just about anyone who comes calling," Sarla retorted firmly, but courteously.

'"I know he's a big man, but I am determined to meet your father, I know all about *Sita Swayamvar*...Baba has told me the story...I have some new ideas..."

'I tried saying something, at that moment, but my gaze was trapped by the obstinacy of the fellow – at how, he wouldn't give up the argument.

'Sarla, I suspect, was equally bemused by the boy: "Look, we are quite happy with Dada Saheb's version, but, since you insist, I can, maybe, beg him to give you a tiny role," she smirked.

Just then, a shadow passed us by. "*Hujha nav kay ahe? Apan kuthon alat?* (Who have you brought along? Who are you?)" Dada Saheb, a staggeringly tall man in his early fifties, craned his neck and enquired.

'Sarla impulsively pressed the oily vada pao she was about to eat into the boy's hand, pushing him onto the elevated platform we were rehearsing on. "*Ikde, ikde, ikde* (here, here, here), eat this first; you look utterly famished, how can you possibly impress anyone on an empty stomach?"

'The boy glanced gratefully at Sarla and smiled his thanks.

'"I believe my daughter has let you in." Dada Saheb's booming voice made our hearts race.

'"What to do? He just keeps standing and watching us all day. He insists he wants to become a playwright, like you; claims he too directs plays," Sarla bit her lower lip, hiding a smile.

'Dada Saheb considered him frankly, for a while. The boy didn't drop his gaze. Dada Saheb was amused.

'"It's a lonely hell, this stage, *mulagā* (lad). Ask me, Natya Samrat Joglekar – a man who has existed in its shadows since I was a young lad, like you, inheriting this *kala* from my father, the eminent Vishwas Chandra Joglekar. You need nothing to come here, son, if you're willing to go the distance. Money, fame, love, lust, loss, greed, ambition...every emotion exists here. But, can you surrender your earlier life? Survive this craft? Stay hungry forever?"

'"I can do anything I set my heart on, sir, and hunger is an old friend..." the boy replied.

'Dada Saheb paused and studied the boy again. "*Hmm*, he has something…Report for rehearsals tomorrow at six in the morning. You can begin with helping with the set. And you may stay in my camp tonight. In case you have no place to go."

'When Dada Saheb left, the boy ran his greasy fingers through his curly mop, jumped off the stage, and walked up to Sarla. "And, your name is?"

'"I'm his daughter, Sarla Joglekar…" she answered haughtily.

'"Well, I'll call you Sarlu…" the boy grinned back. "By the way, I'm Amitabh, Amitabh Kulasheshtra, and *my* father is a clown in Ganesh Circus…the only blind clown in the circus…"'

◈

Almost all the news channels featured Kulasheshtra. I was surprised that the accidental death of an old theatre stalwart had taken precedence over the wedding of a Mumbai-based billionaire's only son in Paris. And the kidnapping and brutal gangrape of a six-year-old girl in a suffocating Dharavi slum. The police had only managed to nab two of the eight accused.

I sprung up restlessly from the comfortable leather recliner and walked out onto the roof-top garden dotted with bonsai plants in bright ochre pots and interspersed with marble statues of nubile, Grecian goddesses. The tips of their breasts glistening in the distant shimmer of the city lights. My fingers reeked of nicotine. I had been chain smoking.

I punched Maya's number again; telling myself this would be the last call. It was 11 pm. I could hear the TV in the distance. A repeat of the 9 pm news bulletin had just started with Arunava Ghosh:

'"*...Memory is overrated. People forget. Everyone lies. Lovers move on. Marriages rot. Kids grow up. Wrinkles appear. Breasts sag. Sex drives slow down. Parents age. Plants die. Jobs change. Money runs out. Boredom sets in. Holidays don't last. Fashion changes. Leaves fall. Night sets in...*

Till, till, you wake up one morning...thinking where it all went.

That thing you had.

That feeling, that fight, that life..."'

Okay, so that's where she was. I watched the TV screen reflected in the glass terrace door as the camera zoomed in on Maya's heavily made-up face, sans any trace of emotion, as usual.

'*...These lines are famously attributed to Amitabh...the news of his...I mean, Amitabh Kulasheshtra's death is indeed sad and shocking. The stage will unquestionably be a darker place, without him. But then, people forget, right? They have to; it's how we live. Move on. Make new memories. Substitute pain with pleasure...As Kulasheshtra wrote in his autobiography: "Happiness is the art of training ourselves to forget...*"'

She sounded utterly fake.

I took a deep breath, filling my lungs with as much air as I could. Kulasheshtra's mug-shot flashed on screen as various stalwarts from the theatre world in Mumbai and other parts of India shared their views on the strange manner of his death. A panel of experts debated whether he had really been suffering from Alzheimer's, or if his slow fading away from the stage was an after-effect of his earlier head injuries. Kulasheshtra's achievements in the world of modern Indian theatre were conveniently overshadowed. A *supari*-chewing Rashtriya Dal leader, one of Amol Rawat's men no doubt, also a part of the same panel, smugly rambled on and on about how Kulasheshtra was himself politically corrupt, labelling him a 'Congress *chamcha*'.

The photograph of Kulasheshtra they intermittently flashed was from fifteen years ago. His face, just the way I remembered it: a sturdy, selfish gaze. The dark cleft on his chin. The arch of his shoulders. The grizzled salt-and-pepper beard that covered his gaunt cheeks. The manner in which he always wore black…

◈

'So, what makes you think you are qualified for this prestigious institute?' An obese man on the selection committee had questioned me after a gruelling four-day workshop. I had set my heart on joining the National Centre for Drama. I had cleared the preliminary exam in Kolkata and was now hoping to make the mains. The workshop was part of the assessment as we were required to perform, sing, dance and discuss a long list of plays sent to us, beforehand.

The Delhi skyline outside had been overcast with dense fog.

'I don't know, exactly. I mean, films have never really been my cup of tea. Neither is acting, honestly. I'm not interested in the struggle of a side hero,' I'd said, knowing that this casual banter would be critical to my selection.

'What brings you here, then?' a lady in a peacock green silk sari had interrupted, catching me off-guard.

'I want to direct. I have a totally different take on theatre; I want to make it more commercial. Rope in corporate sponsorship for street plays, for instance. It's why I am here. I believe theatre needs men like us; directors who are game-changers. Ambitious, young blood who can envision production on a larger scale; chart out a better plan of action, something way bigger than a few shows here and there, a snatch of an award, distant critical recognition. I want plays that run for seasons, not a week or two; to popularize experimentation in the field, discover alternative methods of storytelling…' I coughed.

'Go on…' a distinctive baritone dispelled the quiet, all of a sudden.

I blinked in the dark, trying to decipher the dark shadow that loomed in the aisle.

'Umm, I *am* aware, theatre is not about quick fame, but, at the same time, I *want* to be famous; to be known for my unique brand of work. I want the good life – I want it for this medium. I want it *in* this medium. I mean, why not? Why should theatre eternally be considered a poor man's craft? Either squalid street theatre, or shallow supper theatre? Why only these two extremes? I want to break the rules; make theatre more mass; make the one play for thousands of viewers, not hundreds.'

'Look at me,' the man had walked up to me and now spoke directly to my face.

I confronted his piercing glance.

'Do you know who I am?' Kulasheshtra looked me in the eye.

'Everyone does,' I said, feeling the sweat drip down the sides of my unshaven cheeks.

'And what if you fail at the above? The exponential rise you talk about, doesn't that also risk exponential failure?'

'I won't…I will win…I have a distinct blueprint…' I spoke fast. The words pressed to each other, like grains of warm rice.

'A blueprint?' Kulasheshtra laughed. 'If there was a blueprint for creative success, would there ever be a dud in the business? What are you talking about, young man? Materialism, or *magic*? Which one would *you* choose, and, why? And if it's only money you want to make, what are your views on social change? What is the message you wish to send out? What is your politics? The colour of your conscience? Your *chetna*...the sum of your soul...?'

'No, sir, I didn't use the word magic, you did, and, as for the colour of my conscience, *chetna* or whatever you would like to label it...let me make it clear here, at the very onset, that I am not political. Theatre is art, true, it *has* a voice, yes, the power to change things, thought processes, but I am not here to start a bloodied revolution. Art, all art, has to sell, at the end of the day...be street-smart, market-savvy, its voice heard by those who matter. It has to change something, fundamentally, agreed, but, at the same time, also possess widespread, populist appeal. The youth need to connect; the elite, who purchase tickets, want to watch something that is bigger than a commonplace *tamasha.* Art that is intellectual masturbation is bullshit...theatre, a *natak*, a play, any play, for that matter, needs an audience...needs patronage, sir...' I spluttered indignantly.

'Theatre is not about winning. Nothing is, in fact, in life. It is the tragedy of humankind that we must deal with failure...' Kulasheshtra countered.

'Failure? Why harp on failure? See, that's what I mean... why this association of suffering with soul, always?' I don't know why I repeated in a shrill tone.

Kulasheshtra regarded me with a level look. 'The greatest Shakespearean plays are about human failure. If failure scares you so much don't bother finishing this interview. If you want to make money and if personal renown and populist propaganda mean that much to you then perhaps theatre is not even your cup of tea. Join Bollywood, become a director of B-grade crap, and don't waste our time here! There are far more deserving candidates...' Kulasheshtra turned on his heel and began to walk away.

'Sir, you are deliberately misconstruing my words, you can't just leave me while I'm halfway through explaining my stance...I have an equal right to be here, you know...I topped the entrance exams...I've travelled to the national capital, from afar...sir, I can do it...I, I will do anything...I am ready to do anything to gain admission into the National Centre of Drama. I have a plan, sir...I want to be someone...' my voice broke.

I heard him laugh in the distance.

I remember that part clearly.

◈

Later that night, I had bought myself a ticket to an amateur play somewhere near Mandi House. Something about the effects of liberalization and inflation on man-woman love. An adaptation of a famous Marathi play by Amitabh Kulasheshtra, a parody, supposedly, one of his lesser-known works.

There were barely any spectators. The jokes were neither laughed at, nor understood. A couple made out in the shadowy back row. Beside me, sat a young, fair girl with green eyes. We made small talk between scenes, sharing a Cola during intermission. She claimed to be an aspiring actress from Manipur who had failed to make it to the interview stage at the National Centre of Drama, again, that year. We grabbed a beer at a rundown bar in Connaught Place before I took her to my aunt's place in Chittaranjan Park. My aunt was away.

I had fucked her in silence. A girl whose name I'd not even bothered to ask. Feeling nothing. Except the way a man does when he asserts himself over a woman; after someone else has asserted himself over him. Revelling in an aphrodisiacal sense of power that only anonymity affords.

'Admission denied,' was all Kulasheshtra who was on the final selection committee of the National Centre of Drama that particular year, wrote in his individual remarks section.

I had grabbed the rejection letter and shoved it in my satchel, seething with contempt.

'*Hazaaron log pariksha dete hain, samjhe, barkhurdar?* Try, try, try again...*angrezi mein kahawat hai...suna toh hoga hi,*' a bespectacled man with hair sprouting out of his nostrils and ears had mouthed patronizingly, peering at me from inside an iron grid.

I stormed off.

'*Kulasheshtra ne band baja diya kya? Arre, agle saal phir se koshish kar lena,*' he called out from behind my back.

By the beginning of next summer, Kulasheshtra had relinquished his advisory position on the selection committee – a post he had held on to for little over a year. One of his most enduring achievements was laying down the outline for the Repertory Company – the professional performing wing of the National Centre of Drama that aimed to promote professional theatre in India. Since then the Repertory Company, had staged over 120 plays based on the works of about 70 playwrights and featuring around 50 directors in several countries, and various cities across the nation.

RK CHOPRA

I woke with a start, the incessant jangling of my cellphone ruining last night's guilt-free intoxication; my mouth stinking of whiskey. I belched loudly, the regurge from yesterday's dinner backing up in my mouth, making me want to throw up. The AC was on full blast, the bedsheets were icy. I felt the satin pillow stuffed between my thighs slowly drop to the floor. The afternoon sun streamed in from behind the dark jacquard blinds casting the hotel suite in a mellow afterglow. Almost the same shade as the whore's auburn streaks; the one I had picked up last night at the rooftop bar, minutes before she went down on me, reprimanding me for not shaving. Asking me where I lived and what my name was.

'RK,' was all I'd said.

The whore had left, just as I had instructed, at the crack of dawn. The last thing I wanted was a fresh controversy. A sex scandal, this time around.

Last night's lay had wanted to keep the television on while we made out. I'd protested initially, before allowing her to tie my hands with my powder-blue silk tie. Popping a Viagra just before she clumsily mounted my half limp member. I was too distracted to care.

My thoughts constantly raced back to the income-tax raid on my Pali Hill head office last week. I'd been forced into hiding after that, with both my apartments simultaneously being searched and sealed, including my sprawling Karjat farmhouse, as also all the three offices of Chopra & Sons, all shut down, indefinitely. Black money spilling over fifty crores had been collected and confiscated in hard cash from them.

The newspapers carried my name and alleged that some of my films had been financed by illegal monies from dons sitting in faraway Dubai, made through narcotics and gold smuggling. In turn, they alleged, the film industry, i.e. me and my friends in Bollywood, contributed glamour and grandeur to scores of underworld parties in Dubai along with gracing functions in Mumbai arranged by the dons and their henchmen. My calls were being traced. A leading political magazine even went to the extent of contending that most of my heroines – women who had debuted under my banner – were handpicked by the 'Bhais' who, also at times, dictated the storyline.

I was advised by my lawyers to stay put, holed up in this hotel, here.

Rakesh Chopra, top Bollywood producer. Wanted for tax fraud. Money laundering. Dealing with the mafia.

RK the pimp.

RK the player.

RK the porn-addict.

My good-for-nothing son, Monty, whose own film career had never quite taken off, was to blame for most of my recent misfortunes. He had pumped a large chunk of my savings into a good-for-nothing film that he had chosen to direct himself. Launching a good-for-nothing woman, he had screwed a couple of times. A small-time starlet, who he'd insisted was slotted to be the next big thing.

I should have known when the film sank without a trace, that Monty was up to no good, and that direction, like acting, wasn't his cup of tea. And yet, I chose to give him a second chance.

I nursed a weakness for Monty. I had cheated on his mother, my first wife, Meenu, with a woman young enough to be our daughter, before she drank herself to death.

Monty had her eyes.

Hits and flops are an integral part of our *dhanda*, I convinced myself. And appeased Bhai. But what I had failed to foresee was how the money flowing in from real estate investments had begun drying up thanks to a slump in the market. Of their traditional sources of income – narcotics, gold smuggling, illicit liquor trade and prostitution – now, only the first remained profitable. And so, especially over the past years, the underworld had turned to us, the film fraternity, and, much like the builder lobby they once patronized and later extorted money from – now bigshot movie moghuls and famous actors happened to be the latest soft targets of dreaded ganglords who demanded their pound of flesh.

The tide had turned, beginning in 1997, when the creator of a 500-crore music company, Gulshan Kumar, was shot dead at point-blank range outside a temple he had built in suburban Versova. Abu Salem, Dawood's lieutenant in Dubai, had supposedly demanded ten *khokhas* (crores). Gulshan, who had started his career running a wayside food-stall in Daryaganj, in old Delhi, had viewed the threat as hollow. I still remember the nonchalant look in his eyes when he had disclosed to me at a music album launch, how he was on the underworld hit-list.

I had volunteered to play middleman and renegotiate on his behalf.

'*Mein kissi se nahin darta*, RK,' he had nonchalantly shrugged his shoulders.

I thought of him now. How his body had been found slumped sideways in a pool of blood. Now I too was being threatened to cough up the enormous losses incurred on Monty's last film. And it was the reason why I had listened to my lawyers and sought police protection, playing along with a cock-and-bull story that claimed I was being falsely framed, thanks to an extortion racket by the D company. That the money recovered from my office premises had been planted by their men, to land me into trouble.

I was on the run from the law. I was buying time from Bhai and my second wife – who had also suddenly hiked up her alimony demands. I even suspected Monty – who was livid that I wasn't going to invest any further in his next film venture – and believed he actually had something to do with the raids.

I trusted no one.

◈

'Advocate Singh,' my cell-phone screen flashed, vibrating loudly. I turned up the television to drown it out. I was still lost in my thoughts when the name on TV, registered in my ears.

Followed by a familiar voice…

'My husband Amitabh Kulasheshtra passed away earlier this afternoon from a massive cardiac failure. Amitabh had been ailing for a while. Following his last wishes, he will be buried tomorrow, at 4 pm, and not cremated. Amitabh was a fiercely private man, and, so, his funeral tomorrow, too, shall remain private. I request his students, colleagues, friends, and the media to kindly respect our privacy. I would like to thank the staff of Kamla Nehru Hospital for their support. Namaste…' Sarla pursed her lips, folding her hands demurely.

I stared at the monitor, tongue-tied. I couldn't recognize her, at first. Her cheeks were gaunt; her dark tresses, gathered in a neat bun resting at the nape of her neck, were streaked with silver. She wore a conservatively styled, full-sleeved blouse and a dull brown cotton sari. Immediately, I thought of the ample breasts beneath that demurely draped nine yards.

I narrowed my eyes and sank onto the side of the bed, grabbing the edges of the crumpled sheets.

The journalists were thronging her with questions.

'*Mrs Amitabh Kulasheshtra*,' I read the caption that ran on the bottom of the TV screen. Repeating her name to myself.

◈

She had always been nervous around her father. That day, when she had walked in for rehearsals, she barely made eye contact with the other actors. I'd been smitten instantly. Though she never smiled freely or tried flirting openly with me, I was certain my fair-skinned good looks and sculpted physique were not lost on her.

I immediately named her 'Banno' in my head. It was my mother's nickname.

Her father was my mentor. Sarat Chandra Joglekar.

A theatre legend in his time; an icon.

I was about twenty-one when I got my first opportunity to audition in Joglekar's theatre troupe in Maharashtra. I was desperate to land a break in acting. I was clear that I would use theatre as a stepping-stone to cross over into the more lucrative film industry. One of my uncles, a distant relative of my mother's, had settled down in Kohlapur after the Partition and started a dhaba that had flourished into a decent, mid-sized restaurant that boasted of the finest *firni* and the most succulent tandoori chicken. I was sent to him to help in the business, to find my way in new India after we had to abandon our ancestral home in Lahore. I was barely thirteen at the time.

I was a good-looking Punjabi boy, *gora-chitta*, as my aunts and cousin sisters often teased me, with wavy brown hair, soft, greenish eyes and sturdy arms: the stuff heroes were made of. I was also quite unscrupulous. I could do anything to make my aspirations come true.

Be anyone.

I had set my heart on being an actor, so one night, I stole my uncle's savings and left his home forever.

A week later, I had joined Joglekar's company, and a week after that I caught a glimpse of Banno in a backless choli.

It was love at first sight for me. She had the most perfectly shaped breasts. I had wanted there and then to place my mouth hungrily over her nipples, gulp her down, swallow her soreness and drown endlessly in her tears. I had wanted to say so much to her, but I was too terrified to even look into her brown eyes; eyes that when they met mine for the first time, glinted with a sanguine, almost sacred strength.

Mitti, the play her father had newly written was inspired by Dalit icon and architect of the Indian Constitution, B.R. Ambedkar's clarion call to fellow Dalits to rise against the ruling class. It wove the explosive story of a married Dalit woman belonging to a migrant community, picked up by a rich exploitative zamindar who eventually falls in love with her, straying outside the designated boundary lines of an arranged, high-caste marriage.

Dada Saheb had been scouting for a fair and tall man who looked 'Brahmin' enough for the part of the wealthy landlord, whose dialogue delivery reflected an aristocratic arrogance and whose body language bore a certain swagger…a distinct disdain for the marginalized. It was how I had managed to make it to the final auditions.

But now I was muffing my lines, as I eyed Sarla distractedly: *'What if I can actually love you…? If I am now begging to live…to be a better man…if* I *am at your mercy? What if there is more to this life?'*

I was supposed to be holding a loaded pistol to my head, to balance on one knee, professing my undying admiration to her, breaking down, for the first time. Instead, I was mesmerized by a faint line of moisture trickling down her cleavage.

'*You ask me what is love, Sahib. I ask you, now, what is death? Who will mourn my demise when I walk out of your sprawling countryside mansion where you hold me ransom? When I will have no choice, but to hang myself from a tree? A fallen, Dalit woman, in tattered clothes with matted locks, whose eyes have not known sleep, such as me? Who will even want to touch my funeral pyre? Tell my story...an unfinished saga of forbidden female desires...*' her pale lips had shuddered.

Her father had frowned, shuffling through the handwritten script.

A dull heat pierced my loins. I took a deep breath and continued: *'My heart, you speak, as if it's all my fault...as if you don't comprehend the weight of my attraction...the fact, that you make me sterile...rendering my whole life impotent with so much as a slanted, sideways glance. You have no right to make me this helpless, you low-caste whore! You vile serpent – how many times, will you destroy me this way, with your reluctance to accept my body, my soul...slow poisoning my senses? How many times, must I prostrate before you? Grovel? What is left of my machismo? Who is the achooth (untouchable), now?'*

My voice cracked as Sarla instinctively grabbed my left hand, pressing it to her chest, giving me the confidence I lacked, telling me with one fleeting touch how she understood my unspoken feelings...that she reciprocated what I feared telling her...in person.

◈

That same night, Sarla and I had met alone for the first time, in a darkened, makeshift green-room; all the raw emotions we had play-acted earlier the same day, suddenly reigniting, as we groped each other clumsily, hungrily.

It was clear from the start that her father would be opposed to our match. We kissed passionately, as she rubbed her soft cheeks against my mine, confessing how it wasn't going to be easy to stand up against her father's will alone.

'You will *have* to tell Dada Saheb the truth about us, you know that, right? Eventually? He's not easy to please, as you may have understood by now...' she had grabbed my shoulders, searching my face...my eyes...

I looked away. Oblong shadows formed on the spacious walls. A lone lantern flickered.

'What will become of this attraction...our love...if he marries me off to a man of his choice? What we share now... this moment,' she had whispered hoarsely, as I'd tightened my arms around her.

'I will tell Dada Saheb everything, soon, real soon,' I'd lied, nuzzling her throat, 'before I whisk you away to our *sapnon ka sheher*...in Mumbai. That's where we belong... There, we will become famous as a couple...you will go on to become a legendary leading actress, mark my words...our future lies in the big city...not here, not the way he believes an artist should subsist, merely on his craft, the way his plays are nothing but long-drawn-out social commentaries...the future lies in celluloid, not another village *manch*.'

Banno stared at me, fascinated.

'This is a *naya daur*...' I propped up her chin, excitedly explaining how the angst of 1950s Bollywood that had mirrored a newly Independent India was officially behind us.

The Sixties were all about colour, optimism and flamboyance.

'*Gaya* Guru Dutt *ka zamana gaya…unnka gam…dhukh bhari dastaan…*have you, watched K. Asif's *Mughal-E-Azam…*heard Shammi Kapoor as he slides down the snow-capped hills of Shimla, roaring "*Yaahoo*"?' I breathed fast.

She smiled, shyly. Shaking her head from side to side.

'I am told I resemble him…' I chuckled, cupping her cheeks, 'I will see to it that all our dreams come true…I want to be together with you…I knew the second I laid eyes on you…I have no interest in inheriting this looming legacy that he promises…I am not Amitabh…'

Banno had covered my mouth with hers in a fervent kiss. Afterwards, she had said:

'I know you are not Amitabh…I don't *want* you to be, and neither do I wish that you live in Dada Saheb's shadows forever. I have no desire to spend my entire life, here, simply being Sarat Chandra Joglekar's only daughter, Rakesh. I felt it too…my beloved…the minute I touched your hand…And, as for Amitabh, whom you will get to know closely, as more time passes – he's a friend, like a brother, almost. I intend to confide in him, about us. He'll never betray my trust. Amitabh cares about nothing, except being the next Sarat Chandra Joglekar…it's why he joined our troupe…forsaking everything. He believes in the same world order…they are strangely similar, my father and he…both of them married to theatre. Amitabh is incapable of loving another person. His selfishness is his armour, it's probably taken him years to cultivate this sort of meticulous detachment…Ami…' the rest of her words trailed, as I dragged her back into my arms.

Amitabh Kulasheshtra.

To think I had once called him 'Bhai Jaan'.

SARLA KULASHESHTRA

I looked up, tired from filling up the lengthy forms. My eyes smarted from lack of sleep. It was just after 7 a.m., the hexagonal clock on a dull grey wall in the waiting area of Kamla Nehru Hospital announced.

I was finishing off the formalities required to get Amitabh out of the morgue. A few of the patients' attendants and family members, who lay asleep on the hard, cold ground on hastily thrown together bedclothes, were stirring sluggishly. Some sat still, numbed by the illness of their loved ones, some others, like me, immersed in the paperwork of death, or in hushed conversation amongst themselves; their heads hung low, their faces lined with worry.

I rubbed my cheeks, fighting a dull cramp in my stomach, scrutinizing the expressions of those around me, one by one. In a far corner, a young mother breastfed her new-born, her light, brown nipples glinting in the fractured light. Our glances intersected briefly.

Someone had increased the volume on the television, near the reception area. I walked slowly in its direction. My Kohlapuri chappals made a flip-flop sound. I located an empty seat, rubbing my eyes. A man in his early 30's in a blue, striped shirt was being interviewed on the news channel.

I narrowed my eyes.

Someone by the name of Tyeb Ansari, the caption on the TV read.

◈

'I can still remember the first play I ever saw of his, on a street, outside Parliament, the year I was on a school holiday to New Delhi. The cops watching in a curious semi-circle, their lathis poised.

'Kulasheshtra's actors were bare-bodied. Their eyes lined with kohl. Their loincloths barely covering their privates; they were enacting a village scene, clutching piles of straw and dummies of malnourished babies.

'I jostled through the swelling crowds. Desperate to get an inch closer to Kulasheshtra, intimidated and inspired at the same time.

'"*What use is the Green Revolution that primarily catered to the rich, large landholding farmers of India? Who are you trying to fool, huh? The small and the lower middle peasantry have almost completely lost their stake…eventually their voice too will be wiped out…this is more than an agrarian crisis…*"

'Flies buzzed over our heads.

'"*Free the farmers, our children are dying, born with their limbs deformed, their bodies twisted out of shape, pass the Bill banning the use of toxic pesticides,*" one of his actors implored.

'A few onlookers clapped awkwardly.

'A pot-bellied man in a grey safari suit suddenly stepped aside, perspiring profusely: "Can't you people see you are holding up traffic, that too when Parliament is in session? *Tamasha khada kar diya hai tum logon ne*; if you have the balls, why don't you contest elections in your own state, concentrate on forming a legitimate political party of your own and then travel cross country, to the capital, to face us, as equals?"'

'Kulasheshtra had walked up to face him. He had been roughed up badly. His left eye was split open, his kurta ripped. "I believe in the unrelenting continuity of the struggle to fight for those lacking the voice to protest. Beat me. Throw me into jail, but leave my art be, it shall always be free; it is my fundamental right to fight for the poor. It is what democracy means to me..."

'"Sir, your eye...would you like some ice water on it? It will bring the swelling down, it's what I learnt at Boy Scouts," I don't know why I blurted, anxious, but filled with a new courage, suddenly adolescent, suddenly alive. I was fourteen.

'Kulasheshtra swerved. Our eyes met. Then he lowered his head. I opened the lid of my thermos, the cold water gushed out, diluting the colour of his cuts.

'A couple of cops strutted forward. "*Yeh launda kaun hai?*" a man with a thick moustache yelled, as more burly men pushed their way in.

'Kulasheshtra glanced up and, sensing trouble, immediately grabbed me, "*Bachha hai yeh...beta jaisa...*" he answered, pushing me away to safety.

'Amitabh's actors closed in on him, as the policemen aimed their water cannons. He looked back at me for a few fleeting seconds, and then he was gone.

'They had been tipped off that there were chances of violence, if Amitabh Kulasheshtra didn't take the Rashtriya Dal warning seriously and went ahead and staged his controversial play in Malegaon, *Mī Jivanta Ahē*.

'That evening, Amol Rawat was in the crowd, as were his goons. They had concealed their weapons and obviously the local police were hand-in-glove. Twenty minutes or so after the play began, in the midst of a satire-laced love scene, these men, who had till then managed to stay inconspicuous, deliberately began creating a furore and disrupting the performance. Before we knew it, a violent mob accompanying

Rawat was chasing Kulasheshtra, hurling abuse in Marathi, one of his men even firing in the air to scare the audience…

'Kulasheshtra tried his best to get everyone to calm down and to reason with some of the attackers, when Rawat intervened, lifting up a hockey stick and threatening to beat him to pulp. Kulasheshtra fought him off, using only his bare hands. When blood gushed out of his head, Prakash Lele, his lead actor, who was close by, stepped forward. In a few minutes, he was beaten to pulp and left for dead. Kulasheshtra did all he could to save him, but Rawat's men who outnumbered him in any case, were too barbaric to overcome.

'They don't make men like Kulasheshtra, anymore.'

Tyeb Ansari stopped and looked directly at the camera, his eyes full of tears:

'In my mind, and many times, over all these years, I have imagined Amitabh Kulasheshtra waiting for me every day at the court; hoping the young boy who was brave enough to give him iced water, will also come forward as a witness. Help him in his battle against Rawat and the Rashtriya Dal. But, of course, I never went. Being a coward needs no extra practice.'

◈

'Sarla Kulasheshtra, Mrs. Sarla Kulasheshtra!' A hospital employee patted my back, gesturing at the public announcement system.

My name was being called out.

I rose with a start as the papers slid off my lap.

'Did you know about his heart condition, ma'am?' a doctor, possibly in his mid-thirties, sporting a neatly-trimmed French beard, spoke anxiously, his hand on my elbow, as he guided me down a poorly lit corridor. It was the first time a man had touched me in a long time.

Amitabh's body had not been immediately released because of the post-mortem formalities. The autopsy report stated that the cause of death was a myocardial infarction. A cardiac arrest.

'Even we could not believe it was actually him, ma'am. We tried reviving his heart, but the truth is, he was dead on arrival. He'd already suffered a massive seizure, and then lay unattended in the station for an hour, at least…I mean, we had no idea who he was either…at first…'

There was a confused silence. I moved away.

The doctor was more distressed than I was. 'I mean, how can this happen? It's just so…so gravely tragic…a person of his stature…dying, this way…unrecognized…' he covered his mouth, coughing deliberately. The doctor was obviously a theatre-goer.

'What a stupendous man…legend…a survivor…I mean, what if his wallet wasn't discovered…is this any way to die, ma'am?' he shook his head from side to side.

I stared down silently at a zipped body-bag lying on a stretcher. After a few seconds, the doctor carefully unzipped the plastic cover; a faint stench mingled with the reek of strong disinfectant, made me want to throw up.

'I will leave now, ma'am…' There was a muffled sound of a door closing.

I forced myself to confront his face. His body had obviously been cleaned up. Yesterday, Amitabh had looked the part – dirty, derelict, and deceased. Like, our memories, like, the rest of us…His beard was missing in places, patches of blood had dried up, resembling menstrual stains. There were deep gashes all over his neck and chest. His lips were bruised, his mouth hung open.

Today he looked cleaned up, as if asleep peacefully; a line of stitches on the right side of his scalp caught my eye. In the same spot, he had been hit in Malegaon.

Thoughts formed and melted.

I ran my fingers lightly over the wound...

'Being a coward needs no extra practice,' I replayed the television footage in my mind. The man called Tyeb Ansari who had quoted Amitabh.

The last line of his interview that wasn't his.

I shuddered and suddenly felt faint, gripping the side of the hospital stretcher to steady myself, my pallu running out of me, like a raging midnight river.

I gazed down at my dead husband's face:

'Did you hear what they said, Amitabh? The doctor? The Press? The theatre-walas? They called you a hero. A legend. You a hero? Can a man like you be a hero? Now? Ever? Can a man like you be forgiven? Can betrayal ever be painted as bravery…?'

No tears flowed from my eyes. I don't know how long I remained like that before I stood up to zip him back up. In death, Amitabh seemed so very ordinary. I pulled up a plastic chair, after a few seconds, sitting uneasily beside him, biding my time, waiting for the next fifteen minutes to pass before I, the dignified, grieving widow could respectably leave her husband's side for the last time.

I fanned myself with my pallu, feeling my head spin.

A tall man with broad shoulders was slowly walking in my direction.

Was I seeing things?

I rubbed my eyes. The way I had.

Forty years ago.

The day Amitabh had let me down for the first time; the day his blind ambition had first broken my heart…

◈

Rakesh and I were lovers by then.

One evening, as I lay with my face buried in his chest, I decided to broach the uneasy subject: 'Just when do you intend to tell Dada Saheb, Rakesh? I have heard my mother bring up the prospect of my marriage, at bedtime, many times. She keeps saying that at 23, I am too old to be living with my parents and that people are already talking about me having acted in a few plays…that no decent boy will want an actress for a wife…I am worried that -'

Rakesh kissed me ravenously, pulling me over him, cutting off my words.

As ususal, I had made some excuse about leaving rehearsal early that evening; something I now did regularly, deliberately bunking the monotonous, late-evening regime of reading the classics with Dada Saheb and Amitabh, a custom he and I had both grown up on. A rigid discipline that Dada Saheb insisted was integral to our development as theatre-walas. Amitabh was always present, always, before time. Those days, we were discussing the Mahabharata – war and fratricide, placing it as Dada Saheb always taught us, against the changing socio-economic topography of India.

I lifted up my head to search Rakesh's evasive eyes:

'Are you apprehensive he might say no? Bring up the difference in our communities? Are you threatened it could lead to you being thrown out of the troupe?'

In answer, Rakesh kissed me on the mouth again.

A month or so later, Rakesh suddenly accosted me in the exact same spot. Dusk was descending. Fireflies flitted over us. 'Do you love Amitabh, Banno?' he had grabbed my shoulders, roughly, his breath acidic.

I had been thrown off-guard. I clasped my chest. 'Well, you know how we have grown up together, I mean, he's been living with us now for eight years, since I was fourteen…we've eaten the same food, lived in the same house, he understands my mixed feelings for my father…he is my fiercest critic, as I am also his…so, of course, I love Amitabh…' I composed my thoughts further: 'He's the only man, after Dada Saheb, whom I have been exposed to, so constantly, so closely…my father trusts him implicitly…he's been the ideal son in so many ways…'

Rakesh's eyes were bloodshot. *Had he been drinking?* He snapped: 'You could have at least lied…just say you don't love him…instead of this gut-wrenching, bloody tribute…'

'I have no reason to lie, Rakesh, there is nothing I hide,' I'd answered truthfully, my eyes filling. 'I love him, but, I can never love another man the way I love you. The way….'

'Amitabh is my brother too, Banno. But Dada Saheb is perpetually relying on his opinion and ideas, what he thinks of everything – prop placement, lighting, lines. There is talk that he is soon even going to allow Amitabh to direct his first play independently. Govind Bhai also mentioned something of this to me…everyone talks, here, you know…Amitabh is the centre of Dada Saheb's universe…the protégé he always wanted…and it's perhaps just a matter of time, before he gives you away in marriage to legitimize the revered *guru-shishya* relationship,' he stalled, looking distant, all of a sudden.

I tried reaching out, my pulse racing. 'Dada Saheb *needs* Amitabh, Rakesh, but I don't…' I held him desperately.

'What do you want, Banno?' he barked, trying to extricate himself from my embrace.

I kissed him over his thick stubble, and rested my head on his chest. For a while, we remained like that. Then I spoke: 'I want to be your wife. Travel the world with you. I want everything that you say I can have…I dream of acting in films, with you as my hero…of making passionate love to you every single night…'

Rakesh tried saying something…

'I like making you jealous, sometimes. I want to be loved, in a way…that makes me feel indispensable to someone…I want to belong, completely…just to you, Rakesh…' I pressed myself into him.

Rakesh caressed my forehead, grazing his lips on the sides of my neck.

'Oh Banno... *how*? How are we going to get what we want? The life we dreamt of...how can you be sure we can trust Amitabh? That he won't betray us?' his voice was strangled.

Later that night, we made love. It was desire doused with desperation. Our movements were frenzied. Like we were scared of being pulled apart by unseen forces. All I wanted was to be touched...tasted...to come alive, repeatedly.

At dawn, Rakesh promised he would speak to Dada Saheb. Tell him everything...

I too swore that I was prepared to elope if I had to, in case it was our last resort.

I remained distracted all of the next day, and went home only late in the evening, wary of being discovered; prepared to bear the brunt of my mother's ire, who always looked at me with suspicious eyes.

Dada Saheb didn't speak to me; his lips tightly pursed, too proud to ask me where I might have been.

'Tell Rakesh to say he was with me, just in case...' Amitabh whispered, pulling me aside. 'I'll make up something, on the same lines. I shall explain matters to Dada Saheb, Sarlu. I know what has been brewing for a while, between you both... why you are so late, these days. The way Rakesh's eyes too guard jealous secrets...Whatever happens, remember just one thing...let *him* take the fall, Rakesh, not you. It's what any honourable man would do, if he truly loves a woman.'

I had thanked him, in all my innocence.

The next afternoon, we were having a full-dress rehearsal for our forthcoming production. There were only three days left for the show to begin.

'No, no, *no*, Rakesh! The scene needs *more* emotional starkness...why can't you just get it, you are a man about to fight a venerable God...you are mourning the death of your only son who was sacrificed to bring on the delayed monsoon rains, that shall end a devastating village drought...you must look more possessed…your eyes can't be so impatient…your grief has to appear stoic…your voice modulation is all off… this technique is not working, your dialogue delivery needs a lot more work,' Dada Saheb lashed out at Rakesh, overtly critical of his portrayal.

We were rehearsing in the open air. The musicians shuffled uneasily, wondering when they would be called upon. At a distance, stood a colossal cut-out of a mythological character.

'What if he doesn't *want* to fight Indra? If he realizes his *real* enemy is the age-old superstitions of the village elders who persuaded him to give up his boy? What if he must take on someone from his own tribe, instead? Fight his brother, who convinced him to listen to the Panchayat Mandali…?' my words trailed, as I confronted my father's ire, trying to defend Rakesh.

'Stay out of this! You aren't the playwright, Sarla, besides, this is about Rakesh's performance, he seems most distracted. Is something the matter?' Dada Saheb cut me short, his tone of voice hostile.

'Umm, I think you are being unfair to Rakesh, and, Sarlu, surely has a point, here,' Amitabh spoke up immediately, trying to diffuse the tension. 'Besides, I think it's high time we extended the scope of these plays to topics more relevant to our generation…make morality more mass… like the Mahabharata…the fight between blood brothers is actually a reflection of the struggle of human conscience… good *vs* evil…'

'Apologies, Dada Saheb... I'll try the lines again…' Rakesh finally spoke, looking tense.

'What if the boy, is, in fact, a metaphor for change?' I don't know why I was relentless, desperate, as if, to push my point; Dada Saheb had never considered my opinion of any worth.

'Exactly!' Amitabh pumped his fist in the air, his mind in unison with mine. I was pleasantly surprised by his open support.

At that exact moment, Dada Saheb looked from me to Amitabh, as if everything was falling into perspective. As if a great truth had suddenly dawned upon him. He darted up all of a sudden from the low wooden stool where he sat and wrapped his arms around me, protectively.

'Amitabh and you seem to share a rare camaraderie, Sarla, something that has skipped my eyes, before…you both see the world the same way…it is important for a man and a woman to be able to do so. Be comrades, before being a couple. It's the one thing that will hold you both in good stead.' He tenderly placed his right hand on my chin and lifted my face: 'It has been this that has weighed on my mind, for many months, now. The reason for my pent-up silence…'

'Get them married, now, Dada Saheb, they make a fine match…besides, you need an *uttaradhikari*, soon!' one of the troupe members, egged him on sycophantically.

'Dada Saheb! No! ...*No!*' I'd shivered, my shoulders caving. 'Amitabh…say something, tell him the truth…you swore, remember? Please...' I looked pleadingly over my shoulders.

Amitabh bowed his head, saying nothing. Not protesting. Not standing up for me.

Breaking his promise.

Rakesh waited for a while, staring at me, accusatorily, before storming off, alone, his face flushed with anger.

'*Uttaradhikari*…' the word wafted in the air.

Like an evil omen.

MAYA SHIRALE

After innumerable calls and much chasing up, I had finally relented to just one 'exclusive' interview on Amitabh. Asking the journalist to meet me at Chowpatty in twenty minutes flat. When I landed up more than two hours late, she was still waiting.

The sun had just set.

I now sat facing Razia Siddiqui, one of Mumbai's senior-most Entertainment Editors who headed *Filmworld* magazine. We were seated in my gleaming black Mercedes Benz. She had not switched on her dictaphone. That had been my first precondition.

As Razia flipped through her handwritten notes, I rolled down the tinted window on my side. My latest Dior sunglasses camouflaged my eyes. Swirly rings of smoke wafted between us, as Razia shifted uneasily in the expensive leather seat.

My driver Alam, a rugged man with a hennaed goatee and a crocheted skullcap, waited outside, glancing back in my direction every once in a while. It was through him that Razia had been able to connect to me, finally, after weeks of hounding me for a proposed lead piece on Amitabh Kulasheshtra. Ten minutes later, she cleared her throat, and pointed a shiny Parker pen, in my direction.

'So, do you come here often, Maya?'

'I come whenever I can…it's probably the only place I visit, by myself…watching the darkness descend…listening to children's voices, wafting in at a distance. The silhouette of waves…this vast expanse of sea…*ek ajeeb sa chain milta hai, yahan*,' I stubbed my cigarette in an ashtray by the side of the car door.

'*Do you think of failure, Maya? Does it scare you, the same way it did, perhaps, at the start of your career?*' Razia leaned in closer.

'Failure?'

'*Yes. What is Maya Shirale's definition of failure? I mean, are you upset by the death of Kulasheshtra, or the spectacle of his failure?*'

'Next question…' I shrugged my shoulders.

'*How would you define failure?*'

'Next question, Razia!' I said sharply.

'*Fine, I'll rephrase that, how have you handled the last years of your life…your choice of films…your personal life…the recent death of Amitabh Kulasheshtra…*'

I pulled down my shades, slipped out of my stilettoes and flexed my ankles.

'*Does talking about Amitabh Kulasheshtra make you nervous, Maya? Worried of raking up yet another controversy…?*'

'Oh please! As if any of you guys expect me to say and do the right thing, at the right time! Maya Shirale has always grabbed eyeballs by being the non-conformist, especially, when the media expects her to be playing to the galleries. I am told I'm always giving the Bollywood Press something to talk about. So, debate, second-guess, slam Maya when a big-budget film falls flat on its face, but never write a word when our top heroes make bad decisions, right? Cast aspersions on whom I—maybe—am sleeping with or what married producer or businessman is leaving my apartment in the wee hours of dawn…and, yet, never gain access to *their* wives, nor ever ask them why they still remain married to such *bhadwas*! Honestly, Razia, I've never quite understood the meaning of these so-called "exclusive" interviews, cover-page shoots, news appearances, even hiring a PR agency; I've never bothered having a manager controlling my dates, except Alam who's always been by my side. I mean, who's looking for the soul-stirring truth, anyway, in this industry? But maybe, age, and experience, *ke saath saath, mein bhi kuch sudhar rahin hoon*,' I clicked my tongue.

'Maya, I hear you, but hasn't this don't-care-a-damn attitude already cost you your career? Look at all the new girls in B-town, currently, Miss India winner, Juhi Mehta, or, say, Rajni Gopalan, who's switched tracks from Tamil cinema to Bollywood, or even Lisa Paul, international model turned actress, or, Kaya, daughter of yesteryear actress, Tarana, for that matter...every newbie is intent on usurping your number-one position. Ruhi, in fact, recently replaced you in the Pepsi campaign. Just saw her latest hoardings plastered across the city as I drove up here. I mean, is that the real reason you suddenly agreed to a film like Shabd, *last year, a silent film that turned out to be a box-office disaster...experimentation or desperation?'* Razia frowned.

'Ruhi *bahut khubsurat hai.* She reminds me of how I was in college...She's sexy. Ruhi is hot. As for *Shabd*...it was probably just ahead of its time, I go by the script...'

*'Then, what's with all those top directors – Vikram Bhatt, Ram Gopal Verma, Sanjay Leela Bhansali – replacing you with these PYT's, at the drop of a hat? Five or six films, or is it more? And, why, why on earth, did you just drop out of that Nadiadwala film, days before shooting was to commence, this June, actually, exactly a week after Kulasheshtra's death? You've even returned the full signing amount, one hears...*Mumbai Blitz *broke the news, with a sensational headline, "I need time to heal. I need more than just movies." This coming so soon after Kulasheshtra's whole death drama played out in media...'*

I dabbed the corners of my mouth with a dry tissue: 'It was a good headline, the article too, was well timed...'

'The *Maya Shirale, tinsel town's longest-standing, lead actress who demanded a fee equal to heroes – a feat hitherto unachieved in an overwhelmingly patriarchal industry, delivering back-to-back hits, for so many years, in a row...why this sudden urge to heal? Heal from what? Amitabh Kulasheshtra? The memory of what you both supposedly shared? Also, the* Blitz *piece, as you may be aware, quoted industry insiders who claim you are refusing to entertain script-reading sessions and...there are strong rumours about you pulling out of the first-ever International Indian Film Academy Awards in October in London, where you were slated to receive a Lifetime Achievement award. And, even if that news hasn't been fully confirmed, let's face it: Except for a few blink-and-you-miss-them appearances in some random, page three parties, where have you been these past few months, Maya?'*

I supressed a yawn. 'Rumours are our *rozi roti*, keeping us pertinent in public memory, even when our films fail, affairs sour, when our lip jobs and liposuctions go awry. Scandal sells, like sex, Razia. Besides, let's face it, my personal life has always created sensational headlines...the same rumour mills went into overdrive when I moved in with a younger man, an angry, rebellious, debutant Bengali director trying to make off-beat films in Bollywood. You know, when they saw Avi welcoming guests at my house-warming...three years ago. A guy who couldn't get through NCD, a director with no past records, with a massive ego...who, days after his debut feature, bagged a National Award and went on to declare at a packed press conference that he's interested only in dark, hard-hitting cinema...calling himself the *baap* of India's noir revolution, claiming big stars too, will have no choice but to look him in the eye, in years to come. Avik even went on record to call Satyajit Ray overrated, as is Mr. Bachchan! Smirking at anything mass...'

'Wait a minute, aren't Avik and Kulasheshtra similar, in that regard? Is that why you chose him, Maya?' Razia cut me short.

'Who? What are you talking about?'

'Avik Dasgupta, I interviewed AD, days after he bagged the National Award for Anubhuti, *which he mockingly dedicated to Kulasheshtra, by the way. He said if Kulasheshtra hadn't flunked him in the final stage of interviews at the National Centre of Drama, given such a negative feedback, he wouldn't be where he was today. Kulasheshtra's rejection shattered his self-worth to pieces, supposedly hardened him, making him immune to criticism, failure...It's all over the Net,'* she pointed at my cell-phone, lying on the seat between us.

I picked it up, leaning forward. Razia looked away, embarrassed at my generously displayed cleavage...

'I hate the internet, Razia...it's fucked up this world, our sanity, our privacy. I can't for the life of me understand why Avi needs to be constantly wired to it. He insists it's his oxygen. Staring at his laptop for hours on end, glued to his tab, watching films, always on the phone, networking constantly. I've even started calling it my "*souten*" it's, it's a joke, really...' I laughed.

'That's *filmi!*'

I winked. 'Well, I *am* like that, I suppose. *Filmi.*'

My cell-phone vibrated just then. I disconnected the call, pushing my sunglasses over my head. Razia stared back at her writing pad. I watched her in silence for a while, how her *kurti* rode up over her thighs, the way she crossed her knees, defensively, every few seconds.

'Maya, would you also agree that AD and you defy the conventional norms of celeb couple-dom? In the way that both of you lead separate lives, for instance? She cleared her throat.

'Conventional?'

'I mean, isn't that the biggest grouse your critics bear against you, that for so many years, and, even as you ruled the box-office,

reigning over commercial cinema, the real guys, so-called serious directors, never gave you as much of a second glance, calling you superficial and sexy, hardly an actor, more a performer? In fact, your contemporary, Sahana Mukherjee, who debuted a couple of months after you and was your fiercest rival at one point, has today gracefully graduated to becoming the face of alternate cinema in India. Maya, weren't you jealous when AD mentioned in the Bombay Times *front page interview after he won the National Award that Sahana was exactly his kind of heroine...you guys had already moved in together, by then? Still, he preferred Sahana, casting her as the lead in* Anubhuti.'

She was trying to get me to react.

'Sahana is more suited to the kind of roles Avik envisages. And, I've always gone on record to say that Avi has a keen eye for casting. Think it's to do with his theatre background... the way he doesn't confuse commerce while characterizing,' I calmly clarified, applying a fresh coat of lip colour.

'*Talking about theatre, Maya, wasn't Amitabh Kulasheshtra also planning to cast you in a film he was to allegedly direct... almost a decade ago...?*' she quickly put in her next question.

'It was a long time ago...'

My phone buzzed again on my lap.

'It's Avi...he's calling again...' I muttered, distractedly.

'*Do you love AD, Maya? Is Maya Shirale ready to settle down with Avik Dasgupta? Is that what you meant by wanting more than movies?*'

'Avi hates that phrase "settling down", Razia. He finds marriage regressive and stifling...His own parents had a sort of long distance marriage that he seldom brings up. His dad was in the army. Avi says there was hardly a time he saw his folks do anything together, as a couple. Guess it's why he lacks a substantive memory of them as a family. At least, it's what I tell him, hoping, perhaps to explain his insistent hatred of anything conventionally or socially "pleasant". Avi's cynicism is far too deep-seated,' I tried to explain.

'Like...like your own arrogance, Maya? You know, dodging reporters, arriving late for commercial shoots, quoting sky-high rates, walking out on producers at the last minute, asking them to rewrite scenes as per your wishes and even insisting they drop top heroes; forcing directors to reschedule overseas shoots citing something as basic as a migraine, demanding first-class air tickets and hotel accommodation for each of your support staff...this crazy addiction to sleeping pills and chain smoking, that is widely publicized...a sort of self-annihilating lifestyle...is it also a deep-seated reaction to something, something deeper, perhaps?'

'Everyone has heard stories of my past. It's all related to my father, Razia. What he did to me, all those years ago, in that squalid housing colony in Pune...' I was tiring of this tirade.

'Is that all, Maya?'

'Isn't that enough? I don't understand what more you want out of me, Razia...this is the truth, or, at least, as close to the damn truth that I've ever got with a media person. Besides, you have had a lot more than twenty minutes,' I said emphatically, hoping to wind up the Q&A there and then.

'I know, and I am grateful for the audience granted, Maya. But, all this on your father has been quoted earlier. It's public information, where you're concerned, since you've always been explicit about your past...' Razia was relentless.

'So? What makes you question it now?'

'Because, I don't think you came here to forget that pain, Maya...this sea, this expanse of nothingness that you watch so carefully, studying it like a lifeguard...this eerie silence...when someone likes you removes her masks...one by one...it can't be only for what her father did to her,' she looked intently into my eyes.

'Let's talk about all this, some other time, Razia...' I waved out at Alam.

Razia watched him start the car.

Then, just as I lit my last cigarette, she pursed her lips again: '*Maya, look, I'm going to be as blunt as I can. Were you involved in a romantic relationship with Amitabh Kulasheshtra, as was speculated almost a decade back when he had allegedly walked out of his home, and marriage? Was Kulasheshtra actually coming to Mumbai, to see you, two months, ago, before this unfortunate incident? Did you know he was on his way here the day that he died?*'

AVIK DASGUPTA

I watched Maya sleep, her lips trembling every now and then, her left hand resting lightly on her chest. I planted a gentle kiss on her forehead, careful not to wake her. It was 10 am. Maya had missed her aqua aerobics class at the Bombay Gymkhana Club. Her discarded negligee lay casually dropped on the carpeted floor. Its colour flaming red; its length short – like she was wearing the day our paths first crossed in Filmistan Studios, almost three years ago.

I remembered our first encounter distinctly. I was visiting the sets of *Benaam Mohabbat.* The Second Assistant Director was a friend of mine. Srinivas had promised to introduce me to his producer who was supposedly taking the leading lady out for dinner. It was a late-night shoot at Mehboob Studios. When the shot was over, Maya sauntered up to me, a complete stranger. 'Was the shot okay?' she had asked smiling coquettishly and walked off without waiting for me to reply.

'Frankly, you could have done better,' I called after her, raising my voice on purpose, acting as if I didn't know who she was, and that I cared two hoots for her so-called celebrity status.

She had stopped, turned around, and walked back to me. Then deliberately leaning in close she reached into my shirt pocket for my mobile phone. She gave herself a missed call from my phone, and handed it back to me, bringing her lips close to my ear: 'Save it, and call me so I can get some tips from you next time, *babumoshai*...' she had whispered throatily.

Srinivas had looked thoroughly embarrassed, trying to introduce us, clumsily. Maya didn't acknowledge him. She just waved at me and walked off.

I didn't call her, of course, though I ensured that I saved her number in my phone book, seconds after she sashayed away.

I next saw Maya a few months later at an awards ceremony where was I Srinivas's plus one, and, later at the after party organized by the same film magazine. I didn't talk to her during the party, and neither did she make an effort to greet me or make eye contact, and yet there was something that compelled me to follow her, wordlessly, into the VIP enclosure where her Mercedes was parked, post-midnight, as she exited all by herself, unescorted; a rarity in Maya's case.

Her regular driver, Alam, she mentioned later, had called in sick.

Maya too was running a slight temperature.

I closed my eyes, thinking back to how we'd paid off the *badli* driver in a rush, making torrid love in the backseat. Maya was as smashed as I had been. She didn't even bother asking me my name. It probably was just another one-night stand for her, I told myself. But we couldn't keep our hands off each other, even kissing desperately in the lift after I drove her home, her thighs wrapped tightly around mine; my fly still undone. It wasn't the first time I was having sex with a total stranger...and yet...

Now I stubbed out my cigarette and studied Maya again. She was sleeping on her stomach now. The curve of her buttocks made me hard instantly.

My first film-shoot for *Anubhuti* had commenced approximately eight months after that one night of passion with Maya, and I had left for Ladakh. I'd made no attempt to contact Maya, to inform her of the same, and nor did she reach out to me, to thank me for driving her home. Anyway, it was the night of the last outdoor. It was snowing heavily. I'd never experienced snowfall like that before. It was so starkly white all around, I felt incredibly alone. Like this hole had opened up inside me…

I don't know why, all of a sudden, I began missing my father, missing him physically, after years. I was utterly desolate, somewhere my heart was breaking. Then out of the blue, I dialled Maya.

A part of me was anxious that I had blown my chances with her. Or, that she had in all probability, either forgotten, or never really registered me. I mean, Maya Shirale had quite a reputation…

Now, I reached out and gently stroked her hair. I had never told Maya why I had called her from Ladakh, in the middle of the night. The same way I had never brought up my dead father or spoken of my actual feelings for her.

It was a kind of silent pact we had. We would never discuss our past. Dissect our mistakes.

We still didn't…

Just then Maya turned on her side, slowly opening her eyes, and wrapped her arms around my waist. 'What's the matter, *babumoshai*? You look unhappy after last night's sex. I thought you liked doing it that way? Want another go?'

I was peeved. 'I hate it when you make it sound like that, so damn vulgar.'

'Vulgar? C'mon, Avi. Stop behaving like a little boy. Sulking again, bad day at work, last night, huh?'

'I thought you liked me acting like a little lost boy. Isn't that what you had called me after dumping my script for *Anubhuti* in the dustbin?'

Maya propped herself up against a satin cushion: 'I just love how you Bong men are always so agitated! Come on, it's going to rain any minute. I want you inside me. I want you deeper…one more time. But go shave, first. I have scratch marks all over my cleavage.'

'Whatever you say, madam, it's your house, after all,' I said irately, and got up from the bed.

Maya grabbed my arm: '*Uff!* Okay, sorry, baba…Avi, stop…tell me…what were you trying to say? Earlier? You mentioned you needed to talk…'

'Well, that can wait, but shaving obviously can't. Besides, look at the state of my Bong manhood!'

'Just talk to me, please. I know you've been trying all of last week…I'll get you aroused again, no problem. I know what works.'

I sat down with a sigh. 'Okay, I give in.' I turned to look her in the eye: 'Maya, is everything okay with us? Between us, I mean, and I am not talking about this shit.'

'Calling sex shit? That's the best part about us; that no matter what, we always manage to get the formula correct in bed! This shit always gets better with us! C'mon, *babumoshai*, you must agree?'

'And is that all it is, Maya? We've been seeing each other for a while now and still I have no clue about your whereabouts when you leave for the day. You switch off your cell for hours. Knowing that I will worry and stay up just staring at the door. Do you know how many times I called Alam all through last week?' A part of me was furious at how I was beginning to sound like the whiny woman in our relationship.

'I must've been tied up with something. C'mon Avi, you're pretty preoccupied yourself. Besides, it's not like I've stopped giving you *just* the kind of the attention you like the best.'

'I hate it when you generalize stuff…'

'Then what is this about, all of a sudden? The morning after we fuck like rabbits?'

'Must you always be this graphic?'

'Oh, stop with your self-righteous crap, Avi, and tell me what is *really* going on, huh? What's on your fucking mind? Is it that *Blitz* article that seems to have suddenly become the talk of town?'

'Perhaps it is. Why did you take Razia Siddiqui from *Filmworld* magazine to Chowpatty, Maya? Hiding even that simple fact from me? And what was that about Kulasheshtra being the love of your life?'

'Alam – that bastard has been talking to you again! I'm going to fire that swine. He's gotten too big for his boots. How dare he two-time me, bloody *chutiya*!'

'Why, Maya? Why will you take away his job, just because he was honest with me, when I kept calling to check on you, to just make sure you were okay, after the production team told me you had left with Razia after wrapping up the shoot? Who's at fault here? Alam, because he cares a helluva lot about you, or me, because I care more?'

'I, Maya Shirale, happen to pay Alam's salary, Avi. He better do what I say! Even if that means keeping his mouth shut. *Saala namakharam.*'

'And what does that make me? Am I now another Alam in your life? A recipient of your mega-star status? Your mercy? Your money? Your mood swings?'

'Well, I don't recall having ever asked you to wait outside my car, or pay my bills, or get my laundry hand-delivered, have I now, Mr. Avik Dasgupta? In fact, if memory serves me right, you were practically living off me, till a year and half ago when your lot slightly improved, thanks to the National Award.' Maya tried to stop herself: 'Please, Avi, don't get me started…'

'You're the one who started this, Maya.'

'No *babumoshai*, you did. I was just happy to suck your balls.'

'There you go again!'

'Balls *bola toh*? Big deal! You men are all fucking hypocrites. Want the shag and yet can't take it when a woman spells it to your face.'

'No, Maya, I still love the way you suck my balls. But, sometimes, *just* sometimes, a real conversation would be appreciated. Agreed, we're both busy people. This damn industry also demands so much out of everyone. Our time, our bodies, our brains…our contacts…there is no end to the networking. And yes, you're right about another thing, I *have* gotten busier with my next film's casting…maybe, the Filmfare Critics Award recognition has worked…and I am emerging out of the shadows. But, in all this, there are times I want *only* you, Maya. I want to share my life with you. I thought we were supposed to go to Rocky Ratnani's calendar launch, followed by the charity dinner at JW together. I waited a lot, Maya, before finally calling on Alam's cell. And, just FYI, he didn't pick up at first, either. He messaged saying you were in some meeting.'

'Maybe, I was actually in one, Avi? I don't remember every detail of my day.'

'Babe, I trust you. The other day too, I knew you were going to be tied up till evening. That's why I never dropped by on the sets of the Lux shoot. I knew you had said yes to that just for the money that you had to return to Nadiadwala. I also know it was partly because you had promised to pump funds into my film, in case I don't manage a decent producer. I know the pressures on you, Maya…maybe that's why I was feeling bad too…guilty, restless. I just wanted whisk you away, somewhere...anywhere…'

'I hear you, Avi, but I don't need whisking away. Now is there something you'd *really* like to discuss, other than this long-winded spiel about our relationship? I have an appointment with my cosmetic surgeon and I need to shower and get going. So, can we do this later?'

'What's gotten into you, Maya? Another surgeon? I find you super-hot...so, if this is about us...'

'This has nothing to do with us. This is about my life, my face and my body, Avi.'

'In other words, my opinion doesn't count, right?'

'Cut the guilt trip, kid. It's not like you were planning to spend all morning tucked inside my blanket. Going in and out of me.'

'And what if I said I was? What if *I* was the unpredictable one, huh?'

'It's not your style, Avik Dasgupta. That's what attracted me to you in the first place. What I find so irresistible about you, still. C'mon, I liked you because you were not awed by my star status, and the fact that I had my own life. It's why I overlooked so much when we hooked up...your struggling status, your empty bank account, your ego hassles – that were legendary, at some level – even your last fling with that small-time TV actress...all of the baggage that a man like you came with...'

'Was it really *that* bad, Maya?'

'No, Avi...and, honestly, I don't keep a *hisab-kitab* of my relationships, analysing every incy-wincy, intimate, disgusting detail, all the freaking time.'

'Really, Maya?'

'What?'

'Is that why we won't talk about Amitabh Kulasheshtra? Even once, Maya?'

RK CHOPRA

I was desperate to see Sarla.

My lawyer, a smooth-talking South Mumbai chap advised me against travelling out of the city till the income-tax officials were off my trail, as were Bhai's *supari* killers. We were talking to ministers and gangsters at the same time. 'It's all a matter of what clicks, first RK.' He texted me again that morning when I told him I had an urgent family matter to attend to:

'Family?' he'd responded, adding a wink emoji.

Monty was in the US. I had managed to sneak him out. My second wife, Pamela, had also been temporarily shut-up, silenced by promises of a heftier monthly allowance and another pent-house somewhere in town.

I ran my hands over the crumpled sheets.

For all the hundreds of women I had slept with, Sarla was the only woman I had ever loved. I fell back on the bed, eyes clamped shut. 'Banno…' I moaned, imagining my head pressed between her heaving breasts.

Dada Saheb had not been impressed with my audition for *Mitti*, a politically provocative tale of a Dalit farmer whose land is encroached upon by an upper-class landlord, and who is subsequently asked to give up his wife – for one night of fun with the landlord – to get his land back. When the farmer refuses, the exploitative landlord kidnaps the wife, but eventually falls in love with her. The woman too slowly develops feelings for her kidnapper – their forbidden love challenging caste boundaries, questioning the sanctity of marriage, the wife of the Dalit farmer, equally oppressed, her body, her bane. The first time I met Sarla, and Amitabh Kulasheshtra…

◈

'You look too affluent for the role of the Dalit…which is why I considered you to play the *zamindar*…you have the height and build I am looking for but it seems to me that you are probably too young, too restless…' Dada Saheb shook his head, disapprovingly, seconds after I had finished reading my lines.

A young man, probably a year, older, walked in just then and sized me up, saying:

'The age of the *zamindar* can always be altered. I mean, his physique is compelling…also what if we can make a change to the script; what if the landlord's young son abducts the daughter of the Dalit farmer, instead? The son who has just, maybe, returned from England? His diction, age and looks fit the part perfectly in that situation…it can be more of a second-generation tussle and we can always show the daughter as being newly married?'

I was caught by the intensity in his gaze.

The man turned to me and offered his hand: 'Amitabh…I assist Dada Saheb…'

'This is a scorching satire, son, set in a poor village in Maharashtra's Marathwada region, not a flippant love story…Our intention is not just to agitate, but provoke us, the casteist audience. *Mitti* shall lend itself to the rise of a new cultural genre...chronicling tales of oppression that were never talked about openly,' Dada Saheb frowned, looking around at his other cast members for approval.

'Besides, we haven't auditioned for a young woman... who will play the part of the young daughter?' Govind Bhai, a regular in all Joglekar productions, interrupted; probably trying to please him as well.

I folded my hands and prepared to leave the stage.

'Wait!' Amitabh commanded, adding impatiently, 'Where's Sarlu? She was right here, reading the lines...Sarlu will fit the role of the young Dalit woman...In fact, she looked too immature for the earlier part...and she happens to be a very emotive actress. She has a resilient strength, and her build is perfect for the role...can we at least see how they look together on stage? Will someone fetch her, please?'

Dada Saheb looked a little taken aback by this direct challenge to his authority, but he didn't protest. He spoke in hushed whispers to Govind Bhai, as I shuffled my feet, waiting silently for the final verdict.

Just then Sarla came back. 'Sarlu...where did you disappear? Here, go on, here, read *these* lines...quick...' Amitabh pushed her on stage and thrust some pages into her hand.

Her simple handloom cotton sari clung to her broad hips, her face was reddened from the dull heat outside. Her hair was managed in a lengthy plait, decorated with a solitary white flower, tucked neatly behind her left ear.

'A man like you cannot love a woman. A man like you can only destroy,' her lips quivered, as she mouthed the lines Amitabh had quickly changed. Getting into character with complete ease. There was no overacting. No histrionics. The lines as she spoke them shone through with a rare integrity.

Dada Saheb stood up in a huff. 'Anger, rage, resentment...I need the revolution, understand! Not a whimpering, lovesick woman,' he hollered.

Amitabh calmly told Sarla to continue reading from the script he had given her, in the same way she had been emoting, and then gestured to me to continue:

'What I feel for you has nothing to do with my father...what I feel for you is more than passing lust...' I thundered, lunging forward, my chest heaving. My throat was parched.

Was I still clumsy in my dialogue delivery?

Sarla brushed aside a strand of hair from her eyes. Stepping forward, she straightened her back, returning to the script:

'The colour of my skin is different from yours, Sahib. As is the texture of my hands...hardened from toiling in the sun all day. My hair is matted, stinking of cow dung...These breasts that you stare at lust-ridden now, are shrunken with the load of the harvest I carry in the evenings...my body belongs to this parched, brown soil...I cannot be separated from it, at any cost, from my people, at any cost. If you want me, you must make me a promise first...' her eyes glittered provocatively.

Dada Saheb appeared stunned, sifting through his hand-written script.

There was pin-drop silence.

'You must kill your father...avenge the death of my forefathers, the usurpation of our agricultural fields. Drink water from the well that shades my courtyard...become one of us,' Sarla placed her hands on my chest.

I was mesmerized. I couldn't take my eyes off her lips, as they slowly opened and closed, the way she swallowed hard, after each line. The force of my attraction towards her made it difficult to breathe.

'This war will be bigger, more dangerous,' I mumbled self-consciously, slipping my fingers in hers, making a tight fist.

'The war has been ongoing, Sahib...My flesh is marked with ugly scars for every woman your people raped and murdered; for every child who was forbidden to drink water from a temple well;

for my father's land that he tilled till your people snatched it away from him, forcibly; for the river you forbade us to bathe in; for this skin, that you hunger for...I am a Dalit woman, Sahib. This war is in my womb...' Sarla closed her eyes, I took a step closer, till our mouths were almost touching, her cheekbones glistening in the half-light.

We both held our positions.

Transfixed, like everyone else present.

'What do you think of it?' Amitabh's eyes scoured Dada Saheb's gaunt face.

'*Mitti* is about Dalit assertiveness and the perpetual power struggle in Maharashtra between the landowner class and the subdued class. We are here to challenge the larger system, son,' he answered tersely.

'Challenge, how?' Amitabh raised his voice. 'What use is art, if it does not deal with real people? If we will hide the social injustices real men and women are facing behind silent Gods and buxom Goddesses? When we can't show crude human emotions – when a woman is still depicted in dance and not as an unapologetic warrior? The world is changing, and theatre, *natak* needs to adapt...political means people!'

Dada Saheb had placed his hands on his hips, his brow creased into a menacing frown.

'The battle in *Mitti* is just not against upper-caste people, per se, it is against the prejudice that arises from casteist thinking. What if the term "Dalit" is an umbrella phrase that includes not just people belonging to the so-called Schedules Castes, but tribals, transgenders, women...like her... discriminated sections who lack a voice or representation... who live on the fringes of popular and political consciousness and conscience. Remember you had told me the story of *Uncle Tom's Cabin*, right?' Amitabh threw his arms up in the air, adding, impatiently, 'the author wasn't an African American. Does that make the story any less authentic? Aesthetic integrity in voice matters more than identity conferred at birth.'

Sarla was quick to defend her father, hoping perhaps to camouflage her obvious attraction to me...our instant chemistry, on stage, and, in person. Or maybe, she wanted to wiggle her way into her father's heart. Dada Saheb had not bothered to pay her a compliment for her rousing act. How she had switched expressions, expertly, like a seasoned performer.

I was pretty certain that there was more to this than met the eye.

'Why did you tamper with the screenplay, just to accommodate this new actor, Amitabh? You know very well that this was a play about the evils of casteism and power struggles...you can't suddenly alter the entire context! Make it about this woman...her honour...her battle...her body...' Her eyes glinted.

Amitabh bowed his head for a few seconds. 'What if,' he slowly resumed, continuing, as he pointed his fingers at her eyes, 'what if your body...your body *is* that war zone, Sarlu? What if a woman is the one who bears the cuts of any larger mass battle? What if it all started here...here...in the space between your breasts...or the gap between your thighs...in the darkness of your sex...'

We all gasped at the audacity of his words. But even Dada Saheb listened in silence.

'*Can you return my honour, sahib? Can you take my hand, here, in front of all your people? Is my war, now, also, yours? Are we both victims of a larger social oppression? Have you ever lain awake...on ghor Amavasya nights...listening to the beating of your own heart? Wondering whether God divided men? Was he a Dalit? A woman? A wife?*' Amitabh thundered, reading aloud from the script.

There was a slow clap.

Dada Saheb stood up, facing me.

'I have to agree with Amitabh, here. Rakesh suits the role of a younger man, a lot better…maybe, as the England returned son of the landlord, as he proposes…I see a flicker of promise, Rakesh, despite the fact that you don't have much experience in theatre…I'd like you to stay on, at least, for a while…if you commit yourself to the stage, surrender to the medium…'

Sarla clutched Amitabh's forearm, biting her lower lip, the worry lines on her face easing into a slow smile of disbelief.

'And you, show me those rewritten lines from the beginning, will you, now? Only then shall I take a final call,' Dada Saheb indicated to Amitabh to follow him.

They left the stage together. Their heads bowed, already deep in discussion.

From the corner of my eyes, I saw you murmur a prayer. Your cheeks flushed. Your eyes clamped shut.

Whom were you really happy for, that day, Banno?

SARLA KULASHESHTRA

It had rained all of last night. I had watched the showers recede, sitting all alone by the edge of the portico, just after the sun came up. In the same spot where Amitabh and I had shared our last night together – before he had disappeared forever, the next afternoon. On the train to death.

It had been over two months since his passing and I had not come to peace with his death; and I don't mean grief, I mean a seething, pent-up anger. The court-case against Rawat was still pending, even though almost all the witnesses had turned hostile. So much of the hard-earned money that I had stored away as savings was being siphoned away in lawyers' fees without any real hope of closure.

Amitabh had been my father's choice, not mine. But why had I never spoken up myself? Told my father the truth about my feelings? Was I scared to break Dada Saheb's heart – the same way I had silently pined for his fatherly attention, having grown up more as his *'shishya'* than his only child? Sarat Chandra Joglekar's reputation was intimidating; akin to my helplessness, in many ways.

When I fretted about Amitabh's coldness, my mother had said: 'Amitabh is an aloof man; his communication is akin to a sign language, you will get used to it over time. Like your father, that boy is built for fame, just you see…'

For the rest of my married life, she had always made it a point to harp on the fact that Amitabh was so very obedient to Dada Saheb; never buying my logic that he was perhaps just plain selfish: agreeing to marry a woman he had never loved to earn a theatre company in dowry. When I accused her of deliberately destroying my relationship with Rakesh she said, 'I'm sorry. But I think you misunderstood my intentions. You had no future with that over-smart, loud-mouthed, over-ambitious chap. Your father knew that all along, being an astute observer of people, and having also had an inkling that Rakesh and you were up to something. Besides, Rakesh was never cut out for this business. Like Amitabh was.'

And when Amitabh walked out on the 'family business' she had another ready answer:

'Your father, as you know, was heartbroken when Amitabh left his company, but he never held Amitabh's raging ambition against him...in fact, he regretted how the bitterness stayed...why Amitabh never returned, as a son. He always said that you were blessed to have a husband like him. Created for greatness. Born to be famous. Fearless.'

The evening after my father's explosive announcement, I had thrown myself into Rakesh's arms, whimpering as I begged him to publicly declare our love and save me from my impending nuptials.

'He's only agreed to marry me so that he can inherit the legacy of Dada Saheb...Amitabh's nothing but a cunning bastard who's finally shown his true colours. I can't believe how naïve I was...to believe he would ever have any loyalty towards me...first...for introducing him to my father...for confiding in him about us...backstabbing me this way...' I had sobbed, burying my head against Rakesh's sturdy chest.

'No, no, Banno, he's bound by a sacred *gurudakshina*...'

'What? What kind of *gurudakshina*? That demands a woman have no voice...that traps her, lifeless...'

'There is talk…everyone in the company knows as well… Something your father allegedly demanded from Amitabh by offering your hand in matrimony…Amitabh cannot say no to his mentor. Not after all that he has done for him…you all are practically family…me…I, I am the, the outsider…' Rakesh's nostrils flared.

'You think a boy who cold-heartedly stormed out on his own blind father can ever love me unconditionally? Ever be loyal? Rakesh, please, look at me, listen. Hear me out. I don't care what Dada Saheb thinks or feels, all I know is that I don't want to be a sacrificial lamb at the altar of theatre, I only wish to marry you, to love you the rest of my life. I cannot accept Amitabh as my life partner…as…' my words trailed.

Rakesh looked down at me before shrugging my hands off him: 'You are promised to Amitabh, now, Banno... It is not in my hands…you belong to another.'

◈

As a young girl, full of the idea of true love and stories I had seen and performed in on stage, I had never imagined I'd have had such a loveless marriage formalized in a quick, no-frills, government office registration – one that felt like a protest; an agreement entered into sans the emotion of romantic promises. Minus the ties of age-old tradition. The buoyant cheering of loved ones. I had not even worn the customary nine-yard sari. Amitabh had no family. Or friends, in particular.

'Next witness,' the wiry registrar had cried in a peculiar nasal voice, cleaning his right ear with a matchstick, pushing a thick, hardbound ledger towards us.

The *sarkari daftar* where we tied the knot and were officially pronounced man and wife was dimly lit and dirty.

Oversized white fans, their elongated blades laden with dust and grime, emitted a creaking noise. The stairway leading up was wet with spat-out paan juice.

We signed our names in silence.

I bowed my head as Amitabh placed a slim gold *mangalsutra* around my neck. His breath falling over my back. It was a gift from my mother. There were no fragrant garlands exchanged. No sweets fried in desi ghee forcibly stuffed inside our mouths. No photographs of that day. I touched his feet shortly afterwards, feeling nothing.

No happy wedding memories, to look back on…Because that's what Amitabh believed in. Convincing my parents that a no-fuss, low-cost, civil ceremony was appropriate for the occasion. That it would suffice. That it was right.

On our way back, Dada Saheb praised him for his principles. 'Sensible,' was the word he used, I think.

◈

In the first few months of our marriage I took refuge in a sullen silence. I hadn't uttered a single word to Amitabh for a fortnight after my father announced our impending marriage before the whole troupe. I searched only for Rakesh in my mind, desperate to blame everyone else for the way things had panned out for us. Knowing in my heart that Rakesh had hurt me just as deeply by giving up on me without a fight. I shuddered every time I recalled how he had remained withdrawn on purpose.

Had he wanted to hurt me back or was he as trapped a victim of circumstance as I was? Torn equally between duty and desire? The night we had made love, slowly faded into a distant, disturbing memory, that only returned in painful, slow waves to haunt my mind. To keep me lying awake, night after night.

◈

After marriage, my days were all the same. Colourless. There had been nothing special or different about June 10, 2002, either.

The day Amitabh died.

In the morning, I had walked to the *sabzi mandi*, at a stone's throw from the house, taking longer than usual to return, holding a heavy bag of vegetables in each hand. I usually did the monthly groceries by the first of every new month. But that particular month I had been a little strapped for cash. I stood in the kitchen preparing the same breakfast we ate daily, before the part-timer arrived. I usually ate my breakfast alone in the dining room whereas Amitabh was sent his on a steel tray to his room. The nurse helped him with his meal. Drinking my second cup of tea, I finished the accounts – a ledger of sorts that I maintained. Muttering the numbers to myself, tilting my neck, as lines of sweat trickled down the side of my ears. I barely noticed when Amitabh told me he was going out. He had a bag with him, which he wanted me to keep for him, but I was halfway through my accounts and didn't pay him much attention.

It was a sweltering June day. I glanced outside at the garden for a few seconds, taking a deep breath. The air felt heavy with showers, and yet there was not a drop of rain. Just before noon, I decided to indulge in a long, leisurely bath, shuddering as the cool water stored in an aluminium *balti*, zigzagged sluggishly over my stomach. My fingers lingered over the crooked line of uneven stitches from my C-section. My heart beating faster, as it still did, at the thought of my dead child.

I draped a rough cotton towel around my shoulders, leaving my wet hair loose, letting it dry, instead of instantly plaiting it up, and made my way into a secluded part of our garden, slowly peeling an orange, the afternoon sun caressing my lower back.

As I dried my undergarments on the clothesline, I heard the sound of the landline ringing persistently. It was my mother, in all probability. She always rang at the same time. So, I didn't rush in to receive her call. The last thing I needed was another showdown or sermon.

Talking to my mother always had a deep negative effect on me; she had always plotted behind my back; wanting to make me that which I wasn't. She claimed to have my interests at heart, since I was a child, but her views had always clashed with mine. Stubborn and perennially focused on social niceties, she had never really allowed me a separate point of view. Always judging me harshly…my mistakes, my marriage, Maya…The pompous way she loved declaring that she was born with a black tongue; making it sound like a power more than an ill-omen. How was it a good thing to be able to predict failure? Sadness? Betrayal? Barrenness?

And yet, she had kept her black tongue in check when my father had married me off to Amitabh.

The phone rang again as I remembered a previous visit my mother had made, soon after my daughter died.

◈

'I have a question?' My mother had said.

'Let me fix you lunch first. It's past two.'

'How do you do this, Sarla?'

'Do what? Fix lunch for my mother? It's simple…see here, here I am getting up and walking towards the kitchen, where Meena-tai is adding the finishing touches to the dal. She's very good, actually, Meena-tai.'

'I wasn't talking about your servant, Sarla. I'm talking about that other girl, in that room upstairs, the one next to the terrace? I've seen her; that chit of a girl who has been walking around your home, for the past few months, since Amitabh was away in Paris...the way you refuse to let her go...telling everyone she has no home of her own...I always find her preening in front of a mirror, mumbling to herself, as if she were possessed. Is she your surrogate daughter now? A fix for your lack of company? I mean, have you even asked Amitabh if he is okay with her staying? Actually, it's this thing you do, this pattern you have cultivated over time, Sarla. Even with that girl, have you ever thought she might be a substitute for the daughter you lost? A *sakha.* Someone to protect, and lean on?'

'Oh, so this is about her, then? The real reason you've came to visit. I was thinking what brought you to Pune, to us, again? What brought you back ever since you left after Maya's death?'

'I came here to warn you, Sarla, about how you are making a huge mistake. There's a difference between an old servant woman and a young, nubile girl on the threshold of womanhood. You shouldn't trust her blindly. Why can't she rent a place of her own and move out? I mean...God knows with what intention she came to meet Amitabh, in the first place? Wake up. Before it's too late. Trust me, I am your mother. I have seen the world.'

'What are you so worried about?'

'I don't want to say it. My father and yours, used to often say I have a black tongue. It's just that I have your best interests at heart...'

'You said the same thing to me after you found Rakesh and me together one night, when I broke down in your arms, confessing to you about how much I loved him, even swearing on Ganpati Bappa. You assured me that you would try your best to convince Dada Saheb that he was my choice. Instead, in front of him, you said I could never be happy with a man like RK, a non-Maharashtrian, that one could never trust

Punjabis; that he lacked Amitabh's loyalty, and talent…I can never forgive you that betrayal.'

Then I had snapped at her: 'Now why don't you just come to the point? It used to be your strong point once.'

'Fine…I will say it to your face: I am sure this young thing will eventually sleep with your husband, seduce Amitabh and wreck your marriage. Amitabh is a man, Sarla, and he's bound to get attracted towards her physically, being years younger and nubile…and, by not sensing this danger beforehand, by continuing to be so naive and not focusing on filling the lacuna in your lives, after little Maya, you are making a colossal error in judgment...'

'Meena-tai, please can you make another hot roti for my mother? The dal is delicious. Another helping?' I was deliberately trying to shut her up.

'No, thanks Sarla, I'm not hungry anymore.'

'But…you've hardly touched your food.'

'Does it matter, if I have? I mean, here I am, going on and on about the dangers lurking around your own house… and you're not even listening! This is the last time I'm going to say it, in any case. You are on the verge of losing the little that you have. Your marriage...Amitabh…your reputation… this…all this…for a chit of a girl. Shameless tramp…actress my foot! Just another common city whore.'

'Get out of my home, Mother. Just leave me. Leave us, alone.'

◈

A hailstorm had been predicted for June 10. A storm that had never quite come with the ferocity it should have. I had finally pushed open the heavy wooden door with both hands, and answered the phone.

'Mrs. Sarla Kulasheshtra...I am afraid there is some bad news,' the man on the other line had said, after I had answered.

◈

Today, August 17, was Amitabh's birthday. I hadn't entertained too many visitors in the months that had followed the immediate frenzy after his death, wanting to make sense of all the noise. The allegations about his illness. His character. His motive in boarding a train to Mumbai. His being away from the public eye, after Malegaon. The way they dragged him and his politics into the dirt. Every discussion about his greatness as a theatre stalwart inevitably turned into a robust television debate or an opinionated obituary.

I turned on the radio. The song playing was an old favourite: *'Abhi na jao chhodh kar, ke dil abhi bhara nahi...*In my mind, I imagined Rakesh singing the song to me the way he did, tipping his beret, copying Dev Anand's signature move. How I used to laugh when he did that.

An old ache rose and fell. I asked myself if it was fair to blame Rakesh or Amitabh for the way my life had panned out? Hadn't I failed, as well? Citing all the same excuses. The way I didn't have the common courage to reveal the truth to my own father.

I had never been able to forgive Amitabh; to trust him, blindly. I had judged him a long while ago. For not protesting our marriage, as he rightfully should have. For hurting me so fiercely when our little child died. For his affair with the girl I had taken in as my own. Amitabh and I had lived under the same roof, but I only knew of his work through media reports. I had never sought to read his writing or watch his plays; I had always been too proud to.

I had never really comprehended, nor quite cared for, Amitabh's deep-seated angst; his seething need to rebel against any kind of establishment or systemic exploitation. The months he spent locked up. Writing ferociously. Or far away from home: meeting starving farmers or wasted whores, living in mud huts and bathing in murky rivers. Desperate to change the way Marathi theatre would be remembered. I never bothered fighting to secure my place in his world, either. Never pleased Amitabh in a way he may have wanted.

Perhaps, it was to teach him a lesson that I played the 'dutiful' wife. I made it a point to ask him what he wanted served for his meals, and yet left the food on the table, covered with stainless steel plates, the rotis, almost always, turned cold, hard. I decorated our home in Pune as impersonally as I could. Everything was clean, but barren. Taking a perverse pleasure in doing everything a homemaker is expected to, but remaining deliberately detached.

I never confronted Amitabh openly about why he accepted my hand in marriage, or thought I needed to talk him out of his decision to take on controversial projects, not protesting either, when he finally broke away from conventional theatre to street theatre; feeling nothing, not even resenting Amitabh his final betrayal.

I always watched, aloof, from a distance, as Amitabh plunged headlong into directing. Committing his life to a form of savage warfare. Becoming Dada Saheb, in a strange way, all over again.

I had never questioned why Amitabh read the books, he read, all day, on some days? Why he had trouble letting go of things. Or felt compelled to try his hand at everything he saw, at once, from miming to martial arts. Being both reckless and reticent. Why he loved walking barefoot, even at the height of summers? Or never trimmed his hair after a point? Or why he slept with a frayed *Gita* underneath his pillow? Or never explicitly asked for children, or sex?

A woman is never taught what she should expect from her marriage. I had never missed Amitabh, in a way I should have: a dull ache that only comes from wanting a man, needing him, inside you, so bad. I never protested the times Amitabh left on another one of his jaunts; preferring the anonymity his absence afforded.

I had not even read his memoir, *Blindside.* I remember how excited he'd been when the first copies came in about two years ago. He had managed to get a small publishing house to put out his work, but they had to withdraw the book when Amol Rawat threatened to sue them, as the court case was still *sub-judice.* I had never read the book because I was not ready to hear his point of view; I was not ready to forgive him.

But today it was his birthday, August 17, and Amitabh had been dead two months. That day, I had finally decided to sort out his cupboard. Amitabh's old clothes still hung inside. I took a deep breath, inhaling his distant scent. That's the first time I missed him physically. The day I acknowledged that I had gradually gotten accustomed to his vague presence; staring at his shapeless black kurtas I fought the same numbing hollowness I had battled with during his sudden, prolonged absences…the new causes he was always eager to espouse.

There was a fierce streak of lightning as I walked downstairs, my breath suddenly rushed. Staring out at the empty hall, I ran outside, barefoot, leaving the front door wide open. The grass underneath my soles, slightly damp. To the small outhouse that had doubled as Amitabh's study.

I had not touched anything in that room since that day. Everything was the way Amitabh had left it. His books. His papers. His study table stacked high with direction notes and set-illustrations etched in pencil. His medicine pouch lay on one side. As did the heavy oxygen cylinder that stood next to his slippers. I hadn't felt a pressing urge to settle his things. Besides, there was always something else. Calls. Letters. Doorbells. Flowers. Journalists. Students. Media.

It was like Amitabh still lived here.

Banished. Yet still breathing.

I pushed one of the windows open, feeling short of breath all of a sudden. Much like the way I had while making my way to Kamala Nehru Hospital, in a shared auto, after being called in to identify a corpse.

I ran my finger down his bookshelf and stopped on a thin volume with a black spine: *Blindside: A Life in Theatre.* I pulled out the dusty book and held it close to my heart. I had never bothered to read Amitabh's autobiography when it had first appeared in print. The first author copy that Amitabh had left on my bedside.

When I opened the book I saw that it had been dedicated to me and to the memory of Maya.

The air, rain-soaked, felt strangely intimate.

ACT TWO

Blindside

MARIE BOURDAINE

BLINDSIDE

Talent is a traitor.

This is something you really know and understand if you have spent your formative years in a moving circus.

Where you see people perform the same old bag of tricks, every night – till the day the trapeze artist, grown immune to the deft strength of his own body, misses the swinging bar; till the day the lion-tamer is mauled by his favourite lion; till the day the circus clown realizes his jokes are on him...

Nothing changes, till the day it changes finally, and forever. The faces, the faeces, the fights, the flings, the fire-eaters, the funny parts...the same tricks to impress the same kind of audience.

No one is really expected to excel in a circus or earn recognition outside its narrow boundaries. What's important is that the crowd claps; that the tickets sell.

The performers are not given any special treatment, either, treated as just another species of performing animal.

Everyone comes in with a set role, a routine, a standard remuneration.

No one bargains in a circus.

No one expects brilliance or creative genius, either.

Those who shine more than the others, leave, chasing bigger dreams.

My earliest memory of my life in Ganesh Circus, is of the makeshift tents where I slept on the bare ground in a large group of people, our limbs entangled in the cramped space, dipped in dry mud, flies swarming over our heads. Fighting for space, our stomachs flat, famished. The air reeking of animal shit.

As a matter of fact, the animals were treated better than us. Fed more generously. Given an occasional second helping, bathed every fortnight in the peak of summer, their bowls always filled to the brim with cold water. They even had coats for winter.

And yet, there was one thing the animals had in common with us. They never slept much either. At night, the sound of their shuffling feet, their deep grunts and lengthy howls rang in our ears. Together we twitched in our disturbed sleep, a slumber from which all dreams had given way to nocturnal terrors.

These disturbed nights providing a sense of continuity, even as towns formed and melted. Crooked train lines disappearing behind tall tree tops. The trapezes dismantled; the sight of slow-moving caravans as we crossed yet another dusty milestone.

The only person I liked in that motley crowd of small talents and stunted people was Manju Bhabhi, the voluptuous wife of our circus manager, Prateik Master. She had no children of her own. She was always dressed in gaudy Georgette sarees, her pallu neatly folded, lengthwise, flopped from her shoulder down to her protruding belly button.

Manju Bhabhi was from Kashmir, a delicate rosebud of a woman. She was very fond of stories, but being unable to read herself, she depended on me to do the needful. She possessed a large treasure trove of books with colourful illustrations. I think Pratiek Master had bought them in a sale from the kabbadi. I would choose a new book, every day. Manju Bhabhi liked nothing better than to lie back in bed, while I sat at her feet, taking gleeful pleasure in correcting my pronunciation, though she herself was semi-literate.

I myself had been taught to read by my mother when I was five and now, at fourteen, read to Manju Bhabhi in the hot afternoons;

the harsh summer sun casting porous patterns on her waist and cleavage, on the exposed parts of her body. As I struggled to look away – a knot forming at the base of my stomach – she stretched herself, moaning suggestively, her blue eyes drooping from the languid torpor of the summer heat and the sound of my adolescent voice that was beginning to crack.

As always, I squatted by the edge of the bed, where her fair feet dangled, the silver anklets riding upwards, as I struggled to glance down. Focus on the chapter I was reading from, modulating my voice, slightly embarrassed at the way it squeaked on occasion, despite me trying all I could to take on the accent of each of the characters. Manju Bhabhi squealed like a child every time I modified my tone, working doubly hard at getting the impersonations right. Sometimes, Manju Bhabhi would bend down, her heaving cleavage in my face, as she gripped my fingers, tracing them over the individual letters...her flawless skin, supple, sensuous...like a memsahib, like those white women with small tits and large eyes.

In my mind, Manju Bhabhi was no less than a movie-star.

Years later, when I met Marie, her porcelain skin and her big, beautiful eyes reminded me of her.

Marie Bourdaine was French.

Like Manju Bhabhi, she was also feminine, fantasy, and forbidden.

◈

Evening was slowly descending over Paris; the bright, laser lights on the Eiffel Tower gleamed incandescently. The Seine shimmered in the distance. I put down my glass of brandy, wiping the corners of my lips, studying the fine lines that now crisscrossed my mouth, in the ornate mirror on the wall of my room in Hotel du Champ de Villiers. The same room that I had first visited Amitabh in. Room number 654.

I ran my fingers over my copy of *Blindside.* A mid-sized, much-thumbed, battered hardback with a black cover, holding it close to my lips. My heart sinking the way it had, when the news of Amitabh's gruesome death had first played out on French national television. His intense stare, the colour of the thick veins on his dark hands, his brooding silences, haunted me for months.

My breath rose and fell, as I slipped my hands inside my lace negligee, weighing my breasts in my palms. I closed my eyes, feeling his touch once again. As vividly as I had then, almost a decade and a half ago.

The project Amitabh had travelled to Paris for was of a magnitude never dreamed of before. It was to be an epic production with a cast of two hundred people, we were informed, as the mega three-month auditions culminated; the French Press going overboard when, for the first time ever, over a hundred entertainers from faraway India – clowns, acrobats, trapeze-artists, percussionists, classical singers, actors, mime-experts, technicians and even snake-charmers – arrived on a long-distance flight, helmed by a man with a name that was difficult to pronounce – someone called Amitabh Kulasheshtra: a dark, brooding, tall, theatre director, probably a few years younger than me, in his early forties.

He was here to stage a legendary Indian classic, penned by an ancient bard, Kalidasa, a sweeping tapestry of love, loss, friendship and betrayal – the test of a woman's fidelity and the wrong-doings of the man she loved. Whose child she carried in her womb. A mighty king, a man of the world, a virile warrior – *La Legende de Sakuntalam* – was to be performed under an open sky, a historic Indo-French artistic collaboration; a magnum-opus of a scale both countries had never before witnessed.

I was chosen to play the role of Sakuntalam – where my fame as the foremost opera singer in France meant that I led the entourage of performers from my nation – in a rousing musical adaptation that would blend the lost traditions of both.

The first week was an orientation of sorts. The Indian contingent was jet-lagged and was having trouble adjusting to the time difference and the starkly divergent food habits. Communication was another grey area. Most of us spoke French, with a smattering of English. While most of them used their own regional language, a smattering of Hindi, and almost no English at all. We shared little in common, except the man who manned this unwieldy ship – who didn't make any extra effort to go out of his way and get familiar with us, his resistant silences and cryptic answers, casting a veil of suspicion, making us unsure of what we had signed up for, in those early days, before we started rehearsing.

The ice was gradually broken over some elaborate team dinners where we were introduced to cuisine from our respective cultures and went on sight-seeing tours together. To foster intimacy, a cultural bonhomie, as it were.

Again, I saw him in my mind's eye, sitting by himself, at the end of the double-decker bus that had been hired to take us all out. 'You, you don't seem to be much interested in history,' I tried striking up a casual conversation with Amitabh, that day, stiffly extending my gloved hand, having walked back to the tour bus by myself to grab a drink of chilled water. He had declined to get off the bus at the various tourist attractions, where it stopped, immersed in making final changes to the script.

Amitabh didn't answer. His head was deep in his manuscript. His well-built arms held it close to his eyes, as he read to himself. His untrimmed, tangled, salt and pepper tresses billowed across his weather-beaten face as he leaned against the window.

'Everyone wants to see the Eiffel Tower...you should too. It is a French treasure,' I broke into a smile.

Wordlessly, Amitabh took off his dark-rimmed reading glasses. Staring at me, intently, he said, '*Man is born free and everywhere he is in chains*...have you read Jean Jacques-Rousseau, Marie?'

I sat down on the empty seat next to him, '*Oui*...my father was a teacher and he made sure my brothers and I studied Voltaire and Rousseau; he insisted on mastering the great thinkers of the Revolution.'

Amitabh absorbed this, nodded briefly, and returned to reading.

'There was...there *seemed*...' I recomposed my sentence, clearing my throat to add, 'there seemed to have been some trouble in India? We were told you might not be directing the production, after all, due to some personal problems? I mean, we almost thought this play would not take off...your name kept coming up...but, I...I mean, we were not really sure you would actually come...and, I just wanted to say, I hope things are better for you...on the home front...'

I drank a large sip of water. Amitabh stared at me over his glasses, but didn't respond.

I soldiered on: 'It's not easy, Monsieur Kulasheshtra, to mount such an ambitious production...to gather so many men and women of so many diverse creative traditions...to think of recasting a classic this way...using performers from a country so very far away from your own...to be able to imagine such a sweeping topography...it requires tremendous vision and, and sheer genius...to get it off the ground...everyone talks of your brilliance here...I pray your problems...I mean, the troubles holding you back, are resolved...' I paused expectantly, wondering if I had said too much. A loose curl kept coming in the way; I shoved it aside, as our eyes met.

'There was a death,' Amitabh said shortly.

I swallowed uncomfortably. 'Oh, I'm so sorry, I didn't know, forgive me for being so insensitive…so direct…' was all I could manage, my throat parched.

'It doesn't matter; I…don't want to talk about it. Tell me about your village instead, Marie. About your first snowfall…your first song…your first kiss…I would like us to know each other better. I cannot kindle the character of Sakuntalam in you until I know who Marie is. Marie Bourdaine…'

I was unsettled by his presence so near me. I gripped the seat in front.

'Yes…' I shook my head, continuing, as my thoughts raced, 'I too need to know more about Sakuntalam to be able to portray her with utmost starkness. Talk to me about her. Tell me the colour of her eyes, how she slept at night when the moon played hide and seek, how her voice sounded, if she had any friends? If Dushyant, the king she signed her heart away to, was the first man she made love to? I want to know everything, Amitabh,' I don't know why I switched to using his first name.

Amitabh finished his cigarette and stubbed it under his toe. 'I am in the hotel across the street from where you all are being put up. I can't seem to get the name, right…Room 654, meet me there this evening and I will tell you all you want to know.'

'Hotel du Champ de Villiers…' I laughed lightly, adding in a soft voice, 'Would you like me to see you alone…tonight…after the official dinner, that is?'

Amitabh touched my face. His slender fingers tracing patterns down my cheekbones. My face powder left a trail on his fingers. 'This has to go,' he dusted his fingertips. 'Sakuntalam was a child of the forest, untamed, completely natural, without artifice…she decorated her lengthy tresses with hand plucked blooms…'

That night I knocked on the door of his room.

'How did you hurt your head?' I asked impulsively, minutes after entering inside, after he had taken my coat, tossing it casually on his unmade bed. Gesturing to me, that I be seated there, if I so wished.

'Ballav Salve,' he replied cryptically, sitting next to me, his tanned arms brushing my thighs, making me strangely restless.

'Ball…Salve? What is that?' I asked naively.

'Not what, *who.*' Amitabh corrected me. 'Salve was a militant union leader in India chosen by a majority of Mumbai mill-workers to lead them in a head-on conflict between the Bombay Mill-owners Association and the unions. He orchestrated a massive strike, forcing the entire industry of Mumbai to be shut down for over a year. Approximately 25,000 workers went on strike and more than 50 textile mills were closed in Mumbai permanently.'

I was carrying a bottle of red wine and two flimsy paper cups. I poured us each a drink.

'I had rallied behind Ballav Salve since I believed that he was predominantly fighting for greater pay and better working conditions for the workers, whereas, in reality, Salve and his allies were just looking to capitalize and establish their stronghold on the trade-union scene in Mumbai. I staged provocative street plays all over India, portraying their pitiable conditions, openly sloganeering against the Congress government. The Congress Prime Minister, Mrs. Indira Gandhi, who perhaps considered Salve a serious political threat, tried reaching out to me, hoping to use my influence to persuade the warring mill-workers. While the meeting proved inconclusive, the government's taking a firm stance of rejecting Salve's demands and refusing to budge despite the mammoth economic losses suffered by Mumbai and the industry, rendered a false impression to a lot of people, especially in the theatre circuit, that *my* involvement, was, perhaps, nothing but a political gimmick to gain cheap publicity. As the strike progressed, Salve's stubborn militancy in the face of government persistence led to the failure of any attempts at further negotiation. Disunity and dissatisfaction over the strike soon grew rife, and....'

I drank in silence.

'Our views were different and so we parted ways eventually,' he gulped down his drink.

I kicked off my black pumps and leaned back on the pillows. 'You mentioned there was a death...?'

Amitabh's face took on a look of anguish. He held out his glass and I poured him some wine. He walked up to the window and gazed out. He spoke after a long time:

'Maya was my daughter. An angel, so pure...only two when she died. It was my fault. I never realized that she was so sick. Even the night she...' he stopped, and turned to me, taking a deep breath... 'She had trouble breathing...I scooped her up in my arms, kissing her, trying to calm her down rather than rushing her to the hospital, as I should have. She turned blue, after a while. So many times, Sarlu had reported this same symptom to me...suspecting something being amiss...always complaining of her breathlessness... how she tired easily and passed out twice while playing...I always told her it was nothing. Playing down her fears...the times I was home, nothing of the sort ever transpired...and so I blamed it on Sarlu's compulsively worrying nature... how she wanted things to be the same...'

He drained his glass. I took the cup from his hand and refilled it, without his asking, this time.

Amitabh gulped down the whole drink in one shot, his ears reddening. Saying nothing else.

'Sarlu, your wife, I presume?'

Amitabh sat down beside me and switched on a bedside lamp. For a while, he gazed at the tiny specks of light reflected in his drink.

'Sarla, actually. My wife was the only child of the man who was my guru, my mentor, my father, in many ways…the man who taught me all I know about the stage…educated me about the world…' he poured me a drink, then. Some of the wine spilt over, staining the white sheets.

Amitabh stood up, restlessly. 'I have not done right by Sarla. I've let her down in ways that I can never forgive myself for. It's possibly why I'm so defensive around her… she never forgave me for marrying her. Because I was her one friend and confidant; the only one who knew she was having an affair with someone else. But what could I do when her father asked me to accept her hand? I know Sarla blames me…but she is too proud—like Dada Saheb—to ever bring this all up…she probably thinks I agreed to marry her just to inherit her father's theatre company, but what she has never realized is that marrying her made me feel like I had been bought. I was equally stifled, I felt unmanned. I should have been selected as the man replacing Sarat Chandra Joglekar in the *Natya Mandali*, which is what his theatre troupe was called, because I was worthy of it, and not because I was to become his future son-in-law. I have questioned my own conscience, umpteen times…wondering how Sarla thinks of me…I have always admired her…the way she was always so upright…I knew what a lot of people in the company also whispered, back then…that I was nothing more than a greedy suitor who was handed over the family business in a sort of dowry…it's why Sarla resented me…why she never spoke a single word to me on our wedding day…nor the months after…never quite understanding how unworthy I felt… still feel... around her.' Drawing the heavy silk curtains, he glanced back over his shoulders, once more: 'Mind stepping out? These sort of places stifle me.'

I put the cup by the bed.

'You can just turn off the lights, if you wish…I do that a lot, in places where I feel vulnerable…the darkness offers a sort of anoni…how do you say it...' I bit my lower lip, 'anonymity…' I struggled with my English.

Amitabh sat on a couch, away from me.

'You and your wife, are you saying you didn't fall in love with her?' I restarted the conversation.

Amitabh rubbed his eyes.

'I didn't fall in love, no. Not in the manner, you Westerners possibly interpret man-woman love…a physical union, almost always coming first. I grew up with Sarla…and over the years, I grew to love her. Not so much as a woman of flesh and blood…but as a comrade…as someone who I looked up to and looked out for…and, was even responsible for, in a way. It is possible to, you know. But Sarla has never trusted me; she's not once spoken to me about Dada Saheb's arbitrary decision to get us married; not once, in all our married life. Sarlu gave up acting soon after we were wed. I didn't insist that she continue, either. I began writing and directing. Leaving her father's legendary travelling theatre company and Kolhapur where he was based, to build our own nest in Pune. Sarlu didn't object to the relocation or talk me out of it, selling off her wedding jewellery to fund my plan. I founded my own theatre company. I hired the actors and technicians I wanted. I travelled more. Sarlu opened a dance school at home. And, so we survived our fate, I guess. No one really prepared us for the stubborn transition from theatre artists to life companions. It's something that I had always known…when she signed her initials, below mine, in a crowded government office. When the registrar called her Mrs. Amitabh Kulasheshtra, for the first time. It was the end of something. And, perhaps, at, some level, the start of something, bigger…much bigger. It scared us. Both…' his words trailed.

I stared at his silhouette, a part of me craving to reach out to him.

'Pardon, Marie, I don't know what got into me…this is the first time I have spoken to anyone…about all this… Maya…*Sarlu*…me…' he shuddered, trying to raise his head.

I untied a silk scarf that I was wearing around my neck. '*Viens ici et dors*…go to sleep…' I patted his forehead.

Amitabh shrugged his shoulders.

'I, I can't…I just can't sleep, Marie…ever since…' he stammered, looking spent.

I loosened two buttons on my silk shirt, saying nothing else. Then after a while, I carefully lifted his head, placing it on my chest. Running my right hand lightly over his eyes, I hummed softly: *'Au Clair De La Lune…'*

'By the light of the moon?' Amitabh murmured, slowly looking up, searching my face.

'*Oui*…an 18th century folk song, a lullaby my mother sang to me. When I had a bad dream…' I steadied his back.

Amitabh hugged me, clumsily, our lips brushing each other's. 'Don't stop, Marie…please…stay here, with me, don't go,' he moaned, his nails digging into my flesh.

SARLA KULASHESHTRA

BLINDSIDE

Maya, our beautiful daughter, was born on a stormy September night, around midnight. It was a difficult birth. The doctors finally had to perform a Caesarean section after Sarlu underwent twelve hours of painful labour. Insisting on a natural birth.

'Here she is, Kulasheshtra,' the obstetrician placed the new-born in my arms, wrapped in a pale green cloth, her tiny eyes clamped shut. Nothing had prepared me for the overflow of emotion I had felt as I cradled my child for the first time. I could barely take my eyes off this tiny, perfectly formed human being, at how she clasped my finger. I thought of Baba as I kissed her forehead tenderly. I missed him then; in a way I hadn't ever missed him before.

Maya opened a flood in me. I had never felt love like this ever before. It gushed out from my heart like fresh blood from an open wound. I held her close to my heart, thinking I could never let her go.

But the gods had willed otherwise.

◈

For fifteen years of our marriage, Sarlu didn't conceive and then, miraculously, she was pregnant. I'd never known her to be happier. She wrote to me: 'I know this comes at a difficult time, but I have saved enough for the expenses this will naturally bring…I want this child, Amitabh, I want us to have our own child...something we created together...something as joyous as a new arrival... something hopeful...to look forward to again. To dream a new dream...the way we once did.'

I remember reading the last line, again and again, trying to imagine the changes in Sarlu's body, as the months passed; I imagined her battling morning sickness, the way I grew up seeing the women in Ganesh Circus throw up into the open drains that ran past our tents, their faces contorted, their bellies bloated. I wondered whether Sarlu would experience hunger pangs at night; crave ripe mangoes and sour pickles...

I wrote back:

'Dear Sarlu, can you believe we have completed a decade of being man and wife? Is time a traitor, Sarlu...or a teacher? Is time on our side, Sarlu? I have asked myself many times in these years. I couldn't be happier, at the news you shared...though I am selfishly plagued with thoughts of how I shall fare as a father. If I am worthy of the unconditional affection a child is known to bestow? If I have it in me, to wipe away my past...if I can, in loving my child back, forgive myself for being an unworthy son? I shall be back, soon. Look after yourself...I want this child, Sarlu, I want us to have our own child. To dream a new dream.'

After wrapping up my last production in Nagpur, I took the night train to Pune, buying pink roses for Sarlu on the way and a brand-new Narayanpeth sari. It was the first time I was buying anything for her, without telling her beforehand or calculating the expense. The shopkeeper made me buy matching glass bangles, as well. They reminded me of Ammi. My mother. My exquisite, educated, Muslim mother, who had taught me to read and write. Who always dreamt of better. Sarlu slipped on the bangles before lunch, rotating her wrists in a semi-circular fashion, as she served hot vegetarian food in a brand new steel thali.

'Our daughter is to be named Maya,' I said, when she stood beside me, to remove my plate.

Sarla mused, 'Maya...Yes I like that, but what if it's a boy?'

'It'll be a girl, Sarlu, I know it will.'

Sarlu ran her hands over her stomach. The afternoon light casting an incandescent glow to her face that looked fuller, happier, younger...Like the Sarla of old, the impulsive girl who had risked bringing in a rank newcomer in her father's towering presence, hurriedly feeding me a vada pao, the first time we met. Forging an uncanny camaraderie.

I had almost forgotten who Sarlu really was.

'Would you like to visit your mother? Spend these next few months in her care? Go back home?' I caught her wrist as she moved away from my side, turning to go towards the kitchen.

Sarlu's eyes moistened. 'I would have, if Dada Saheb were still alive...now there is no point...' she pursed her lips.

I ran my fingers tenderly over her waist. 'I'm sorry,' I said in a low voice, 'I should have taken you to visit them when we got news of his illness, you should have been with him when he died...by his side.'

Sarla nodded. Then before I could say anything, she pressed herself against me, 'I am scared, Amitabh. This feels so strange, so surreal, at some level. I know we have never spoken about a child before, or even tried particularly hard for one, but when I found out I was pregnant I felt as if a giant emptiness in my life had been filled...I feel complete...the way I have never felt about myself... selfishly guarding my own happiness...it's why I didn't write to you, sooner...or my mother, for that matter...what if it doesn't last...what if this is all a lie...this unborn child...'

Tears clouded her eyes.

I pushed back the chair and pulled her onto my lap and placed my hand on her midriff. 'Maya, born of illusion, my baby daughter...Amitabh and Sarla Kulasheshtra...our first joint production...' I murmured into her ears.

Sarlu rested her head lightly on my shoulders. She looked frail, all of a sudden. Her face had hardened from the years of struggle.

Her thick plait of hair had thinned and yet, in that one moment, she looked so vulnerable.

I rubbed her back gently, where the hooks on her blouse began.

'When is the next show?' Sarla moaned, not opening her eyes.

'I am not going anywhere...I will be here...with you, in this house...I will wait...for Maya,' I pulled her closer, feeling her heart race, like mine.

The next six months were different. I stayed in, reading a lot, watching Sarlu as she continued diligently with her dance classes, never demanding a day's rest, even as her feet swelled up and she had trouble walking up the stairs. I broke the only fixed deposit I had, that Sarlu had insisted on us opening, and employed a fulltime house-help. Meena-tai gradually took over the kitchen, washing utensils and clothes, besides mopping the rooms, in the last months of her pregnancy. Being an elderly woman, she substituted the absence of an elder in the family. Often telling Sarlu what she should eat. The spices to avoid. Tying a black thread on her left ankle to evade 'buri nazar'. It was nice to have someone else in the house...between us...I pitched in, when Sarlu was advised bed-rest in the last two months. As I hung the wet clothes out to dry or lent Meena-tai a hand with the groceries, I marvelled at just how Sarlu had managed to do all of this, by herself, for as long as she had. Never complaining. How I had never asked her if there was sufficient money for groceries or bills. How she had taken it solely upon herself to manage the life we lived.

How I had let her.

◈

Sarlu lay asleep on the hospital bed with her infant child. As I watched them both, my pulse raced. It was the most complete experience of my life, thus far...and, at the same time, the most anxious...as I grappled with the enormousness of the responsibility I would have to henceforth shoulder...how Sarlu could not be alone, any more, how she shouldn't have to be. Alone.

Ever...

Looking at Sarlu made me visualize my own mother, Ammi, biting the edge of her torn dupatta as I had denounced her in public...Baba, my father, who had lost his sight and never left the circus, whom I had heartlessly abandoned...Dada Saheb, Sarla's father whose troupe I joined after leaving Ganesh Circus, days after Ammi died...what would I tell Maya about her lineage?

My past...

Who was I, in the end?

A boy who walked out on his blind father? Who called his mother a whore in a fit of rage? A rebel who married the only daughter of a theatre stalwart? Who agreed to a marriage of convenience? Who was hardly ever there, in it?'

Sarlu was worn out after the delivery. The stitches from her C-section were horribly painful, as she tried to get up from bed to go to the bathroom.

'I had a dream,' she wheezed.

'Rest now, it's been a difficult time,' I said as I guided her back to bed, my arm around her shoulder.

'I dreamt we were standing on the bank of a large river, Amitabh. The colour of the water...it was so clear, crystal blue. We looked so young again...like we had nothing to fear, like we could dive into its ripples immediately. You were bare bodied...you, you looked so happy...' she touched my cheeks.

I caught her hands.

'I am happy,' I gestured to the crib beside me.

Sarlu cupped my cheeks.

'No,' she interrupted, adding, slowly, 'that happiness was different. It was the kind of happiness that didn't weigh you down with obligation...that set you free, in the end.'

I listened to Sarlu.

'Get some sleep, please…' I whispered in her ear.

The next morning after I had fetched her some tea, she looked me in the eye. 'When do you leave?' She asked, sounding washed out.

I was taken aback at the question.

'The mill-workers' agitation in Mumbai…what are you going to do about it? It's been on your mind these past few months, Amitabh,' she asked me point-blank.

I had forgotten just how much of an equal Sarlu was to me, always.

'I…umm…I will have to travel…I wish to start a series of street plays that showcase the horrific working conditions all over India, Ballav Salve has been doing a lot. I have expressed my interest in the movement, my solidarity with the agitation…I have been writing on those lines,' I answered.

Sarlu was wide awake.

'Go on,' she urged.

When Maya was eight months old, I had left Pune accompanied by my newly recruited team of actors and technicians.

Looking back, those months I spent with my daughter were the most beautiful months of my life. Helping out with Maya, bathing her, changing her, warming her milk bottle, singing her odd lullabies at night, waking next to her at dawn, checking on her. Rocking her through the night trying to put her back to sleep. Sitting beside Sarlu, as she breastfed our child.

As I boarded the night train, I imagined Maya sleeping soundly beside Sarlu. It was the safest I had ever felt.

Like standing on the banks of a great, big river.

Sarlu's river of dreams…

Unafraid to drown.

◈

I closed the file, my insides trembling. My anger spent. Why had Amitabh and I had never once brought up Maya's death? Why had I let all these years pass…thinking I was the only one who had suffered when clearly Amitabh had been aching too? In the months after Maya passed, there was always my mother or Meena-tai present between us. And I had been determined never to let Amitabh see me break down, either. Somehow, I told myself, I couldn't show him my weaker side. Maybe being angry at Amitabh, blaming him for Maya's death, was easier than dealing with my deep sense of loss.

I had hated on Amitabh all over again, for asking me to wait till he returned from Mumbai to show Maya to a specialist; I held him squarely responsible for the deterioration in Maya's condition. Directing my anger at him instead of sharing the loss we had both suffered, helped me cope with the raging current of grief that threatened to literally sweep me away. I was incapable of engaging with anyone, or anything. All the resentment I had harboured for Amitabh slowly solidifying into a cold, unmoving detachment.

It was easy to keep him away from me, as I had preferred in the past – holding out my heart, in a rehearsed, unrelenting silence.

After Maya's death, I asked myself the same questions, repeatedly. The same way I blamed myself for my cowardice in confronting Dada Saheb at the time of my marriage. Why had I not insisted on taking Maya to the hospital?

Why did I not read the signs that Maya was gravely sick? What scared me? Why had I not trusted my gut instincts? I lay awake, night after night, watching the gnawing shadows on the walls.

Had I expected Maya to fix me?

My marriage?

Had she failed?

I picked up the book again, searching for answers.

◈

BLINDSIDE

After Maya's death, I was distraught. I envied Sarlu, to be honest. How she had managed to get her life back in perfect order; how she had carefully cultivated this world she inhabited, like an oasis of calm. A life so opposed to the one I had. The chaos, the causes, the crowded places that camouflaged my own cuts…

How everything in Sarlu's world seemed seamless, untouched in a sense, like it was before: a respectable dance academy; a modest, one-storied house with a decently-sized front porch, a small, but well-manicured garden strewn with clusters of roses; a perfectly-run kitchen, a well-managed, well-stocked household; Sarlu's little puja corner devoted to the gods. I hated the way the house smelt, like a temple, all the time. Incense burning everywhere…

A strong odour of jasmine oil permeated the interiors, similar to the one she used in her hair, parting her tresses carefully, segregating the silver strands with her fingers.

From time to time, she'd rotate her ankles, stiffened after years of rigorous dance practice, balancing herself on her toes. Her kohl-lined eyes, strangely calm, her hips jutting out. Her purple, silk sari starched. Faux zari dripping down its pallu. Pleated in a neat, rectangular fashion, as she squatted on the hard, cold mosaic floor, clapping her hands and clicking her tongue.

The clamour of children's voices, hushed whispers running down the elongated corridor, the banging of doors, the constant sound of ghungroos, amidst the backdrop of thickly-accented South Indian songs, the drone of dialogue.

Hands folded, breasts upright, covered from head to toe, pious, Like someone who could do no wrong. Who seldom retaliated, whose strength lay in her studied silences.

◈

Except for that terrible night when Maya had been declared dead in the emergency room of a local hospital where we had rushed her – when Sarla had howled like a wild animal bereft with grief, mourning for her dead in the most primal way – I had never seen Sarla cry openly. We never really grieved Maya's loss as a couple. We weren't really trained for those sorts of rituals, in any case.

I had carried Maya in my arms to the crematorium, watching as the saffron flames leapt up, as Sarlu refused to accompany me on the final march, listening to her mother, who insisted that women should not go to the shamshaan ghat. That it was ordained so in the shastras.

Sarlu accepted her fate resiliently, for the second time, not overtly blaming anyone; never holding me directly responsible for the life I had given her, never asking why I was the absent parent, the one who left her, travelling overseas to Paris, in the months that followed Maya's death to direct the most ostentatious project of my career.

Our letters to each other were curt, customary details of the household and the seasonal changes in Pune; we never pined for each other or craved each other's company or made promises to return by a certain time. How I longed to tell Sarlu everything about Marie, how what I felt was not pain. But hurt…

'I'm going to the Arya Samaj, there is going to be a reading from the Upanishads. Swami Gurumurthy will be reciting sacred shlokas,' she said, one day, her eyes bloodshot, a month after I returned.

Was it from lack of sleep? I had wondered. Did Sarlu too, have dreams? Like me? Nightmares? Like last night, again? Did she too, hear a child cry, endlessly?

'Tell me what you want for dinner so I can tell Meena-tai…

'I want a simple fish curry…steamed rice. Just, plain, steamed rice,' I spoke, after a few seconds.

'You can't, not today, Amitabh,' she cut me short, crossing her hands staunchly over her heart.

'Why? You just asked me what I'd like to eat!' I snarled.

'How can you…' her lips quivered, slightly.

'How can I?'

'How can you eat non-vegetarian food? Today is 16th September…the day she died…Maya…' Sarlu looked at me.

'September…16…5.50 pm…' I muttered, glancing at the wall clock.

The corners of Sarla's eyes were red-rimmed.

I should have reached out to her.

Said something. Wept in her arms. Held her close. Made love. Made a promise…

'Fine, then the usual dal will do…' I shrugged.

'You like the amti dal she makes, right?' Sarlu called out just as I turned my back, wiping her eyes.

'It'll have to do,' I raised an eyebrow, swallowing my own tears.

And just like that, we became strangers again.

Invisible to each other.

◈

I pushed the book away. My thoughts travelled back to Amitabh, the day he told me about the Parisian project over lunch, a month or so after Maya's death. It was raining heavily. I listened, barely touching my food. My mother was staying with us.

'How can you leave her after such a tragedy?' She had hissed at him.

Amitabh had stared at my face. 'Would you like to come, Sarlu?' He had asked softly.

I looked at him through dulled eyes. 'No, I plan to resume the dance classes, Amitabh, I'm going to call up my old students…' I pushed a bowl of rice in his direction.

My mother frowned. 'Why don't you just go with him, like he's telling you to, the change may be good for your mind and body,' she butted in, adding sarcastically, 'You should listen to your man.'

'Sarlu will do as she pleases, she is no longer in her father's house and has to do no one's bidding,' Amitabh had interrupted her, brusquely.

I pushed back my chair, excusing myself.

A part of me wished Amitabh would force me to accompany him, like any other husband. The kind of man who is scared to leave behind a woman he loves. Another part seethed with pent-up anger at Dada Saheb and Rakesh… at all the men in my life who had always placed their own wishes before mine.

'It is going to be a long trip, maybe a year…maybe even more,' Amitabh added, as soon as my back was turned.

I stood still, for a few seconds.

'Maybe, that's what we need,' I had responded, clearing away the plates and storing the leftover food in a second-hand refrigerator.

'Need for what?' I heard my mother holler agitatedly.

'Maybe, we are both better off healing, alone,' Amitabh had retaliated in a raised voice, speaking on my behalf. Coming to my defence. Protecting me, strangely, even when we were the farthest apart.

Or maybe, it was the only time we were close.

So close that we failed to see we were broken…in exactly the same places.

MARIE BOURDAINE

BLINDSIDE

The question of morality often plagued me. Even in the years spent with Dada Saheb, who taught a poor, semi-literate son of a clown to challenge the very world order he wanted so desperately to inherit. Even when our ideas clashed, he let me rebel, naturally, assuming possibly, like any aging sire, that the son in me would always return.

Not knowing that there was a part of me that always held out. That trusted no one. Least of all myself.

I can recall the first time I expressed an interest in starting a parallel theatre company to Dada Saheb.

I had just turned twenty-one. Many of Dada Saheb's old cast members had left or were leaving. Times were changing everywhere. Like the moving circus, theatre in villages and small towns was being replaced by more formidable forms of entertainment. Movie halls…The audience wanted to laugh. To see a good-looking couple's romance. A fight. A song.

My interest in petty village affairs and make-belief mythological tales had dwindled. I was more focused on what was happening in the country. On the social issues that plagued it.

There was news back then that farmers were dying thanks to the use of deathly pesticides. Many children were born deformed. Their limbs painfully stunted. Some, the lucky ones, were stillborn.

The farmers' angry pleas fell on deaf ears. The State Government, unmoved, like the Centre, that was numb, not so much by choice, as by convenience. Slave to new-age fertilizer companies that had possibly funded their election campaigns – the ones who simply offered hefty compensation packages. The media a pimp that hustled for any side that offered them cash.

Some of the families accepted the money, quietly wiping their tears, swallowing their regrets, as more children died.

I had written a play called Charkha, *based on the same theme, which questioned where India's future lay – how the Green Revolution had actually strangled the agrarian economy. I wanted to use puppets and miming.*

The world around us was changing, and, I was keen to be a voice, a conduit, and not just a passive, make-believe storyteller…

'What use are our plays, if not to question human justice?' I'd once challenged Dada Saheb and the seniors in the troupe, when they had labelled my writing 'extremist'. 'I don't care to be popular, all I care about is the human revolution, if I can't direct Charkha, *in this company, I will leave it, and do it on my own,' I raised my voice against them for the first time.*

Dada Saheb had stormed off the stage.

'You didn't mean that, did you?' Sarlu had hissed, mortified at my outburst.

RK stood behind her. We were like brothers back then. 'Yaara, maafi maang le. *You have to stay in this profession…unlike me, who can't wait to join films,' he'd winked, slapping my shoulder.*

I turned to Sarla, grabbing her by the arm: 'Did you like it? What do you think of my writing?' I always depended on her approval.

'Araam se yaara…*you could hurt her,'RK reached out and removed my hand. I knew what they both were up to. Sarlu had been gone again last night, her bed unslept in, her slippers missing.*

In the morning, RK was late for rehearsal, saying he wasn't feeling well. He was lying. They had both been lying.

Now Sarlu searched his face for a few seconds. Before turning her gaze to mine. Looking softer, at dusk. 'What's all this about breaking away from Dada Saheb? How can you, after all he's done...just because he doesn't approve of one of your infinite new thoughts...you know how your words will break his heart...' she clenched her jaw.

I was struck by how beautiful Sarlu was when she transformed into her own.

'What if I am not built to be loyal?' I snapped.

RK stood behind her. Their bodies strangely aligned. I watched them with a guarded jealousy.

Sarlu said nothing more.

Later that night, as I squatted at Dada Saheb's feet, I contemplated apologizing for my earlier demand.

'We seek immortality, son. We demand that people remember our body of work. We hide behind human arrogance. We are narcissists. We wait for the slow claps to pick up momentum... But, our job, Amitabh, as directors, is bigger...more than just telling one story...we must search for the next one...Amitabh, you cannot afford sadness, or attachment or anger. It is the true purpose of art, and of this stage. You belong to no one. You are a mere sutradhaar. *There is nothing you can take from me that is not already yours, son...'*

I buried my face in my hands.

'I understand your impatience; it was the same with me when I started craving my own company...it is a generational thing, to seek an inheritance, and so you shall, too, but, before that I will ask for my Gurudakshina...one day...' Dada Saheb spoke slowly, lifting up my face.

'I'm sorry. I have never been a dutiful son...you must know that...I always let my father down...Nor was I a faithful son to Ammi. What if I am not built to be trusted, Dada Saheb? By anyone...' I broke down.

Dada Saheb didn't stop me. When I was through he said, 'Turn off the lights...'

I did as I was told, studying the shape of his shrivelled ankles. Imagining them to be Baba's.

I wondered if he was alive. A knot forming in my stomach as I imagined him searching for me, groping the darkness. Calling me by my pet name.

Bijli. Meaning lightning.

A month later, Dada Saheb, called me aside, one evening.

'Our next production will be Charkha*...I will step down from directing this one,' he pressed down on my shoulders.*

My heart raced.

'But, there is a price, Amitabh,' he continued, as I helped him sit under a large banyan tree, 'I want you to marry my daughter.'

'What? No, no...I am not suitable...no...I cannot marry Sarlu, never...I mean...' I protested vehemently.

Dada Saheb cut me short: 'I know exactly what you are thinking...Sarla is my only child...I have a sense of things, Amitabh...though I have not ever pulled her up or insulted her by asking her about her personal affairs. She is fully grown now...maybe, it is something I deliberately ignored, as her mother constantly blames me for...maybe, I should have sensed Sarla's needs as a woman, and not just as my daughter, or a fellow artist...' he was breathing with difficulty.

Before I could speak, he stretched out his hands, 'Marriage is a puzzle, son. Maybe one that will take you an entire lifetime to decipher. This is the gurudakshina *I want from you...'*

I moved closer. 'You don't understand. How will I feed Sarlu? Besides, I cannot afford any attachments at this stage...especially, now, that I am to direct...take charge...Sarlu will always occupy second place in my life...I am not cut out to love a woman...I am devoted to the stage. I, I want to leave behind a legacy, like you...' my face was flushed.

Dada Saheb patted my back.
I tried saying something.
'This is *the legacy, son,' he gripped my shoulders.*

◈

Room 654. Hotel du Champ de Villiers. I ran my fingers over the Room Service bill. Having difficulty reading the letters, in lower case, without my spectacles.

Over the years, I had always made it a point to stay here whenever I visited Paris, in the same room, where Amitabh and I had first met. As man and woman. Where we would return to, unfailingly, every single night, after the team dinner concluded, where, at the end, as etiquette dictated, I leaned in and kissed his cold, stubbled cheeks. Amitabh would nod. Never saying more. Opening the door to his room, the same way, barely, a minute or two, later, always flinging my coat on the bed. Before I made it over there.

The French tabloids had lapped up our newfound interest in each other, labelling us a 'couple.' Carrying a photograph, or two. I never asked Amitabh if he understood the implications of our growing proximity, which, at some point, I presumed, would naturally tempt us to explore each other, sexually. Now and then, Amitabh would sleep with his head on my chest, never pushing the boundaries, or as much as indicating that he wanted more out of this. I was immensely drawn to him, physically, and, yet, something scared me. Or, maybe, there was something inherently respectable about being with a man who desired you, and yet maintained his distance.

Amitabh Kulasheshtra did what no man had done before. He made me feel safe. Maybe, I did the same for him. Maybe, I told myself, there is a love that is never spoken. A love, so unselfish, it didn't fear its own silences.

I kept a copy of *Blindside* on my bedside table, reading from it every night, before I retired to bed. It comforted me to hear his voice. To imagine him in the life he once lived. To see myself sharing the years of his existence, before he came to me. Amitabh had been my '*âme sœur*,' my soul mate.

I draped a light woollen stole around my shoulders, staring at the glass window, overlooking the River Seine that now reflected the cluster of stars in the midnight sky. I turned a page.

◈

BLINDSIDE

Over time, I became something of a regular feature at Manju Bhabi's olive tent, often even bunking my lessons to spend languid afternoons, reading to her. Sometimes resting my head on her stomach, her Georgette sari riding up to her knees, where we lay on the untrimmed grass, a drone of flies swarming over our heads. Sometimes Manju Bhabi would fall strangely silent, staring listlessly into the distance. Never answering when I asked her the question: whether she was happy, here. Rumour had it that Prateik Master had taken on a new mistress in Nagpur.

'What will you do with all these storybooks? What use do they have, once I have finished reading them to you?' I placed my hands over hers, clumsily.

'These books are my only constant. The stories they contain make my spirits soar, and you my darling boy, are the only way I can access them…'

I wiped my newly sprouting moustache.

'Darling,' I chuckled, adding cheekily, 'you, rich people use that word a lot. It was also there in our English textbook, in some of the short stories or, maybe, in one of the poems; darling meaning lover, right? Am I your lover?'

Manju Bhabhi blushed.

Later that night, as I lay next to Baba, dead drunk himself, with his clown makeup intact, I fantasized about her, imagining Manju Bhabhi in a cramped loo, covered by a makeshift asbestos shed, only her spine visible as she scrubbed a pile of dirty underclothes in insipid colours.

As I turned lethargically on my side, I tried suppressing a cramp in my lower abdomen, my organ stiff as I visualized her lips opening and closing, a thin line of sweat travelling down her cleavage divided by a thick gold chain interspersed with a series of tiny black beads. My feelings for Manju Bhabhi trapped somewhere between loneliness and lust.

I insisted she watch my first-ever production – the story of a magnificent lion in a great, big circus, whose greatness lay in tamely obeying instructions, over the years. Jumping through circular rings of fire and growling when his trainer cracked the whip.

I wore a mask I had hand-painted, jumping at a great height, on her bed.

'What happens, next?' She pulled me closer.

I grabbed her hips.

'A terrible fire breaks out in the circus, the same year. The lion – a fool – watches the circus burn to ashes, taking refuge in his cage, like a coward. Frightened by the very prospect of the freedom he so desperately longs for. A mighty heart thwarted by time…'

I panted on purpose.

Manju Bhabhi sat on her haunches, on a cotton mattress.

'Darling,' she dragged me into her arms.

For a while, we remained like that. Then before I could say anything, she asked me to kiss her over her mouth, her breath tinged with supari – her addiction. I spent the rest of the night, lying beside her, stark naked, as she instructed me, matter-of-factly, telling me what to do next. I told her someday I would be a famous man. Not a mere manager, like her husband. How I wanted to direct, own a stage…

At dawn, I left.

'You have a talent,' Manju Bhabhi groaned, as I walked away.

I liked the word.

'Talent,' I pronounced awkwardly, a couple of times. The way it made me feel. Like I meant something…that I was someone.

The next night, I was back outside her tent: 'I want to show you something else, this time…another type of natak I have written. You said I was good the last time? That, that I had a talent…I found your note…I believe you…' I professed, as she covered my mouth, suspiciously glancing over her shoulders and dragging me, inside.

I followed, transfixed, her passion intoxicating as she unbuttoned me urgently, pushing her tongue desperately inside my mouth and pressing her sex over my organ…gyrating deliciously, as I clumsily held her hips…

When I got back, Ammi stood waiting for me: 'What were you doing outside Prateik Dada's tent, again, at night?' she reprimanded sternly, emptying out the contents of my frayed satchel.

It was the last show in Solapur, where we had been stationed for all of last month.

'I was there to read Bhabhi a new natak *I have written. She's the only one who understands these things. She's also more refined than the rest, here. She is my darling…' I bragged.*

'Focus on your studies, this woman, she seems desperate…' Ammi hissed.

My blood boiled: 'And, what were you *doing out again, at night? What's to say you weren't desperate, like her?' I pushed back Ammi's rough hands, speaking in a cold, dispassionate tone.*

◈

Six months later, Prateik Sir fired Baba. Throwing our things out, as Ammi pleaded before Manju Bhabhi and him with folded hands.

'Where will we go, now? What great talent do we ordinary folks have?' she sobbed, collapsing on the ground.

'Spare us the drama...we know just how talented you all are...' Prateik Master sniggered, clicking his fingers.

Ammi covered her face in shame.

'And your son...that is, if he even has a real father...he's way more talented than you all put together.... Up to no good, here... where's the money to feed all these extras, anymore? The glory days of the circus are dead...' he raged, even as his wife attempted calming him down.

Baba who had been listening silently, all this while, outstretched his hands, as if he was trying to say something.

'Why don't you be plain? Tell us the real reason for throwing out my father, who despite his blindness, still performs the fire act, with brilliance...people come from far and wide, just for this man, here...' I stood defiantly between Ammi and Prateik Master.

'Bijli...' Baba shuddered, calling me by the nickname he used to address me, covering his shrunken chest.

'What do you mean, plain? Talking too much, you son of a...' Prateik Master shoved me back with his hands.

I grabbed his collar.

'Why don't you confess to your pretty, innocent wife how almost every night even you sneak out...tip-toe to the animals' feeding area, how you go missing conveniently just to...' I gritted my teeth, adding in a menacing voice, 'how you ask my mother to suck your swollen cock...dragging her into an empty tent... at the farthest corner of the field...and fuck her all night... free of cost...how you exploit women like Ammi, here, daily...

besides having another mistress in another town…how you take advantage of our poverty? Our dependence on this circus…'

Prateik Master's face was flushed.

'I…I don't know what's gotten into this boy? Who's been filling his head with such filth? Forgive him his foul mouth, please, Dada…' Ammi cried apologetically, trying to disentangle my arms from around Prateik Master's burly chest.

'Just leave me, Ammi…I am sick of you all, this damn life… the constant pretence!' I retaliated as Prateik Master swerved lower and removed his sandals.

'And you…what are you doing watching this spectacle with this sorry face of yours, huh? Go on…tell your husband how you have been luring me, on purpose…how you can't get enough…how you teach me things…pleading with me to come to your tent, alone, on the pretext of making me read books, just any excuse to be touched and tasted…speak up, I say! Enjoying this tamasha, aren't you?' I hissed, pointing accusatorily at Manju Bhabhi who placed her hands over her ears, her cheeks reddened.

'He's deranged, this lad! Been drinking that cheap country liquor again, or what? All I did was listen to some play he had written because he literally begged me to…something about a lion in a burning circus…juvenile stuff, really, I, I mean…' she stuttered nervously, trying to evade my fierce gaze.

Ammi fell at Prateik Master's feet.

'Tell me what I have to do, to atone for this misdemeanour…I am willing to send him away…I have a cousin, close by…I can do anything…but, but, please don't take away our jobs…this circus, is our life, my husband's sole existence…where will he go, from here? You know he can't see…' she begged, weeping copiously.

Prateik Master was fuming, his eyes enflamed. His chest heaved up and down, along with his misshapen paunch.

'Mumtaz…' Baba interrupted all of a sudden, clumsily walking up in their direction.

Ammi shot a desperate glance over her shoulders. It was the first time I had heard him call her that in public.

'Is it true, what Bijli just said? Everything...?' he questioned, sharply.

Prateik Master laughed out loud. 'Maybe we should introduce a new segment to your act – the sordid sex lives of you poor, desperate losers! Bet that will be a sell-out!'

I slapped him hard across his face, just then.

'Darling...' Manju Bhabhi shrieked, lunging forward to hold him in her arms.

Prateik Master glanced up; his lip cut open. Blood gushing out.

'Tell her the truth, rascal...tell her what you do to my Ammi every night...speak up, you loser...instead, of blaming it all on us...you...your wife...all of you...all you privileged people... you are all the same, selfish, sadistic,' I rolled a fist, pointing threateningly at him.

Some members of the circus had gathered around us by then. They stared, shell-shocked, whispering amidst themselves.

Prateik Sir was shaking, his shirt drenched in sweat. 'I...I...' his lips trembled.

'It's all my fault...' Baba spoke out of turn again, taking everyone by surprise, adding, as I breathed heavily into Prateik Master's face: 'Forgive my son; I...it was on my instructions that Mumtaz...that she...I mean...the money that was stolen last summer...it was me...I stole it from Prateik Dada's tent...I needed it desperately...the alcohol, it is the only thing that makes me feel sane...accept this condition that just wouldn't go away...I was petrified Dada would discover it was me...it's why I sent her, every night...hoping he would forget, maybe get distracted...stop suspecting a blind clown, like me...it's all my fault...Bijli...I made my wife a common whore...I used Ammi to survive this trade...I had no other way...I am not talented, like the rest.'

Manju Bhabhi let out a lengthy wail, as Ammi clasped her chest, looking stricken.

Tears gushed out of my eyes.

'Talent...' I mouthed stiffly, swallowing with difficulty, my thoughts going back to the summer our bags were searched thoroughly, one morning, the thanedar giving all of us a severe warning about the five thousand rupees that had gone missing from Prateik Master's tent. Fingerprints had been taken. Rumours made the rounds that it could be one of us.

In mounting horror, I remembered the sudden spending spree we had briefly enjoyed. 'Here, take these; these books should serve you well, now you don't have to complain that you have to share your things with all the others...promise me, you will study well, from today,' Ammi had said one day, bringing me brand new textbooks.

Just then there was a thud.

'Mumtaz...' Baba howled.

Everyone huddled around Ammi who had collapsed to the ground, clutching her chest. Some urgently splashing water on her face. Others running helter skelter...the dust flying. I stood a few feet away from where Ammi was. Removed and detached.

'Bijli...here take this, some warm rice, eat well, and, then study, and keep an eye on Baba...I will take care of the rest, I am here, for you, son,' I remembered her words from last night, before she'd melted into the darkness again.

By the evening Baba and I had buried Ammi:

'Na jayate mriyate va kadacin nayam bhutva bhavita va na bhuyah ajo nityah sasvato 'yam purano na hanyate hanyamane sarire'

Baba recited the same passage from the Bhagwad Gita over and over again. His hands trembling as he threw the last fistful of dry mud over her grave.

◈

'I'm talking to you!' Amitabh yelled ferociously at me one day, during the last week of stage practice.

It was a supposed to be a dress rehearsal.

'Sorry, sorry Monsieur…I was, was just asking if we could do another take,' a young man, who worked as translator, stuttered, petrified at Amitabh's ire.

I coughed, rubbing my eyes. The ostentatious Indian bridal finery made it difficult to breathe. I shuffled through the script, wondering if I had forgotten my cue. We had been through so many stages of improvisation. Each day, there was something new added only to be removed or altered the very next day. Amitabh's obsessive need for perfection made him one of the most demanding directors I had ever worked with.

'Is this what I have taught all of you? Is this a *film* we are shooting? This, this is…' he clenched his jaws, holding up his copy of the stage notes…'this is theatre, the stage…it's sacred…I can't have my actors coming to work, unprepared. It's a sign of disrespect! Towards me…towards our audience…towards the very craft, we worship. Do you understand? I cannot have you all treat this space like a film set! No one has the right to! Not, not even you, Marie Bourdaine, despite your star status…it's high time you remembered the revised cue…' he hollered, shaking his finger at me.

'Also, you are playing Sakuntalam, a woman forgotten by the man she loved…a powerful king, whose child you now carry in your womb…where is the pathos in your singing? You are not a prima donna, Mademoiselle, you are at the mercy of your lover…a man who has walked away…'

I stepped forward into the spotlight, my head lowered. We'd been rehearsing for almost eight months, away from home, cooped up in a tiny, airless hotel room, overlooking the Seine.

A strange river, a lonely river, a river that divided my heart, between the man I had been engaged to and a married man who had suddenly come between us, all the way from India. From a tiny city called Pune, in a swarming state called Maharashtra. Like my village, on the outskirts of Paris, and yet, in the heart of France.

As I stood in Amitabh's looming presence, my eyes filled, feeling insignificant, the leading lady…and yet…no less than a woman scorned; much like the character I was essaying. Suddenly, fighting the suffocating distance between a director and an actor.

'She is not too well, let's just do it one more time please,' a crew-member from our contingent tried diffusing the tension.

'Listen, Patrick, my mother had her menstrual cycle for ten days every month. She was *always* bleeding. Most women in our part of the world are like that, anaemic. But that didn't stop her doing her job every single day. Marie is not going to get any differential treatment…just because we are close, because your silly gossip columns seem to think we are a couple…' he shouted, his face creased into a scowl.

'I'm sorry, I, I did not mean to upset you, in any way,' my cheeks were reddened from being screamed at this way in front of the whole cast. And yet a part of me felt reassured.

It was the first time Amitabh had actually acknowledged what we shared.

The walls we had built. And broken.

When I went over to his room, as was, by then, habit, Amitabh was fervently scribbling notes on the side of the bound, hand-written script. Lost in thought. The same hotel room suddenly felt strangely distant. The bed, where I rocked him to sleep, somehow, uninviting.

'I just couldn't get you out of my head...what we shared last night was transformative...I mean, the way our bodies melted into one another...at dawn...when you entered me...all these months of...I want you so much, so badly,' I confessed, awkwardly, avoiding direct eye contact.

'We have to stop seeing each other, Marie, this has to stop, whatever this is,' Amitabh's eyes scanned my body.

I hadn't changed out of the heavily sequinned, Indian *ghagra choli.* My eyes were heavily lined with kohl. A *bindi* etched on my forehead. My arms were heavy with transparent glass bangles of myriad colours.

'Why? Just because I was distracted today? One day? Or, because, you are threatened that by the fact that a woman can actually openly desire a man? Does my attraction emasculate your manhood, Amitabh?'

'Listen, Marie...' Amitabh cut me short, pointing at my eyes, 'I come from a really poor country, and I mean really impoverished; poorer than you can ever imagine, any of you French people. My father was a blind circus performer. My mother was a trapeze artist who once dreamt of being an actress, a dancer...she slept with anyone who would have her, for us to stay alive...for food...books...warm clothes...for my sake...

'The last few years, I've worked tirelessly to put our craft on the international map. Struggling to stage performances, working night after night, to apply for grants, literally begging for money at times, staying hungry, fighting against giving into sponsorships...staying away from home, for months, fighting the battles of the marginalized...being hit, arrested, accused of being a traitor, a rabble rouser, anti-social element...all in the hope of giving the have-nots a voice, that can be heard outside...that travels widely...Do you know how hard that is, Marie? What my life has been... before I came here...I have put a lot at stake by taking up this project...I can't allow this mega production to fall apart just because *you* are lovesick, all of a sudden.' His shoulders were shaking.

I stood up. My eyes smarted. 'Are you saying people can't fall in love? That they don't in India?' my voice echoed in the silence.

Amitabh removed his vest. 'Love? Who said anything about love? I was talking about the production, the costs we have incurred to stage this magnum opus...Kalidasa's eternal love ballad *La Legende de Sakuntalam* to be performed as a grandiose French opera...going back to the start... song and dance...caricatures and costumes...the reputation of my country...the deadweight of expectations...on either side.'

'I'm in love with you, Amitabh, I have been, since the first night these arms held you...watched over you as you slept...and every single night, since then...I know there is a lot at stake...and I didn't plan on things changing between us, either...but, they did, and I am not escaping from what I feel,' I ran out of breath, wiping my eyes, to add, weakly, 'I know this is true love, Amitabh...and love in its full form is free from any expectation or preconditions...it never dies... it must never be allowed to...'

'And, what about Henry?' Amitabh quizzed, sharply. Stepping into the shower.

'Who?' my right eye itched, the bleeding kohl having entered inside.

'The man you were supposed to marry...the one you ran away from, coming here, to Paris, instead. Henry, your childhood sweetheart, the man who loves you...back...the way you want him to...' he turned on the tap.

Steam steadily rose in on us.

'I can't love Henry, anymore...not, not after what we shared, last night...all these past months, I have never felt so deeply connected with anyone my whole, entire life…' I spoke passionately.

Amitabh traced the outline of my lips with his thumb.

'I have betrayed a lot of people, Marie…there is blood on my hands…' he pulled away, slowly.

I pressed my face on his back, laden with droplets of moisture.

'Maya's death wasn't your fault, she was a sick child… very sick…' I added gently, planting tiny kisses all over his shoulders and neck.

Amitabh had closed his eyes.

'I promised Sarlu we would get her to see a big doctor…I was sure it was nothing. Later, that night, when she developed breathing trouble again, Sarlu ran out to call our neighbours. I held Maya close to me. 'Go on, get dressed,' Sarlu screamed hysterically. 'She could be dead…'

'It was too late, I was too late…Maya was declared dead on arrival…it was my failure, Marie…I failed as a son, once…and now, as a parent…I wasn't enough…a man like me is never enough...' Amitabh pushed me away from him.

That night, we slept on separate sides of the same bed.

Like total strangers.

The lights over Eiffel Tower strangely muted.

◈

I sat up with some difficulty. Switching on the bedside lamp, I opened my personal diary. Flipping through the pages, I finally found Amitabh's last correspondence to me. A handwritten note, penned to me, on the last day of the production – *La Legende de Sakuntalam* that had played for two whole months, touring practically all of France, before travelling also, to some parts of England. The small, white envelope that I had found neatly placed on this same bed, where I now lay, by myself, would have been the last time I spent alone with Amitabh.

My last memory, of us.

Beloved Marie,

I'm sorry I checked out from the hotel before the official dinner and felicitation ceremony was to commence. I hate these functions, anyway, as I've said to all of you, many times, this last year. Besides, my French is not as proficient as your English has gotten since we started rehearsals.

Anyway, so, I said to myself, save yourself the embarrassment, Kulasheshtra. My team will represent me. They are good at making excuses on my behalf. It's an Indian art form; we call it 'bahana' back home.

I know you'd understand not seeing me tonight...you always did, Marie. Even when we spoke in two diverse tongues.

You know, I've asked myself why a woman like you would want to be with me? How was it so simple? After you walked into the bus, striking such an affable camaraderie? Remember that moment? Our first, alone...

I'd never seen someone more perfect, Marie. It was as if you forced me to take notice, as I did. Unlocking my hotel room. Holding your coat in my hands, feeling fur, for the first time. Touching a foreign substance, defying the distance, between us...

I know I have failed you, Marie. Failed myself. Failed what we had...what we could have. Failed because I didn't try hard enough. The way I must walk away, now, without even putting up a decent fight, knowing I will carry the burden of such a cowardice, all my remaining years.

The sense of being vanquished by the man I could have been. The man you made me want to be, Marie. The man you chose.

You, Marie Bourdaine, were not just my Sakuntalam on stage... but my soulmate. You helped me grieve. Move on, in some measure.

The one time we made love…the many months we waited…were real, Marie. Make no mistake.

You, Marie, were the first woman I ever fell in love with. Not loved.

I know thus that you will not question my decision to return to my country. To my wife, Sarla.

PS: Jusqu'à ce que nous nous revoyions (until we meet again).

Henry, my fiancé, and I were married later the same year in our village chapel, where he now lays buried. We were married for fifteen years before he was claimed by cancer. Henry was a good man, and he loved me, deeply. Never betraying me.

'Au Clair De La Lune…' the words inscribed on his grave.

'Au Clair De La Lune…' I softly whispered, kissing the yellowing page, watching as the letter disappeared into the impenetrable darkness. Floating, lithe. The way I had felt, when Amitabh had entered me, sans words.

I shut the window tight.

The way I had, the night he went away.

Understood in his silences.

SARLA KULASHESHTRA

Amitabh's memoir had recently been re-published and now everyone was reading it. I could not help being bemused by the attention death had brought him. As if dying had lent his career a new lease of life. His book was now selling on the pavements. There were so many events to honour his memory. Every theatre group worth its name was trying to cobble together an event using his name as a branding tool. I refused to attend any of them.

A few months ago, I had turned down an opportunity to speak at the Prithvi Theatre Memorium in Mumbai. A part of me knew that I had possibly risked the chance of being misconstrued. In the same way that Amitabh's silences had always been judged and dissected by his critics, fans and the media – especially, in the years after Malegaon. The pressure on him to take a stand had never quite abated.

I was cynical about this new-found recognition because I had witnessed my husband turn into a shadow. How Amitabh had grappled with a gnawing hollowness – a mounting disbelief in basic human goodness, transparency, and the legal system of this country, qualities and institutions that he had sworn by all his life – eating away at his mind. After every court hearing and press interaction, Amitabh seemed more self-defeated, as witnesses suspiciously switched allegiances, as newspapers tainted his intentions and involvement, depending on the colour of their conscience, as judges floundered, as the case dragged on. As Amitabh blamed himself – not so much for the price of his art, but the nature of his resistance.

The thought that shallow caste and communal politics, which he had fought against and discarded all his life, now chased him everywhere he went. He was a man, not just grappling with his own vision – the projection of it, the purpose of it – but with a dangerously changing nation.

Amitabh wanted to reach out again, but wasn't sure how to anymore.

He had lost relevance, I suppose.

◈

I had just come home from a prolonged meeting with Amitabh's lawyer, who advised me to quietly have the case closed. Now that Amitabh was dead, he insisted that there was no point contesting the charges of sedition that were levied on him more than a decade ago. To go on and on about Malegaon.

'Rawat is all set to launch his own party, Mrs. Kulasheshtra. Let bygones be bygones. At least, this time we can capitalize on public sympathy for your late husband, settle matters, discreetly,' the lawyer had swallowed uncomfortably, adding: 'That's the thing about death. It brings a sense of closure. Maybe, it will be good for you too. I mean, how long will you keep responding to mechanical court summons, travelling in the hot sun, selling your pots and pans to meet mounting legal expenses…and all for what, huh? It's not like there will be any new witnesses, at any point. Rawat, the main accused too was let off long ago. *Kahani ko abhi aap* the end *kar daliye*…this is India, where even gang-rape cases take forever to resolve...this is the time for you to relax, Mrs. Kulasheshtra. *Jitna* footage *iss case ko milna tha, mil gaya*...why waste time on ideological warfare, at this point? Activism was Kulasheshtra's thing... in any case. *Aap bas apni* retirement *ki sochiye*...think selfishly, Sarlaji...*kabhi kabhi* compromise is the best...'

The doorbell rang just then, breaking my chain of thoughts. I opened the door a crack and saw a familiar but not particularly welcome face.

◈

Facing me on our modest cane two-seater sat veteran Marathi theatre actress, Anupama Apte, a ghost of her former self. She was one of Amitabh's most well-known 'finds' who had gone on to carve a unique place of her own in regional theatre, even starring in a few Hindi films, in small side roles. I knew she had always been infatuated with Amitabh and couldn't come to terms with his lack of interest in her.

Anupama had lost a lot of weight; her voluptuous body now hung loosely on her frame. She wore a long cotton skirt and a plain off-white kurti. Anupama lived in Dadar, Mumbai. She had a daughter who studied in a boarding school in Lonavala, from her first marriage to a director who failed to make it big in Bollywood. An FTII pass-out. Her second husband was a film distributor. Also, a decade younger. She was trying her luck in both Hindi and Marathi serials, she mentioned. She had been out of the country for a year on some film assignment and so couldn't visit earlier.

Apparently, she had come to condole.

'Amitabhji was the one who told me to start focusing more on emotionally strong parts, to take up roles I could never dream of executing. I was always a director's actor…I loved him too, you know,' she put her cup away, leaning closer towards me, wiping her eyes, for effect.

'I remember crying *so* much after he narrated the script, Sarlaji. The way he described Maya, as a flesh and blood character – a young woman with gaping wounds, who wants to get even with her father.'

I listened patiently as Anupama went on with her memories, telling me of the time she had auditioned, and had subsequently been rejected for the role of Maya, by him.

'Sarlaji, Amitabhji sat me down and said, "It's a very demanding role, one that needs emotional starkness and complete surrender. Maya is complex, and, yet supremely childlike…you need to work much harder on your expressions. Learn to give in to the character, completely. Give up on who you are, don't hold so much back," he told me. I was stung. "Are you saying you don't trust me as a performer? That you doubt my capability, all of a sudden?" I had interrupted. "Everything I say is not about me. Or my feelings, Anupama," Amitabhji reprimanded me.

'I caught his hand, at this point and pressed it against my cheeks. "Is it true, then, about that Parisian actress? Everyone's talking about her role as Sakuntalam, about this thing you shared…Amitabhji…Sir…was it true? Or was it the effect of the time you spent in Mumbai…I mean the Ballav Salve fiasco…?"'

Known in theatre circles as a loudmouth and trouble-maker, Anupama looked at me sideways, trying to gauge my reaction. I should have known her vested interests in raking up the past. After all, she had been the one to first tell me about Amitabh's fling with Mrinalini. I pushed open a window, allowing the cool evening air to enter the living room. It had been unused for a while.

Anupama pretended to wipe her eyes again sorrowfully with an embroidered handkerchief, before continuing:

'Amitabhji lifted my chin, slowly. He said, "Try and get into the skin of the character, Anupama, this is all too superficial, get rid of this dark eye makeup, trying to look old…"'

She turned her face in my direction. 'I felt so bad, Sarlaji. I shouted: "Why can't you be plain with me? You are a coward, you know. Shit scared to get involved with an actress, here, in India, in Pune, huh? Especially now that everyone is pretty sure you had something with that French opera star?" I was on the verge of bursting into tears. Amitabhji stood watching me, his hands on his hips. "That is exactly the kind of pent-up anger, Anupama, a seething rage in your body language…why don't I see it on stage, more often?" he searched my eyes…'

Anupama paused dramatically, perhaps to assess if I was bowled over. Seeing my impassive stare, she went on, gulping down the remaining tea in her cup:

'Sarlaji, I told your husband: "Everyone knows why you are directing this play. This dark satire that explores the fractured relationship between a father and a daughter…a cycle of abuse and hate…"

'"What are you talking about, Anupama?" Amitabhji had asked me, frowning menacingly.

'I laughed. "I'm talking about her: the one and only, Ms. Mrinalini Shirale…. Your wife's adopted daughter…All the guys in your troupe can't stop raving about her…"

'"And what do they say?" Amitabhji had clenched his jaw.'

Anupama cleared her throat, turning to face me, directly; her eyes glowed, with leftover anger:

'Sarlaji, *aap saanp paal rahey they…woh bhi apne chhat ke niche*,' she spoke fast, all attempts at sounding concerned having left her voice. 'That Mrinalini Shirale was the worst kind of two-faced creature. She *destroyed* your home, and lured your husband away from you. She repaid your kindness by biting the hand that fed her.'

I looked away, hoping to convey the message that I had had enough. I'd never liked Anupama, in any case. And here she was, playing her old games, as was her second nature.

'You remember our last meeting?' she added urgently, whispering thickly, perhaps hoping to convey a fake sense of concern. 'You had the *saddest* eyes. Ever since you lost the child…people said you were never the same again... that the *randi* broke you…something like that…'

I stood up. 'I'm tired, Anupama, and you better leave, thanks for your visit, but I want to lie down now.'

As I shut the door on Anupama, an old memory rose, of the time she had visited me, once before.

◈

'How are you, Sarlaji?' Anupama had barged in all those years ago, much like she had today. Her makeup was tarty; her cleavage generously on display in her small choli.

'What brings you here, Anupama? I heard you were moving to Mumbai? Heard you are tying the knot, soon? Hope you will not discontinue acting?' I tried to be civil.

'I should've called first, *na*? But, but I just thought…it's my duty to tell you…everything. Right from the start, before I left Pune,' she had declared, dramatically narrowing her eyes.

'So, things between Amitabh and you soured after he didn't select you as the lead actress for his new play, *Maya*? You're not the first one to make these allegations about him, you must know that, Anupama…' I had remarked, matter-of-factly.

'I know, but this is not about us,' she had snapped.

'Then don't waste my time, dear. I have a dance class waiting. Besides, I have to take Mrinalini to the doctor later,' I called out for Meena-tai.

Anupama clicked her tongue. 'This is in fact about her; *your* Mrinalini, the one you now think of as your daughter,' she had retorted sardonically. 'Yes, you heard right, Sarlaji, this is about Mrinalini – the girl who calls you "Aiyee".'

'What makes you think I should react to every rumour you report? Why do I have to listen to your crazed drivel, Anupama?' I had replied angrily.

'Because, this time, you have no choice, Sarlaji, you are just as powerless as I am, as we all are!' She had stared back into my eyes. 'Look, I just want to be a friend to you…a well-wisher; only a woman can understand another woman's heart,' she had tried reaching out.

'I have no friends, Anupama,' I cut her short, 'I have lived this way since I moved out of my father's house. Also, Mrinalini is my child. *I* took her in, not Amitabh. So, I would appreciate it if you leave her out of these petty politics and mindless allegations. She's a talented young girl and, will, I know, make her own place under the sun. And, as for Amitabh, he's a man many admire. To confuse admiration with attraction would be dangerous…for you…so get out of my house. I don't need you and your poisonous mind to taint everything that is pure. Get out now!" I had lost my temper.

Later, of course, I had witnessed the truth with my own eyes.

I had caught Mrinalini in Amitabh's room.

His head rested on her bosom. She rocked back and forth. Their eyes were closed.

The room too was shadow infested.

I shuddered at the memory of that dark night. The way our lives had been altered irrevocably. Anupama had known something I couldn't fathom, even when it was happening under my nose. I flopped down on the cane two-seater, feeling drained. The cushion was still warm from her presence. Wiping the sides of my neck, I flipped open to the page I had been reading. Hoping to find some solace in Amitabh's words.

Hoping to understand why he had done what he had done. Hoping for answers as to why he had wronged me, again?

Why did he always have to destroy the people I loved?

First Rakesh, then my baby girl, and then, Mrinalini.

The girl I had taken in and nurtured, and started to care about.

MAYA SHIRALE

'Goodbyes are gruelling. Goodbyes are greedy. Goodbyes are gullible. Goodbyes are guilty. Goodbyes are greeting cards. Goodbyes are girly. Goodbyes are ghosts. Goodbyes are gruesome. Goodbyes are gimmicky. Goodbyes are gritty. Goodbyes are guesswork.

Goodbyes don't mean a thing.

Except...goodbye...'

The lines blurred in front of my eyes. I felt completely hollow these days, so empty inside that though Amitabh's memoirs made me cry, it was a relief to feel *something*; anything that wasn't anger and hysteria and frustration. Since the day the news first came...

My cell-phone had been vibrating incessantly. I had been ignoring it all morning. I groped under the icy sheets. Avi was gone too. His boxers lay by the edge of the bed.

I put the phone on loudspeaker. It was the journalist, Razia Siddiqui.

'I've got a new job.'

'*Accha, toh?*'

'I wanted to meet you once Maya, we could go to your favourite spot...?'

'I had something else planned, Razia, a prior engagement, I'm sorry... '

'But...'

'I've got to hang up now…someone's on the other line…' I fabricated.

'Please, Maya, at least let me text you what it's about, then you decide.' She messaged me saying she was trying to put together a longer and more indepth article on Amitabh Kulasheshtra as the more she read and heard about him, the more he fascinated her. His professional triumphs and his personal failures. Trying to understand his flawed genius. His creativity and his conflicts. His convictions and his contradictions.

I decided to meet her.

I guess I owed him that much.

Or, maybe I needed to feel closer to Amitabh; for I felt so far apart now.

◈

Razia was waiting at the exact same spot where I had last met her in Chowpatty. She had probably been waiting for a while, but I didn't care. The sky was overcast with pregnant rain clouds. The sea, unusually tempestuous. It was also high tide.

I asked Alam to park at some distance from Razia and then asked him to tell her to come inside the car. It wasn't dark yet. And I was reluctant to be spotted.

I turned off my cell.

Razia slid into the seat next to me: 'Thanks for texting and coming down, Maya, and answering my call earlier.'

'Only because you said you were working on a piece about Kulasheshtra. For Amitabh's upcoming death anniversary…'

Razia turned on her recorder: '*Maya, I am here to ask you what transpired that night between you and Amitabh Kulasheshtra, when his wife supposedly walked in on you both, in the dark, in the bedroom of their Pune house…as she later told leading Marathi newspaper,* Samna, *almost a year and a half later. Alleging you ruined their marriage. Claiming you betrayed her, most of all. A woman you even called...'*

'Aiyee...I called her Aiyee, as in mother. The thing is, I loved her, more than even my own mother, perhaps, Razia. The way she looked after me...It was because of her, that I got to meet Amitabh, to become Maya...*his* Maya...'

'I assume you are referring to the sensational play, Maya, *here...Kulasheshtra's first work, after Paris...and... Marie...?'*

'Amitabh caught me sneaking around in his room a few months after his return from Paris. I'd been living in their home for almost a year by then. Aiyee had taken me in when I'd taken up position outside their gates, after running away from mine. Aiyee and he slept on separate floors. In my desperate eagerness to catch his eye, I'd often sneak inside, look through his things. It was on one of those days that I happened to discover the script of a play he was supposedly working on, almost accidentally, really, and it blew my mind. It was as if he had written *my* story. When he caught me, the first thing I blurted out was: "How do *you* know how a child who has been molested feels? A girl raped by her own father, almost every night? Did, did she tell you? The character in your new play...?' It was the first time I actually stood in his presence – a man whom I had obsessed over for so long.'

'Wasn't he upset you had looked through his script? Kulasheshtra was known to be famously private, especially about his writing?'

'He was. But I was so immersed in the script that I immediately said: "I know this is wrong, a big mistake, even coming here, to your home. But, please will you answer me. How did you know all this about my life, the entire thing? Did Aiyee mention something?" Amitabh looked at me quizzically as I continued: "You know, that...that my father touched me, every night, almost...till I ran away from home...decided it was enough.'

'What happened next, Maya?'

'Amitabh listened to me without saying a word. I went on: "Aiyee told me about your daughter. She said ever since her death...you've changed...you won't talk about it, she claims...it's, it's exactly the way I feel, too, you know, about everything...I can't talk about it," I wiped my face, adding edgily, "Maya...was your little daughter's name, *na*?...Is that's why you've named your lead character after her? This *is* a new play, right?"

'"Sarlu told you that? Even that?" Amitabh finally raised his voice.

'"No, no...Aiyee hardly mentions your work. She only talks occasionally about Maya. She's so lonely, Aiyee...'

'Was their marriage over, by then? Did you take advantage of the void in...'

'It was Amitabh's decision to cast me as the lead in *Maya*. He was looking for a fresh face, and perhaps my personal history also influenced him. The day before the play opened, I spent the entire night with Amitabh in the Pune house, in his room, rehearsing my lines. The last scene, in particular, I broke down: "I'm scared my father will come and watch this play. And...and see me. I've, I've managed to hide here. Even now, after all this time, I can't sleep without feeling his breath on my shoulder. The way he'd casually brush his hardness against my buttocks. Before he grabbed my breasts. Tearing at my t-shirt. Pulling off my panties. I, I have tried so hard...to forget..."

'"Take a pull on this," Amitabh had passed me a half-smoked bidi.

'"I don't like hiding things, from Aiyee," I pushed his hand away.

'"Hiding is what you've been doing all your life, by your own admission," he took a lengthy drag.

'There was an awkward silence. The room was stinking of tobacco.

'"As a performer, tap into that primal fear and use it to your advantage. Fear is what keeps us alive. The fear of being found out, of being judged, of being unloved. It's why we try so hard, constantly, to be this other person, to wear a mask; to keep love out. Perhaps, abandonment and abandoning, are the same thing…in the end," Amitabh placed his hand protectively over mine.'

'*There was obviously an attraction, Maya. I mean, the guru-shishya paradigm slowly polarizing into more of a man-woman thing? Was it the same as what transpired between Marie and him, in Paris? Was Sarla punishing you for someone else..?*'

'As per tradition, Pune was where we staged the final show. *Maya* was Amitabh's most awaited production after the international success of *La Legende de Sakuntalam*,…it was a massive success, the play, lauded for openly tackling sexual abuse in modern Indian homes. A topic a conservative society like ours shuddered to confront. *Maya* catapulted me into a theatre sensation overnight; critics lauded my no-holds-barred performance, blown away by the emotional starkness of the character; at how sexual abuse was used as a metaphor for a regressive society, and how unsafe the girl-child was in a sexually closeted culture. The play was essentially a monologue that used a lot of shadow play, and it had Amitabh enact a brief role, the first time he acted in his own creation, essaying the role of my father, the one whom I murder in the last act. It was our only scene together on stage. I had never spoken to anyone about my own father, before Amitabh, before this play.

'On the night, after our final performance I was completely overwhelmed. I hadn't bothered to remove my make-up. Amitabh had consumed a lot of alcohol. Most of the men in the troupe were sloshed as well. We'd also organized an impromptu party, it wasn't really planned, or anything. After we reached home, I guided Amitabh up to his room, helping him to change out of his kurta. Aiyee was sleeping downstairs in her part of the house. She never attended any of his plays. "It will bring bad luck, if I come…" she used to say, a little darkly I thought, each time I pleaded with her to come and see me perform. I always felt she was being unnecessarily superstitious.

'"Turn off the lights after you," Amitabh had commanded, as soon as I was done.

'I did as I was told. "Thank you…for giving me a chance of a lifetime…" I said tremulously, as our shoulders brushed.

'"You could have performed much better, you know,' Amitabh removed a bidi from behind his ear, flopping down on the bed.

'"I'm sorry, if I didn't live up to your expectations…' I said, turning back and sitting down on the floor by his bed.

'"Mrinalini,' Amitabh propped up my chin, 'you've got to bury your father. You can't get away with not killing him, in your mind, each time."

'I covered my face with both my hands, "I feel so dead inside…soulless…the little girl who shivered every time she heard a door being opened, lights being turned off…who bore the brunt of a stale marriage, a paralyzed mother and a father who couldn't retain a single job…paying the price…" I swallowed my tears.

'"We're all dead, inside. It's why we love this stage so much…it's the only place we get to be completely alive. Tell our own stories, pretending to be someone else. Live a different life than the one you ran away from, the one that still haunts you daily. It's exactly why you failed today… you just couldn't be her, the woman who wanted to stab her father, desperately…the pervert who abused her every night. The hatred…I didn't see it fully in your eyes…that vengeful wrath…you should have been consumed with…"

I couldn't look into his eyes. "But…it was not in the script, either. I was meant to drop the blade and walk away at the end," I feebly tried defending myself, wiping my eyes.

'Amitabh stubbed out his bidi. "Then what are you doing, here?" he grabbed my shoulders, all of a sudden.

'"I was scared you may slip and fall down the stairs… you, you were drunk…" my heart raced.

'"I've been walking alone up those stairs, every single night of my life, Maya…I will not fall," Amitabh tugged at my shirt.

'I was wearing a chiffon blouse. The top button popped open.

'"Don't," Amitabh held back my hands, stopping me from fixing my buttons.

'"Why? This is all *so* wrong…Aiyee could wake up, any minute…she, she will…" I couldn't control my tears.

'"What are you so damn scared of? That I will touch you? Here, in my room? With my wife sleeping, downstairs? Why do you hold back from me in this fashion? The same way you do on stage? Why couldn't I see that madness in you? Why were you scared to stab your father? What frightens you? His shadow? His stare? His seeing you as a piece of flesh… why do you allow all the men in your life to treat you the same way? When will you stop running, Mrinalini Shirale? Where?" he leaned closer, his breath covering my lips.

'It's true then? "Kulasheshtra's head sandwiched between your breasts…"'

'Nothing happened between us that night, Razia. Actually, Amitabh was dead right. Every man I had ever loved…fucked…was to my mind, a guy resembling my father. It's why I always left first, wanting them to get hurt, to suffer perhaps. Seeking retribution…"You, you must sleep…it's late, let me help you lie down, please, it's been a long night…" I gestured at the made-up bed.

"Tell me the truth. why did you barge into my house, the way you did? Stay on, for days?" Amitabh ran his fingers roughly through my hair.

'"It feels safer, here, with Aiyee….' I had answered.

'"You really love Sarlu, don't you? In your own, childish way? Grateful that she took you in, that afternoon? I have heard about the way she nursed you back to health…the way she never let you out of her sight…Sarlu took me in, too, all those years, ago…she has a kind heart, despite her outward facade…Sarlu can't watch someone fall…she has never let me fall, I'm one of her projects, as are you…' he spoke in an icy tone.

'Then before I could say anything, he added, "Anyway, promise me…that you'll keep this name, from now on. You will be Maya. Maya Shirale, not Mrinalini, anymore."

'"Maya belongs only to Aiyee and you…she always will. I have no right to be her, after tonight, it's not my place," I kept my voice down, on purpose.

'"No…you don't understand. Everyone has taken my Maya away, my memory of her. Sarlu, especially, hates it when I say her name aloud. It's what we've been doing, both of us. Playing hide and seek with each other. Maya…Maya was the purest part of us. She was so small, perfect. My daughter. I miss her. I miss Sarlu and the way she looked during her pregnancy…"

'I touched his mouth. Amitabh fell forward, his body limp; he had passed out.'

'So, it was his fault, then? Maybe, Amitabh Kulasheshtra wanted to seduce you?'

'I cradled Amitabh, steadying his back. It was pitch-dark, except for a tiny sliver of light. From outside.'

'Sarla!'

'Yes. She saw me and assumed the worst. I wrote everything in a letter to Aiyee. Told her what he had said to me. I lied only to Amitabh. Saying I had won a spot in a prestigious beauty contest in Mumbai that I had concealed from him while we rehearsed and performed the play. Telling him I couldn't wait to be famous; to see my name on billboards, eventually, start acting in commercial, Hindi films…make a lot of money…be like the men, you know… be a hero…I boarded a bus at 6 am. Leaving the way I had come. With nothing.'

'So, Sarla lied then? Made up facts in the sensational Samna interview, just to frame you, falsely? To perhaps get back at Kulasheshtra…Mrs. Sarla Kulasheshtra…not quite the woman the world believes her to be…'

'No, Razia. Aiyee never lied. Aiyee never lies.'

AVIK DASGUPTA

BLINDSIDE

Interpretation is everything in theatre; unlike cinema that relies on neat conclusions, happy ones mostly; the stage begins and ends the same way – in the pulse and thrust of darkness. The measure of which changes constantly.

For a long time, I tried understanding what I was doing. Trying to seek an explanation of my craft through the eyes of others. Each time, I took a risk. Taking up a cause. Each time the media and my colleagues wrote me off. Criticizing my seething need to re-invent the rules of how the world was being trained to view the stage. Fed on an elitist, bourgeoisie diet. Theatrewalas who'd constantly try to compete with cinema, instead of discovering a new idiom of stagecraft. Reach out to our glorious Indian past of storytelling. Returning to the simple village chowk that was the first 'rang manch' in a way…glorious indigenous folklore, pertaining to everyday heroes who exemplified goodness and championed the people of the soil. Dancers, musicians, puppeteers, and magicians, whose language of expression, was the source.

My techniques were constantly debated….

◈

My cell-phone buzzed madly, falling out of my hands, toppling the copy of *Blindside* that I had been re-reading the whole of last month. I ran my fingers slowly over the cover, after bending down to lift it up. Thinking of how the past year had played out…how we had all made an uneasy peace with Kulasheshtra's passing away.

The tiny fairy lights on Maya's sprawling rooftop garden gleamed at a distance. Resembling those on the 35th floor of JW Marriot, Juhu. One of the city's plushest five-stars, that was packed to the brim with guests, stars and media.

I closed my eyes, again. My thoughts travelling back to the biggest night of my life. And how Maya had let me down again.

◈

I had been smoking, non-stop. My eyes were bloodshot. Shirish Kulkarni, my first Assistant Director, kept coming up to me every few seconds, wanting to say something, before walking away, his hands inside his pockets. Finally, he thrust a copy of *Bombay Times* into my hand and stabbed his finger at a small write-up.

Payal Shah, a small-time TV actress I had once dated, before I ran into Maya, with whom I lived together for some time, had made it to the back page of *Bombay Times.* It was supposed to be a tribute to Kulasheshtra on his death anniversary. The article came with a small disclaimer from the newspaper editor stating they were in no way looking to malign Kulasheshtra's image, and that Payal's remarks were hers, alone:

'AD is just using Maya Shirale and she him. There is no love lost. I have my doubts Maya will even surface today to give the mahurat clap for AD's big-budget, second film, Nirmaan, at the glitzy press conference that has been organized by his producers, Eros Entertainment. I am not saying all this because he dumped me for her or because I haven't been invited. I am saying this because today is bound to be a manhoos day. Kulasheshtra, also died, today, exactly, a year back, right? Aaj ka din hi manhoos, hai. AD will never forget June 10.'

'Maya is *not* coming, AD.' Shirish had said emphatically. 'Rosy called. She is suffering from a severe attack of migraine. Rosy is giving her medicines, but has been instructed to leave her room, as Maya insists she wants to sleep,' Shirish cleared his throat, glancing at me, apologetically, walking closer to add in a muted voice, 'Maya doesn't want any calls.'

I lit up again.

'How can she do this to you?' Shirish glared angrily, before throwing up his hands, 'Media, *aap dono ko saath dekhna chahti hai. Waise hi...bakwas likhti rehti hai, aap dono ke bare mein.*'

I flung my half-finished cigarette away. Looking up my speed dial to inform the Publicity head of Eros Entertainment, wondering what excuse we could give to the Press who had been patiently waiting for Maya.

'*Umar mein woh badi hai, aap se...kaee saal. Usske* against legal case *hai...Sanki woh hai!* Time *usska bura chal raha hai,* your star, your star is on the rise!'

I didn't respond.

'What shall I tell them downstairs?' Shirish had raised his voice, probably waiting for my reaction.

I shrugged my shoulders, heading towards the elevator, in silence.

'Maybe, she *is* really unwell, she does have an issue with migraines,' I wiped my mouth, checking my wristwatch.

The event was scheduled for 7 pm. It was now 8.46 pm.

'It's your first commercial film, a big break!' Shirish held the elevator door, 'This *is* a huge deal...a two-film contract with Eros, the most sought-after production house, here. Besides, Maya could do with the positive coverage too! I mean, for the past year, the media has only been interested in raking up garbage about that Kulasheshtra fellow and her, as if anyone cares anymore. This is the 20th century. Everyone's doing someone, in this industry! How long can she ride this unsaleable image of hers? Sit on her high horse! How can you just let Maya off the hook, so easily? What kind of a man does that?'

His eyes were turning red. 'You deserve better, man,' Shirish muttered under his breath.

'Maybe,' I turned to face Shirish. 'Maybe, so does Maya. Everyone deserves better, Shirish. Maybe, even Kulasheshtra!'

It was the first time I had spoken of Kulasheshtra, this way.

'Has Maya ever spoken to you about Kulasheshtra?' Shirish quizzed, sounding suspicious. 'No one really knows if they were in touch, and if he was actually coming here to Mumbai to meet her the night he died.'

◈

'Maya Shirale Ditches Live-in Boyfriend, Avik Dasgupta at the Much-Talked-About *Nirmaan Mahurat*,' the Bollywood tabloids gleefully reported the next morning.

My team was unusually silent.

The very next night, we left for Rajasthan for the gruelling outdoor shoot of *Nirmaan.*

A full month passed before I tried Maya's number again.

I had been shooting non-stop. The last few months before I had left for the shoot had been especially difficult. Every time, I'd made plans, she'd inevitably disappeared, sans an explanation or citing an attack of migraine. Occasionally, on the rare days when she was when she was available, I was away on location or in meetings related to production. Talks were also on with Fox Searchlight Pictures for a new deal as they were planning to launch their studio in India with four breakthrough Bollywood directors.

Maya never asked me when I would be back or how my day was, or if I had missed her. Or surprised me on sets as I used to, when she would be shooting, earlier. She had been drinking a lot, of late, as well. Alam would report back, making me swear I wouldn't breathe a word of this to her. Some nights, Rosy would call too, her voice laced with anxiety. I drove around town like a maniac. At dawn, when I entered the apartment I'd find Maya curled up on the couch with her designer heels still on. I would be livid, and yet, there was something so fragile about Maya this past year, especially.

Between us…

Something I was so scared to touch.

Or, maybe, I knew it would take one bad day.

Just one last fight…

◈

'Maya…Maya, what do you mean, leave the room? Do you have any bloody idea what time it is?' I smashed the glass on the floor, as Maya removed her make-up, smoking constantly, asking me to leave her alone. Citing the same excuse: migraine.

'Stop screaming, Avi, *mera sar phaat raha hai*…just leave…this house has four bedrooms, Goddammit,' she walked towards me, her footsteps unstable.

'Migraine, huh? Bullshit, Maya,' I pushed her shoulders roughly, losing my cool, 'Alam called me, an hour or so ago…saying your cell which you gave him in the morning, has been buzzing, nonstop, and that you asked him to not take any calls. To just tell people you are out of the country, or something. My phone hasn't stopped ringing, either, Maya…it's always the same…every time, the same crap…I am summoned, probed on your whereabouts, as if I am your bloody, personal secretary…Maya, are, are you…talk to me, Maya…just how much have you boozed?'

'Turn off the lights, this is my house. Do as I say,' Maya fought off my advances, flinging the cigarette away.

I covered my nose. 'Snorting that shit, again, huh? Fuck Maya! Have you lost it, completely? You're doing drugs, again, combined with alcohol. Do you have *any* idea how dangerous this combination is…you could die, Maya!' I tried grabbing her hands.

'I won't die, Avi…please just turn off the lights, now…I can't take the glare…not tonight…let me be by myself…. Please, Avi…get out of this room…this house…leave now…' she rubbed her heavily mascaraed eyes, trying to pull away from my arms.

'Maya…this is getting out of hand. I can't keep rushing back from my shoots, always…thankfully, I was in the country, today…my staff in office…how many meetings have I cut short…to manage your mess…it's started affecting me…my reputation…' I tried gripping her waist, firmly.

'What reputation, Avi? You are barely two films old… *abhi teesri banne toh do, pehle…chalne toh do*…everything you have, is Maya Shirale's. I made you, Avik Dasgupta. Maya made you, *samjhe*? You were nothing, so don't you dare shove your reputation in my face. And as for Alam calling you… I'd told him clearly that I'm not interested in taking calls today…' Maya's eyes glared, her lips quivering with rage.

'Maya, stop yelling. You have had too much to drink.'

'Let go of my hands, Avi...' Maya tried wriggling out, again, her jaws clenched.

'Maya okay...baby, look, calm down, you need to take a shower, sleep,' I pulled her chin up.

'Patronizing me, *babumoshai...*' she chuckled, looking mean.

'No, Maya, that's not what you pay me to do. I am just concerned, that's all. Your drinking has gotten worse in the last one year...and now this...you are back to these drugs.... Maya...I am worried, sick...' I paused, wiping the bleeding kohl from her eyes, 'I...I can't sleep...nights you disappear... when you leave home and I don't know when you will get back or where you are...it drives me insane...I've tried being okay about it, accepting your need for personal space...'

'Stop trying to save me all the time, Avi...' Maya stared back at me.

'Why, Maya? What's wrong if I am saving you or want to?' I was hurting.

Maya said nothing.

'You had a script reading with Romil Ratnam, this afternoon, Maya, he flew all the way from Chennai...and you just didn't show up...he, he called me, so many times, utterly frustrated with your erratic behaviour...Romil is a legend...' I ran my hands over her back.

'Aren't they all, Avi? All you, guys? Directors? Legen.... leg...' she slurred.

I tried getting her to sit down.

'I am Maya Shirale. I will get a million Romil Ratnam's begging me to spare some time. I care two hoots that I spurned him...anyway, this is the fifth or sixth time he's expressed a keen interest in working with me...last time, he wanted me to play that Vikram Sampath's sister...sister... me! The time before that, he wanted me to do an item song... *kamina saala*! He may be a miracle worker down South, but in

Mumbai, I rule…' she wheezed, beads of sweating trickling down the sides of her face.

'Unfortunately, Maya, that's hardly the case,' I cut her short rudely. 'You are getting on in years, and, despite your costly skin peels, overseas Botox sessions and enhancement surgeries, you can't hide your age forever. There are younger, prettier girls, today, in Bollywood…desperate for that one big break…including star kids and Miss India's, who anyway, have an extra edge…so, unlike what you think of yourself and others bending backwards, for you, you actually have to work that much harder, so…Maya Shirale, instead of putting words in my mouth, clean up your act…and…for God's sake…'

'…Sleep with Romil?' Maya smiled spitefully and pushed me aside.

'Must you bring every conversation down to sex? And every man to being a recipient of your sexual prowess?' I retorted as she sashayed away, unsteadily.

'That's what they all say, don't they? That Maya Shirale gets away by sleeping around. C'mon Avi, stop acting coy. They all say I seduced you. That I used you as my toy boy, even that ex-girlfriend of yours, *do takke ki* television…*badi aaye* Bombay Times *mein…*' she shot me an accusatory side glance.

'How do you think such rumours and headlines make me feel, Maya?' I raised my voice, this time, 'every time, you end up doing something out of hand, things are inevitably connected to us? Why don't you tell me what's troubling you, instead? Why I always have to beg? Like the time you didn't turn up for the premiere of *Nirmaan*?'

Maya strutted over the broken pieces of glass, not caring if she hurt herself: 'How many times will you keep hounding me about that, Avi? I had a migraine. Simple,' she turned to face me, directly.

'I was upset, Maya, humiliated...you could have taken some medicine, called me beforehand, stretched yourself for once...knowing fully well that the first clap was to be given by you...fully aware the media would play this up big; straightaway alleging there was trouble in paradise... throwing up muck...' I looked away; the memory of that evening still haunted me.

'*Tumko tumhare* reputation *ki badi padi hai aaj*, huh?' Maya lit up, flinging open the balcony door.

'Yes! Yes! Goddammit! If I say yes...what would that make me, Maya? An ungrateful lover? A cold-hearted, prick or another selfish jerk? Why can't we be just an ordinary couple in Bollywood?' I followed her out, my face flushed with anger.

Maya was drinking again. 'If you wanted ordinary, you should have still been fucking that C-grade chick you were about to settle down with, before you decided to up your game and shag me in my car...thought of "ordinary" before moving in with *the* Maya Shirale...Drinking her expensive single malt and smoking her imported cigarettes.... *ordinary*!' she sneered, the colour rising in her cheeks.

'You are insulting me, Maya,' I shouted.

'No, you are, Avi, because in Bollywood, no one is ordinary. This word, ordinary, it's utter trash. It means nothing,' Maya lashed out at me.

'Is that what I mean to you also, Maya? Utter trash? Ordinary? Is that why you chose me, when you did? Wanting to change my appearance, my wardrobe...share your contacts, freely...ask your driver to drive me to my meetings...Why did you do what you did? Because, you were in love with me, or because you hate ordinary?' I retaliated.

'*Mera sar*, please, Avi...go watch some football, or something,' Maya clicked her tongue.

'Why? What's so bloody special about your migraine, today? Just say it, Maya. What are you so damn afraid of? So, it's been a year already? So, my *Nirmaan mahurat* was on the same day. June 10? It's *manhoos*, right?' I gripped her shoulders, violently.

'How dare you!' Maya widened her eyes, her drink spilling on my shirt.

'How dare I what, Maya? Bring up Amitabh Kulasheshtra to your face? *Why not?* Everyone wants to know what was cooking between you both…if, after he left Mumbai a few months after the shocking *Samna* article by his wife, you both were in touch again? If you reached out to him…and if he was, as is being speculated, indeed on his way to meet you? Why don't you spill the beans, Maya? *It was just a fling, right?* He cheated on his wife with you. He was years older. Your teacher. A *guru. So* what, Maya? You just said it yourself… nothing is ordinary in this industry, no couple is ordinary, so what was so special about Amitabh Kulasheshtra and you, answer me, Maya Shirale…' I yanked the glass out of her hand and banged it down on a small wrought iron table.

Maya placed her trembling hands over my chest.

'Amitabh is not your concern…' Maya grit her teeth, 'I mean, it's not as if you are fucking me to get back at your mentor…a man you looked up to as a role model; who cut short your dreams of being a director in theatre…your first love…everyone knows your issues with Amitabh Kulasheshtra, so quit pressurizing me to play into the hands of the popular press…just, so that you can feel even, after all these years. I mean, why didn't you try to gain admission to NCD, the next year? It's your ego, Avi…even that night I didn't show up at your *mahurat*, it was your same bruised ego. All you men are the same. You pretend to care. But all you want is a version of a woman you can remote control,' she wheezed.

'Go fuck yourself, Maya Shirale!' I clenched my fist, my chest heaving agitatedly.

'And, just where do you think you are going, Avi… strutting off that way, huh?'

'None of your business,' I met her eyes, one last time.

'You're turning a mountain into a molehill, Avi…' she rushed inside.

'No, Maya Shirale, that would be *your* thing,' I banged the bedroom door on her face.

RK CHOPRA

'This Kulasheshtra's childhood is bloody *dilchasp*...' one of my lawyers remarked lewdly, waving a cheap pirated edition of Amitabh's memoirs in my face. After Amitabh's death, the copies of *Blindside*, that had rotted on the shelves during the years he was alive, had suddenly received a new lease of life. Everyone seemed to want to lay their hands on it. On him, in some way.

'Where did you get this from?' I asked impatiently, grabbing it from him, running my fingers slowly over the cover.

'Better buy yourself a copy, to keep yourself engaged, RK. After all, you might have to spend a few weeks in the *hawalat*, in the lock-up, just to make it seem all is fair,' he cackled, not directly answering my question.

I looked away. The case against me was dragging on. It had been over a year since I had got any work. 'Didn't know you were into reading...' I remarked, placing the book on the bed and walking up to the mini bar. I poured myself a stiff whiskey.

The lawyer pointed at the book. 'It's been selling like hot cakes, it seems. Just picked it up from the Juhu Tara Road crossing...*sasta, sundar, tikao*...never heard of this shit, before,' he laughed, scratching his beard.

I hadn't been able to focus on anything, beyond a point. My thoughts constantly travelled back to Banno. A part of me was desperate to just see her once. I imagined her lips pressed over mine. The way she would kiss me, not holding back

'Can I travel out of Mumbai? A day trip?' I pulled myself a seat.

'Nothing before our confidential meeting with Amol Rawat, RK,' Jayant Salve, Singh's junior, a sidekick of sorts, who always carried a shiny black briefcase and faked an American accent, said. 'He's a big man in the party, with close links to the Centre…a king-maker, of sorts, he's the only man who can bail you out of this mess, if he puts pressure on the system.'

Mahesh Singh, senior advocate, who was known for his *filmi* links and who headed the legal team that was representing me, flopped down on the edge of the bed. Flipping open *Blindside*, he smirked: 'Remember how Rawat fucked Kulasheshtra? *Aisa danda mara tha saale ko*, he got such a stick up his ass…No wonder, he ended up being beaten to pulp on that train to Mumbai. He had supposedly misbehaved with one of the ladies, or something…'

Jayant, who was making some notes burst out laughing. Then he suddenly remembered something and turned to me: 'Hang on a minute, didn't you also know this Kulasheshtra chap? I read somewhere that…' he piped in, as I took a large gulp of the single malt.

'Go slow, RK. *Daaru ke paise bhi tumhe hi chukane honge*,' Mahesh rolled his eyes as I raised a toast in their direction.

'Rawat's PA messaged saying he's free this Friday, and will meet us at the Bombay Gymkhana. He will book us a private table. For lunch. We'll manage the local police,' Jayant, spoke out of turn, scanning his sleek, black phone.

I shrugged my shoulders listlessly.

'Whatever happened to that case between Amitabh and Rawat?' I turned to face Mahesh directly.

My phone buzzed. It was my son Monty calling. I put it on silent.

'As expected, nothing much,' Mahesh removed his rimless spectacles, and continued, 'As far as I can recall, nothing came of it, after a point. Rawat had the full support of the Centre, and was a force to reckon with in Maharashtra state politics by then, so he is said to have bought out most of the witnesses, all those who had seen his goons actually bash up Prakash Lele.

'Lele's own daughter also backtracked, at some point, showing keenness for a hefty out-of-court settlement. A few years later, she was given an election ticket by Rawat. She lost, though.

'So, after a while, technically it was just Kulasheshtra *vs.* Rawat. And while the Congress always had a glad eye for the theatre stalwart and his brand of grassroots activism, its chips were down in Delhi, the Lok Sabha polls were also nearing back then, and no one wanted to risk too much. I have heard that the Rashtriya Dal had tried through some fellow theatre artists, to reach out to Kulasheshtra…or, maybe, actually his wife. To strike a convenient truce. They were willing to drop the sedition charges on Amitabh, if he withdrew the counter allegations against Rawat. There was a lot of back and forth, was all I knew. I think the case is still not closed, but due to lack of circumstantial evidence, there was nothing proven on paper. Rawat was innocent, as in, until proven guilty. Kulasheshtra also lost his allies. And while there were protests and some student agitations organized by the National Centre of Drama and the Film Institute, random stuff... some show of solidarity towards Kulasheshtra who tried his best to keep the fight for justice alive... but the incident had taken a toll on him, mentally and financially. He sustained substantive head injuries himself, and never regained his full health. He was also suffering from Alzheimer's towards the end of his own life, or so I heard. Or, maybe it was dementia. There were numerous versions, when he was found dead on that train.

'Kulasheshtra was a formidable force, no doubt. But, a spent force. At some hearings, he was represented by his wife, Sarla…she was always, there, never missing a single hearing, even as Kulasheshtra could not make it. Maybe, there was no point, anymore. Maybe, it was just a case of saving face. Artistic integrity, or whatever bullshit these arty folks are all about! *Bakwas…*'

My heart skipped a beat.

'Hadn't things soured between them, though? I believe they lost a child, or something?' Jayant commented casually, walking towards Mahesh with an open file.

For a while, both of them whispered between themselves. 'Well, it isn't as if Kulasheshtra was any *doodh mein dhula insaan.* Wasn't he shagging our very own Bollywood drama queen, Maya Shirale? At some point, even relocating here, supposedly wanting to make a film with her? She was his "Muse",' Mahesh winked, meeting my fixed stare.

'Maya Shirale, of course, has slept with everyone,' Jayant quipped cockily, pulling open the curtains.

The room was suddenly flooded with the mid-morning sun.

I covered my face.

'Hey, you know what that Rawat's PA, Satish Manjrekar, told me in confidence, making me swear I wouldn't tell anyone.' Mahesh opened a bottle of mineral water, and gulped down a large sip. 'He says Kulasheshtra was carrying some cloth bag with him on that train when the skirmish happened…it was lost in the commotion, it seems. The railway police had it with them, not handing it over to his widow along with his other worldly possessions…he bragged about how one of their men in the force who subsisted on their hefty bribes had sent it over to Rawat…'

I swerved. 'What bag?' I asked in a shrill voice, placing my whiskey glass down with a thud. 'What was in it? Was Amitabh coming here to meet someone in particular? Did that Manjrekar chap say anything more…?'

Mahesh was just about to answer when Jayant who was walking towards me with some documents, looked up in our direction: 'Maybe, it was case related stuff, though I am dead sure he was headed here to reunite with Maya Shirale…his old flame…wasn't she a small-time Pune stage actress, or something, before she became a star, when old man Kulasheshtra spotted her talent? Casting-couch *wala* scene…' He winked lewdly at Mahesh.

'Maya Shirale's quite an item, huh?' Mahesh chuckled, adding in the same breath: 'Tell us, how was she in bed, RK? I mean she debuted with your production house? Bet Monty had the hots for her, too. Had a family threesome, *kya*?'

Jayant who was gesturing to me to sign on the legal papers, hissed: 'Maybe, you should ask Monty that question, Mahesh. Maya wouldn't have spared him. The slut.'

'Is there any chance we can lay our hands on that cloth bag, that Kulasheshtra was carrying?…If we can buy out Rawat, guys?' I changed the topic, clearing my throat, stirring my drink restlessly.

The lawyers looked stunned.

'Are you off your rocker, RK? You know how hard it is to get these income-tax guys off your back? To convince the cops on your trail that you aren't hand-in-gloves with the D company? What we've had to do to ensure you get police protection…a safe refuge, here. *Bahut papad belne padte hain*,' Mahesh snapped, looking offended, adding agitatedly, 'Besides, what interest is Kulasheshtra's cloth *jhola*, to anyone? What's the maximum he could be carrying inside?

He was practically a finished man by then. That Rawat... he's one dangerous bugger. You wouldn't want to mess with him, RK, not after the shit that you are currently swimming in. No one is in this for charity, you know...save your own ass!'

I unfastened the satin robe I wore. Running my hands over my hairy paunch, I let out a stale burp, 'Which is exactly what I pay you for. Buy one, get one free!'

'Noon, this Friday, Bombay Gymkhana. Will have you picked up. Don't fuck this up, RK. Just repeat exactly what we have tutored you to say to Amol Rawat,' Mahesh stuffed the signed papers back inside his briefcase and instructed me tersely, before both the lawyers strutted out of my suite.

'Don't bother jerking off on Kulasheshtra, *woh toh saala mara insaan hai*, RK. Unless you have started fantasizing about corpses, now!' Jayant could not resist making a parting shot, before shutting the door with a bang.

◈

All these months after Amitabh's death, I still hadn't called Banno. There was so much I wanted to say. Things I was sorry for. Mistakes that I needed atonement for. Somehow, Amitabh's death had put everything into perspective. Made me feel we were less invincible than we once thought ourselves to be.

My phone buzzed. 'Cash crunch, Papa. Call back, ASAP,' Monty's text read.

I flung the phone on the bed.

I planned to set up a small business for him and his family in America, eventually. Monty was a good-for-nothing fool, whom I suspected had now joined hands with my second wife. Maybe, they were even sexually involved. Monty had my genes, after all. He needed a woman to warm his bed daily. Constantly.

I dialled Sarla's number. I had sourced her Pune landline in the week Amitabh died.

◈

The phone rang and was picked up. But there was silence on the other end. I knew she was listening. 'Banno, I know it's you. Listen, I happen to have some news…some important news…' I felt myself stiffen, as I brought the cell closer to my mouth, adding in a low voice, 'Amitabh was carrying a *jhola* when he left for Mumbai…I can't say anything more, at this point, Banno…this damn mobile phone, too, maybe tapped. I am in a sort of house arrest situation…'

I redialled impatiently as soon as the line was disconnected.

'Are you still angry with me, Banno? Did you blame me for the life you led – for losing a child, and now your husband?'

I took a deep breath, 'Please, Banno…I want to see you…just once…I am trying to recover that *jhola* bag… Bhai Jaan's *akhri amanat*…I will be the hero you once dreamt of…Banno? Hello, Banno?' I heard was the silent click of a receiver being placed down.

Thoughts raced through my head.

'Pirated…'

'*Sasta, sundar, tikao.*'

'*Dilchasp.*'

The phrases haunted me.

What would I say if Banno actually agreed to see me? If I managed to retrieve the cloth bag Mahesh mentioned? At what cost, this time? Could that turn time back? Help me, move forward?

Did Sarlu know the part I played in his love affair with Maya Shirale, in Mumbai? That I was determined to ruin Amitabh Kulasheshtra, as a man, as a maestro? The fact that I had lived, almost all my adult life, consumed by an all-encompassing need to seek revenge? To punish Amitabh for what he did to us?

I made one last call.

◈

'I need some cash...urgent *mamla hai...ek khokha se kaam nahin chalne wala...*' I spoke fast, lowering my voice. 'I need a crore. My bank accounts are all frozen, as you know. The cops don't trust me even though I have said I am willing to become an official *khabri.* I know your issues with Bhai. I would rather side with you guys, this time. Also, I am meeting Amol Rawat, this Friday. I will see to it that your name is cleared from that Panvel builder murder case that's been dragging on for years.'

The man on the other end of the line listened in silence.

'Rawat is one of our men too...*bahut logon ko tapka diye hain uss se supari le ke...*His son's Lower Parel and Thane real-estate business is also run under our supervision...I will arrange for the money...but if you try to play games and double-cross us with Bhai, then that's the end of you, RK. *Toh soch lo...*Bhai and us have an old rivalry...*toh* double crossing *kism ki zyada hoshiyari dikhaoge...toh seedha upar jaoge...*'

There was a piercing laughter.

'*Waise* Indian *hawalat ki hawa itni buri bhi nahin hoti hai... samjhe, dost...*'

'*Dost,*' I repeated, before hanging up.

Dost.

A codeword common in the underworld. Meaning someone you can trust.

Someone who doesn't switch sides.

◈

I remained restless for the rest of the day. Wondering if the private number I had used to call Chotta Shamim, one of Mumbai's most notorious ganglords. was safe. After all, he was a sworn enemy of Bhai's – and, incidentally, also his younger stepbrother who had fallen out with him when he had abducted and married his second wife. Was I taking on another huge risk? Playing Rawat and Bhai against each other? Not to mention the cops and my lawyers, who were all also on the take? I didn't change out of my nightclothes. Nor did I sext the whore I had made out with the day before. I wasn't in the mood to order my usual chicken malai tikka and butter naan.

Unable to sleep, I picked up Amitabh's book. As always, looking to him to make sense of things.

◈

BLINDSIDE

My father was a much-desired son born after three daughters, to a prosperous cloth merchant, Narayanrao Ghorpade in Ichalkaranji, a small town nestled in the Ghats on the western coast of India, located about 425 kilometres south of Kolhapur in the state of Maharashtra. By the time he grew up, Baba however realized that he had no interest in the burgeoning family business, and dreamt of being an actor on stage – something he could never quite share with his own father, one of the most prominent merchants in the region, also credited with setting up a power loom there that changed the destiny of Ichalkaranji forever.

After he finished his matriculation, my grandfather insisted that Baba visit him in the factory every day, in the hope of initiating his only son into the trade. By his own admission, Baba hated the stifling environs, the way the only talk was of money and business rivals, about the impending marriages of his older sisters, and, how his cunning uncles were perennially conspiring against his father, jealous of his soaring financial success.

Baba aimed to study acting, finding his solace in watching plays like those by Dada Saheb Sarat Chandra Joglekar, whose travelling theatre company was making waves in the whole region. Baba made it a point to catch all the shows, sometimes travelling from village to village to watch them again. Lapping up any book on theatre that he could find in his school library.

It was his passion to join theatre that made him defy my grandfather's wish that he quit his studies and eventually join the business, full-time, midway through his BA. Baba was a satirist, deeply influenced by Tamasha, a form of Marathi theatre that involved mostly song and dance and poking fun at authority. He sang beautifully and wrote all his own scripts, mostly monologues, since he had no money to pay anyone else.

Baba's insistence on going to college in Nagpur, was also linked somewhere to his thirst to hone his craft, meet more like-minded people, maybe even Dada Saheb, who often travelled there.

It was on the train to Nagpur that he met my mother, in his second year of college. A young Muslim girl, clad demurely in a burqa, she had been separated from her family when she had hopped off at the station to buy herself some tea. He noticed her looking lost and had bought her a fresh ticket, escorting her home. On the way, they had talked deep into the night. He learnt she had trained in dance in Nagpur and that she aspired to become a professional dancer someday, if her conservative family allowed her to forgo marriage and motherhood – the fate of every Indian woman.

It wasn't love at first sight. But, perhaps two people slowly discovering a quaint world of their own – safe from the rigid suffocation of their respective families – their own aspirations, their own art. Their fears, somewhat, similar. They met often, after that, in secret, mostly bunking college.

By the end of the academic year, Ammi and Baba tied the knot in an Arya Samaj temple, with Baba taking her home the same day, knowing that she would be disowned and possibly even killed, by her own family. Letting her study, and learn dance had already tested the limit of her personal freedom.

Baba was 21. Ammi 19.

Baba probably imagined his father would be livid at first, but, then, come around, for fear of losing his only son. My grandfather, however, was an egotistical man. He was stunned and shattered by his son's sudden decision. Not even his deep love could stop him from summarily throwing Baba out of the house for marrying a Muslim. He threw him out with his shy bride, simultaneously writing him off his business and in a fit of rage willing it to his daughters, to spite him his latest rebellion, dividing the ancestral wealth between his grandchildren and sons-in-law, with the aim of leaving his only son on the streets.

Baba and Ammi scoured the village with nothing...no money, no connections, no support for their inter-religious marriage, with even friends shunning them for fear of social stigmatization. The next few years proved to be even more torturous. Baba did all sorts of odd jobs to make ends meet, his plays hardly attracting an audience, especially after word got out that he was an outcaste in his community.

Ammi, on the other hand, scrubbed utensils and baby-sat when she could to support him, often concealing her religion for fear of being shunned in an essentially staunch Hindu environment.

My birth within the next year was their greatest mistake. Baba drank himself to oblivion on most nights, especially after I was born. His appearance soon transforming from the handsome, pampered son of a rich seth, dreaming lofty dreams, to a young, haggard, householder, straddled with a wife and child and mounting expenses. Baba floundered to find a stable job, a social unfit of sorts, sometimes a peon, sometimes a handy man. Having discontinued his college education, the world, he so desperately craved for, now betrayed him, as he was faced with its harshest face.

Slowly, Baba sold all his books and material belongings. There was always a paucity of funds. Forced to choose between starvation and sanity, he finally found employment in Ganesh Circus, one of the most famous circuses in Maharashtra that was supposedly looking for a clown. Impressed by Baba's talent in mimicry, the owner agreed to hire Ammi, as well, but she had to train as a trapeze artist, was the condition laid out. Ammi had long given up dancing. She was perhaps just happy to be safe. Have a permanent roof over her head. A fixed salary, finally. Breastfeeding her prematurely delivered child.

Baba and Ammi entered Ganesh Circus. Their sunken eyes hopeful...again.

One night, when I was about 13, I crouched over an open latrine. I had just smoked a half-finished bidi that I had found on my way outside. My breath stank. I stood in the grass, my shorts pulled down, my penis swollen with piss. And watched as a couple made frantic love, their bodies pressed together, at the back of the performing arena, opposite the monkey cages.

He had an ugly paunch. He was not naked.

She was. Her pubic hair, coarse, untrimmed. Her anklets created a soft clamour.

I blinked, a couple of times; glancing down, anxious someone might discover me this way, staring with my mouth wide open.

It was a full moon night.

The woman squatted on her haunches, grabbing the man's buttocks, their movements repetitive, raw. Then the woman was down on her arms and knees as the man climbed over her, entering from behind.

I gasped.

His whip was placed around her neck. The veins on his, protruded. His organ, stiff. Stubborn. Sadistic.

The woman let out a fierce howl, wanting to free herself. Losing the fight, after a while, as the man stuffed the whip forcefully inside her mouth, before pulling her face up by her matted locks. The woman's nipples, caught the light.

I clamped my eyes shut.

Remaining silent. Next to me, lay my father. Once the most famous clown in Ganesh circus, his body now reeked of cheap, country liquor. His lips were faintly painted. His chest shrivelled by the tuberculosis that had almost killed him a couple of years ago.

He stirred.

'You're back? Heard Dada Saheb is touring Satara this time… we must go watch his latest play. It's been so long since I left this damn place…' Baba muttered, placing his hand on my stomach.

I pushed it away, roughly.

'Was she there again?' he spoke after a moment's silence.

I turned over listlessly on my back, my eyes smarting.

'Did she, did, your Ammi look happy?' he asked, all of a sudden.

I covered my face in my hands.

'I don't know. I couldn't see…it was dark…' I answered, gruffly.

The next afternoon, I smoked again.

I liked smoking, I liked smoking a lot.

SARLA KULASHESHTRA

Amitabh's first death anniversary had come and gone. I hadn't switched on the television during those days, on purpose. The phone had rung non-stop. Students, fans, admirers, newspaper editors, channel heads, theatre company directors and festival organizers – everyone wanted to express their condolences afresh.

I thanked them all, politely expressing my reservations about appearing on camera or giving detailed interviews – accepting the garlands and flowers that many of them had personally carried or had sent over.

The living room still reeked with the scent of stale blooms. There were no pictures of Amitabh in the house, though. Amitabh abhorred the idea of worshipping the departed, never stopping to place an *agarbatti* or bow his head even before the portrait of little Maya that hung over my bed. We hadn't slept together in the same room, after I had lost her.

The dead had paid their price, here, in this house, perhaps.

I had politely declined inaugurating a couple of photo exhibitions and retrospectives the past week – knowing I'd be inevitably hounded by the Press again. I had nothing to say to them. Nothing about living without Amitabh was sensational enough, having lived without him, for as long as I can recall, in the same city, in the same house. A man like

Amitabh could never belong. It was probably his greatest undoing.

And yet, in a strange way, for the first time, I missed him in a physical sense, that day. Missed hearing Amitabh clear his throat in the morning; missed watching him catch a quick nap in his room, his spectacles on his chest. Missed ordering his medicines and fixing his doctor's appointments. Missed visiting the courts on his behalf and ensuring there wasn't too much salt in his food. Missed keeping my bedroom light on, until I saw his turned off.

Outside, it had started drizzling mildly.

The doorbell rang, just then. I waited for a few minutes, hoping the person would leave if I didn't answer but the visitor was persistent. Reluctantly, I answered the door.

A man in a brown safari suit stood outside, holding a large packet in his hands. He folded his hands politely, as soon as I asked him who he was.

'Sarlaji, *namaste*,' he said, bowing his head, 'I hope I have not caused you any disturbance. I would have reached earlier, but my driver could not quite locate the address. I apologize for this intrusion. Hope I'm not disrupting your lunch.'

I stepped outside, covering my shoulders with my pallu.

'And who may you be? Mister...?' I narrowed my eyes, inspecting him closely, 'I wasn't really expecting, anyone.'

The man handed me the packet he was holding. 'Please to check if it is okay...' he looked up, gesturing at my hands.

'What's in this? Can you please tell me who you are? Where you are from?' I appeared confused, trying to recollect if I was to receive any parcel from anywhere.

'I was asked to hand-deliver this...only hand it in to you, and no one else. Sir will kill me if it is damaged by any chance or if it lands in someone else's custody,' the man swallowed hard, adding hesitantly, 'You are Mrs. Sarla Kulasheshtra, right?'

I nodded, tearing the transparent tape that ran along the sides of the paper packet. A thick wad of papers sown together by a dull yellow thread dropped into my hands.

'This…this is, it's Amitabh's handwriting…where? I mean…who are you?' I said in shock.

The man stepped back a couple of steps. After fumbling in his trouser pocket he handed me a letter with a visiting card stapled to it.

'I shall take your leave, now, Sarlaji. It is going to be a long drive back, and, looks like the weather isn't in our favour, either,' he glanced up at the darkened skies.

'Where did you find this?' I questioned sharply.

The man folded his hands, again.

'It's all in the letter, Sarlaji…It is what I was told. You are Mrs. Sarla Kulasheshtra, right?' he answered as he rushed off.

I read the typed, unsigned note:

Amitabh was carrying this on the afternoon he boarded the train to Mumbai. Rawat was fearful this might contain some fresh evidence in the Malegaon trial and that's why he had this nixed. I met Rawat, recently, at the Mumbai Gymkhana Club. I was worried he could leak excerpts to the media, or blackmail you, with this, at some later point. Rawat is an unscrupulous man, someone who can resort to anything to get what he wants. He's now gunning for power in the Centre, allegedly even forming his own party, soon. Amitabh was the only man who dared him, in a sense. The Malegaon incident is a dark spot on his reputation, as well. I could sense the unease in his eyes. Amitabh Kulasheshtra is still alive for him...his new party is looking for funds... Rawat called it most secular party of recent times...it was my promise to bring this to you, soon...as soon as I could... somehow...'

'*Cut...*' I whispered, running my fingers over the papers.

My thoughts spiralling back to the gory Mumbai riots, the incessant bloodshed, the sudden news of the demolition of the Babri Masjid – it was all so deeply personal to Amitabh – he was affected much more than an ordinary person.

'Oh Amitabh! This is the manuscript you were carrying with you on that day; the one I refused to look after for you...' I choked, clasping the papers.

Amitabh's face flashed before my eyes. I relived the way I had witnessed a once proud man crumple, especially over the years, as the Malegaon case dragged on relentlessly, along with mounting bills and endless courtroom appearances.

Amitabh and I had lived separately after he returned from Mumbai in the early 90s. After Maya had spurned him. We had nothing to say, or share, except a sense of failed courage...me...here...Amitabh, mostly in his room, in the outhouse...for the first time, our wars were starkly different. I no longer questioned his sanity, never asking him why he had to take the dare to stage such a controversial play in Malegaon. June 1994 changing our lives in a way from which there was no return or redemption.

Tears clouded my eyes, wiping them with my pallu, I returned to the note: *'You see* Cut *is not just Amitabh Kulasheshtra's final work. It is his...'*

I couldn't read further. I held the papers close to my heart, thinking of the last night Amitabh and I had spent talking, just us.

In the garden, outside...

◈

'What are you doing here, Amitabh? Have you taken your evening medicines? What's that in your hands?' I'd demanded.

'I just wanted to see the house, once. The paint...it's all peeling off.'

'No, Amitabh, it's the same, the paint is fine…it's just the rains, the house always looks different after a spell of heavy showers, mellow, somewhat muted...some parts of it lighter...I've got used to it in all these years...it's just that you haven't come out and sat in the garden in a long time at this hour…'

'How come I've never noticed them, Sarlu? Why do I feel the house resembles an Eastman coloured postcard? Even the roses on the front porch appear different.'

'Those are not roses, they are carnations,' I brusquely said.

'Carnations? But, I always thought you loved roses…and, and that carnations don't grow here, something to do with the weather?' Amitabh softly reprised, clearing his throat.

'One of my students gifted me these and they just grew on their own, I suppose. Initially, I never even watered them regularly or cast as much as a second look. I mean, what's the point, I remember telling myself...you start caring for something that is meant to eventually perish. But...then...'

'Then what?' he touched my shoulders, lightly.

'One morning, I was standing alone, pre-occupied. I may have even been sad, about something, when, all of a sudden, these plants caught my attention. Their colour, the shape of the buds I don't know why, but I replanted them at noon, spending the whole of the next day, and the days after, tending to them meticulously, watering them, watching over them, in the afternoons when the sun was at its peak…'

Amitabh walked slowly, towards them. 'Sarlu, how long will you care for each and everything that lives in this house, in this garden…in, in my life?' he suddenly glanced back over his shoulders.

The light was falling. I had a function to attend.

'I don't care about things, Amitabh. I am just scared to watch them die,' I cut him short. 'Anyway, I'm leaving, now. One of my students has opened a dance academy of her own, close by. I had agreed to be her chief guest.'

Amitabh said nothing, at first.

'Sarlu, I have something to ask of you…' he finally said.

'What?'

'Will you promise to keep this cloth bag safely? I know you take care of my stuff, the best. You've always been so careful about looking after my things…always extra watchful not to lose any of it, remembering each date…every bill… every Court summons…every doctor's prescription…every little saving, I could ever manage…'

'That was different, Amitabh. Even if you were right about me handling your things with care in the past, why am I suddenly obligated to help you now? Why this sudden benefit of doubt?' I interrupted, impatiently, checking my wristwatch.

'Sarlu, do you suppose it's going to rain again, tonight? You, you always could tell, just by the way the tiny blades of grass felt under your feet…do you think there will be any more showers in June?' he asked slowly.

'I don't know, Amitabh...' I pushed away the bag.

'What day of the week is it, Sarlu?'

'It doesn't matter, Amitabh,' I pursed my lips.

'Even I do that a lot, nowadays. Pretend, I don't care about days of the week or what time it is, telling myself it's enough, that whatever little I have left, what little memory, that it's all okay, that whatever I can piece back, is enough. Sarlu, please take this and keep it safe, please?' he stretched both his hands out in my direction.

'Amitabh, I hope you realize that we have to meet the lawyer…the date of the hearing is coming up,' I frowned, wiping my face, taking a deep breath, 'maybe, it's pointless to carry on the case against the Rashtriya Dal…Amol Rawat is a seasoned politician today, with deep pockets and has risen up the party ranks in all these years…he even bribed Prakash

Lele's daughter…the Courts acquitted him citing lack of circumstantial evidence…Rawat is a free man…it's almost like Malegaon didn't happen…I am not sure if anyone even remembers that time…'

There was a minute or more of suspended silence.

'What time, Sarlu? You said you had to be somewhere… somewhere else…I, I wasn't even sure if we would meet… if you were home…if you be in the garden, now…' Amitabh broke out into a violent cough.

He had lost a lot of weight. I could faintly see the outline of his ribs. He had been recovering from a secondary chest infection.

'Ami…' I had just started speaking, when he held out the cloth bag in my direction, again, 'are, are you planning to go away again?'

I frowned, confronting his intrepid gaze.

'I don't know, Sarlu. I can't say what I will do, really. That's the thing about this illness…Sarlu, you know what I regret most about this marriage?' Amitabh shrugged his shoulders, losing track of what we were talking about.

'Ours?' I met his eyes.

'What I regret most, about us, was that it was not all bad,' he stared hard into mine, 'we failed, yes, I suppose, we failed a lot, Sarlu. But, so did they. They failed, too. They all failed us. All those who wrote us off…each one who stood watching us take the fall, including me, and you, in some measure. We were all wrong, Sarlu…all we did was to underestimate each other. Like Malegaon… that you feel doesn't matter…that you think is a blip in time…a day that's been collectively erased from public conscience…'

Amitabh wheezed, his eyes gaunt.

'Sarlu,' he moved closer to me, 'Rawat didn't win…just, just because he was allowed to walk free…you must know that…Rawat…the Rashtriya Dal…they cannot win…it's why we must not give up…no matter what happens…to, to this case…to this country…to, to me…'

I settled my pallu.

Amitabh watched me, in silence.

'Just because you can't see things Sarlu, doesn't mean they don't exist…' he took a deep breath, adding slowly, 'Like us…what we were…the things that truly mattered… the edifice of our marriage, Sarlu…Each day, each month, every year…each word I have managed to make a note of…is, really, the sum of us…every sentence we ever uttered…the pent-up silences, my nights locked away in that airless terrace room, your lengthy sighs after we touched…the months we lived apart…the affairs that were sensationalised…Maya, our daughter…and, and, her.'

'So, this is about her, then? I should have guessed where this was going! Love letters to your one-time mistress, Maya Shirale, huh?' I snarled, my words laced with sarcasm.

'It has my manuscript, a new *natak*,' Amitabh's eyes suddenly glinted.

'A play?' my heart missed a beat.

'It's part of the same film script I was once working on, the one I began in Mumbai, the same one I had promised, Maya,' he coughed again, covering his mouth.

'Then take it Amitabh, and, give it to the concerned person. What am I meant to do with all this? I have enough on my plate…' I shrugged my shoulders dismissively, walking away.

'Sarlu, wait, you will know what to do when time comes, just look after it, please…for me...' Amitabh called out, as I turned to go, his voice breaking.

'You're asking your wife to safeguard a script that you penned for your lover? You should thank your lucky stars you're the one who's sick…' my eyes stung.

'Sarlu...'

'No, I have heard enough, Amitabh. It's bad enough that we have this case hanging on our heads...your doctor visits and deteriorating health...your heart con...just take this back, at once. I am not interested in what the bag or the damn script contains. I am done with cleaning up after you. For being the one who listens.' I bit my lower lip, the colour rising up my cheeks, 'Unlike you, I am not interested in looking for redemption, Amitabh, after all this time. And if an evening like this makes you assume we can go back to being the way we were, you are wrong. There is no going back. People can't go back, ever. We had what we had. The bridges we built, we burnt. With our own hands. The way Malegaon finished you, Amitabh. The way you lost. The way you cannot win, everything...over, over everyone...'

I was shaking.

Amitabh held the cloth bag close to his heart. His eyes closed.

'And, and, I want you to understand something. I can never meet Mrinalini, again, all right? Not even halfway. Do you hear me, Amitabh? I vowed never to see her face. Our paths must never cross; even if you are dead. When you are finally...dead...Amitabh Kulasheshtra...'

My lips quivered.

Amitabh stood with his shoulders stooped. Was his leaving Pune, pre-planned? Had he known he was going away?

Did Amitabh have a premonition about his premature death?

Or, was this what I had wanted? All along?

The first time I had spoken my mind.

Stood up. Put up a fight.

Won...

◈

Had I pushed Amitabh away forever?

I re-read the last bit of the note:

'Cut is not just Amitabh Kulasheshtra's last play. It his first love letter, to you, Mrs. Sarla Kulasheshtra…' I read the last line to myself, many times, before removing the visiting card that was attached by the side.

A flash of lightning ripped through the sky. I couldn't believe the name of the sender.

'Chopra & Sons, Towers 1 & 2…'

Rakesh? Had he managed to get this manuscript back from Amol Rawat? *How?* A tear fell on the line scribbled on the first page.

'It's not your fault…we just ran out of time…'

A line I recognized from the first page of Amitabh's memoirs.

Had all of us been vindicated by his unlikely death, in some measure?

Or was he playing the *sutradhaar*?

ACT III
CUT

AVIK DASGUPTA

This was the second time I was going to see Mrs. Sarla Kulasheshtra at her home in Pune. Amitabh Kulasheshtra had been dead for two years.

The first time we met was after she had called me suddenly out of the blue, a month ago. I had flown down the very next day. That's when she told me that, last year, she had got her hands on a copy of her husband's last play, *Cut*; the one he had been carrying with him when he had died two years ago, and which had been missing since. She had refused to tell me who had sent it to her, the price she had to pay to acquire the script, or why it was me she wanted to see urgently on this matter. If she had reached out to others from the same business, my competitors and industry rivals, I didn't know. How long she had been planning this? Watching my career? My films? Studying my success ratio? My reputation? My rates? Was she aware of my history of hate with her husband?

Questions crowded my mind. And yet, I didn't press the issue. A woman like Sarla Kulasheshtra only disclosed as much as she needed to. Something also told me that she didn't trust me fully either; and I didn't blame her. After all, I had mixed feelings too, at this point.

She had said at the conclusion of our first meeting that after much thought, she had decided to entrust the direction of the play to me. *Cut* being the last play written by Amitabh

Kulasheshtra, his answer to his critics, to all those who had taken sadistic pleasure in propounding the theory that he had lost his mind, especially after the Malegaon incident. The play was a refreshing departure from Kulasheshtra's last controversial production. A beautifully etched love story; a tribute, in a sense, to a longstanding relationship; a dying man's declaration of admiration; a last love-letter to his wife.

I was astounded by how clear she was in communicating what she wanted and how much the staging of *Cut* meant to her. And yet, even as I patiently heard her out, I was tempted to interrupt her, ask pointedly what her real intentions were in resurrecting Kulasheshtra to an audience that had turned their faces away; and if she was aware that I had removed myself from the realm of theatre after Amitabh had ensured that I was rejected from the National Centre of Drama. Since her call, I had been conflicted and, at the same time, intrigued about taking on *Cut* and the complex challenge offered by her proposal.

Somewhere, I suppose I felt I would be redeemed by *Cut*; that directing Kulasheshtra's work meant that I was worthy of the stage after all.

That I was his equal, in some measure.

◈

Sarlaji was sitting in the portico when I arrived. She was formally dressed as always. Her hair pulled back in a tight bun, attired in a starched cotton sari. And yet, this evening, she looked different. She offered me tea and a plate heaped with poha, as we exchanged customary pleasantries.

'Are you married, Mr. Dasgupta?' she asked, out of the blue.

'Yes, ma'am, as a matter of fact, I am.' I had married Reema soon after Maya and I had split, a year ago.

'Are you happy? Do you have children?'

'My wife is pregnant. She happens to live in your city.'

'Oh? Here in Pune? That's nice. When is she due?'

'I don't know the exact date. Truth is, we fell out some months back when she left Mumbai, claiming she needed space... She mentioned something about being tired of being "single in our marriage".'

'God, the way you people of this generation deal with relationships. What does that even mean?'

'I'm not sure myself. We haven't spoken since the day she left Mumbai. I am giving her what she wanted...what was most lacking in our marriage...space! Anyway, coming back, to why I'm here, I know you're keen to know what I thought of *Cut* and whether I will accept the offer. I was travelling for a bit and was in the midst of some important shoots...I have just started a new TV production company...and...'

'*Sab ko aajkal* busy *hone ki bimari jaisi hai*...everyone says the same thing. It's become a job, being busy,' she shook her head.

I picked up a spoonful of poha. 'Actually, I have a question, and you must be honest with me,' I leaned closer. 'Do you think I would've been *his* natural choice?' I asked, meeting her eyes. Then, before she could come up with an answer, I added, 'You must know, I have hated Amitabh Kulasheshtra most of my adult life, Sarlaji. Don't mind my saying so to your face, but your husband was an arrogant bastard; he ruined my theatre career...All my life I have wanted to prove myself to him...I thought of him while directing my first feature film, desperate to impress him, and, at the same time, get back at him. Be a rightful contender...'

Sarlaji put down her cup of tea and looked me straight in the eye. 'I am aware of the way he treated you, Avik; do you know what Amitabh said to me a long time after he had interacted with you at the National Centre of Drama? Yes, yes, he remembered. Amitabh always did when he was drawn to somebody; he had been impressed with your passionate intensity. He said rejecting you was actually his way of challenging you; by not giving you an easy entry into the world of theatre he was hoping to ignite a deeper passion in you. To strengthen your life philosophy, and your commitment to the stage…Amitabh knew he saw more than just a spark in you…and, maybe, that frightened him as well…he was in many ways just the way you were, years back, when your paths crossed…Amitabh, as you may know, wasn't a man to be easily bowled over.'

I placed the half-finished plate of poha by my side. I was silent for a long while before I finally said: 'Sometimes, a rejection can dishearten one so much that one might leave the field altogether. Or, maybe, I idolized him way too much. I was desperate to be in his presence…to learn the art of screenplay and stage design…to travel with him into the parts of India that he had the courage to perform in, espouse the same causes…maybe, that's why what I felt was akin to a very deep betrayal…What he did was more than break my spirit. I spiralled into a state of deep depression for *months* after.' My voice shook with anger and pent-up rage.

'Yes, it was a gamble. But it was a gamble my husband was willing to take. That's the kind of man he was, I suppose. Like my father, the legendary Sarat Chandra Joglekar…Dada Saheb was known to goad and rile people; to push them to the limit, just so they didn't get complacent. Even if it meant that they might get hurt in the process. In the way a schoolmaster prepares his best students by being more tough on them. In fact, I remember Amitabh watching a film of yours a few years ago on television. I had come in to meet his nurse, when he turned to me suddenly and said: "Sarlu…have you ever wondered what it would be like to have a son? Maybe, we gave up, too easily."

'He said: "You know, I once met the director of this film many years ago…I don't exactly know why I was so unduly harsh with him, Sarlu…the boy, he had such a radically different vision of what modern theatre and art could mean. It was his final interview at the National Centre of Drama… and I was on the final selection panel that year. He was Bengali…. his name was Avik, Avik Dasgupta. His intense, brooding stare, it was the first thing I noticed, the time we conversed. There was something in his eyes, something that almost brought time back; he was hell-bent on defying me…!"

'"Why did you flunk him then?" I'd asked.

'"Sometimes anger is a mercurial motivator, Sarlu. Sometimes a harsh rejection by the people you emulate or want to be like the most, fuels you; drives you like one possessed, makes you want to prove yourself even more. In the way a piece of carbon is thrust into the raging embers to discover the rarest diamond. I have been avidly following his career, Sarlu. Avik Dasgupta. His first film absolute brilliance! I watched his debut feature, Sarlu…I watched it alone…he has the same irreverence as I did when I was his age…he *will* be a change-maker, that chap…I have wished to say this to him…some day…one day…"'

I was stunned. 'Why…why didn't you tell me this when you handed me over the script, Sarlaji?' I asked, my eyes stinging with tears.

'Things take time, Avik. Intimacy needs practice,' Sarlaji eased into a smile as I stood up restlessly; moved beyond belief by Amitabh's assessment of me. His words of praise meant everything to me; way more than I myself had ever believed possible. It was as if suddenly, in that single moment, all my self-doubt was dispelled; all my struggles validated.

◈

'By the way, have you met her yet?' Sarlaji asked after a while, breaking the silence that followed as we both were lost in our thoughts.

Sarlaji had been adamant that the role of herself be essayed by none other than Maya Shirale.

'Briefly,' I shrugged my shoulders. 'But I am not sure if I was convincing enough. Sarlaji, are you also sure about not letting Maya know that it was you who brought the script of *Cut* to me, calling me here, to Pune, insisting on the phone that it was critical? That it is an absolute requisite that Maya essay this role…And what if she refuses? Have you considered that scenario? Do you think you can forget Maya and move on to another actress, in case the outcome is negative?'

'Moving on is a myth.'

'Why do you say that?'

'Because emotions don't change places, the way people do; this play will *not* happen without Maya. I *need* Maya Shirale to say yes to this role.'

'But, Maya and you have had no contact since she walked out of your life and everything that…transpired here…in this house. Are you absolutely certain that it is a wise casting call…the lead role being played by her, and no one else?'

'Yes, I am sure.'

'Sarlaji, please pardon my forthrightness, but is *Cut* about forgiveness? Am I right in thinking that deciding to stage Amitabh Kulasheshtra's last written work is perhaps a means to forgive the man he was…to you…to all of us, in the end?'

'Honestly, Avik, I can't really analyse all this just yet. Maybe, maybe, there is more to me, too... more left to salvage. Or so, I think.'

'I like that word, "salvage".'

'Reading *Cut* has also changed me, Avik. It's dispelled the bitterness in me, in a way I never knew possible. Sometimes, we do end up hurting those we love, pushing them to a place from where they can seldom return. Maybe, it's how two people survive. Why they are still vulnerable…Amitabh wrote *Cut* at a time when he himself was in the twilight of his life…struggling to piece together his fading memory, battling allegations about his political beliefs, carrying on an ideological crusade. Maybe, what makes *Cut* all the more relevant is the fact that he's not here anymore. Absence is a privilege, Avik,' she closed her eyes, opening them slowly to add, 'Marriage is like a bloodied wrestling match in so many ways, and yet, it's a team sport too. And *Cut* has made me look back on my mistakes as well, I suppose... the stubborn way I held out; how I was always looking for someone to blame when those I wanted walked out on me; how I was unfaithful to Amitabh for far longer…how I wanted him dead…for far longer…how my seething hatred at my own father was paralleled by my deepest respect for Dada Saheb…how I just wanted to be seen as myself. And which is why I am here now, with you. *Cut*, isn't about forgiveness, as much as it is about faith. My faith.'

'It's difficult for me to convince Maya, Sarlaji. I haven't spoken to her in a year, not after our break-up. I married Reema on the rebound, quite honestly. And, the thing is, Reema... my wife... she absolutely hates Maya. She always has. She says I transform completely under her influence. She calls Maya a parasite. She alleges it's impossible for Maya and me to be "just" professional. It's what she fears, I suppose, in some way. That's why she has left me. Reema won't ever accept it if I tell her about *Cut*. In fact, we were supposed to start scripting sessions for Reema's debut feature soon. She's directed some brilliant ad films, before this. I had no clue Reema was pregnant, either…maybe this is her way of getting back at me. Punishing me…'

'Maybe, Reema is the one feeling left out...'

'I have done nothing to make her feel threatened or broken her trust, Sarlaji. Never cheated. Never lied. I told her everything about Maya when we started seeing each other. Reema is being silly and plain jealous.'

'And don't you think she has every right?'

'Sarlaji, I am sorry, but marriage is not slavery. It does not mean there will be no one else...'

'You know what Amitabh said to me once, here, on this portico where we are now sitting and talking? He asked me if I loved him, staring intently into my eyes.'

'And?'

'I replied, "I am your wife. There is always a difference. The method of loving a man, once you own him."

Sarlaji grew philosophical: 'Avik, this is the truth and I owe it to you: Amitabh never wanted me, nor I him, except during the brief interlude we almost, accidentally shared. I wasn't used to his attention, as a woman; nor did I ever seek it, actively. We were never lovers, not in the real sense. So, in some way, I had known we were always meant to end up the way we did, just filling a void in each other's lives. Role playing. Making up names. Everyone needs a wife, Avik, my father would often say. *Ardhangini*…another part…a lost piece. Perhaps, I too hid behind the wife tag, equally, hoping to fit a particular slot, still be inconspicuous, and yet protected. Trying to make a marriage of convenience matter over the years. I didn't leave Amitabh, after all. What was stopping me? Why did I take care of things? Ensure that there was always food on the table. That the bedsheets were cotton and white, and freshly washed. No prints. No synthetics. The way he liked them. That the *dal* had just the right measure of salt; as prescribed by his doctor. That the bills were paid on time.

I lay beside him every night, until the night my baby died, telling myself that a warm, compliant body resting beside a man, night after night after night, would be enough. That I would get accustomed to this gaping wound I carried, one that refused to go away. I allowed Amitabh to leave, when he wanted, never promising when he would return. Never staking a claim on him. It's the kind of marriage I saw my parents share. Functional…and farcical, at the same time. It's what made me go out of my way to see that nothing was ever quite out of place…or, maybe, we were just, just two people fighting fate and living out a patriarch's arbitrary decision, trying to honour our pledge of togetherness, with whatever we had…'

'Is this play something you want to do for yourself then, Sarlaji? To resurrect the memory of a failed marriage, and present it as something else? An image clean-up, maybe?'

'What I now remember, Avik, is our time together… our interlude of affection; the assurance of a once broken promise…that time cannot resurrect…but that teaches you something so meaningful about life and yourself. That one evening with him was the most beautiful, most perfect moment we shared in a long while. Everything felt unspoilt. One moment, I was pruning the roses alone as usual. The, the next, he was there, watching me from afar, standing a few metres away. I don't know why I reached out to Amitabh that day... not wanting him to return to his room, just yet, even though it's what I told him when we began talking…'

'I still don't get it. I mean, how could just that one evening make you take this gigantic leap of faith, Sarlaji? I mean, how can you even remember such a day? What does it have that is so worthy of preservation, given the way things panned out, the very next afternoon? Also, is being wanted and being needed *really* that different, in a marriage?

'Being wanted is like poetry... being needed like prose, Avik...'

'And, what makes you so certain that everything you just narrated happened the way you think it did, Sarlaji? Sometimes, the mind plays tricks…Maybe, like my wife Reema, you're plain jealous of Maya…in denial about the last evening you shared with your husband.'

'I *was* jealous, you are right, Avik, but, not of Maya, as a woman, this time. Not that evening, despite returning the script to Amitabh, and walking off in a huff, leaving him stranded, screeching out my name, begging me to keep his cloth bag, in safe keeping. That night, I was only jealous of Amitabh. I know what I felt.'

'Why?'

'Because of the way Amitabh had made sense of the single most perfect experience of our adult lives... so easily... because of the way he saw us. How our marriage, like Malegaon…like the case he fought for against the Rashtriya Dal, for all these years…that I represented him on countless occasions, was no different than Ganesh Circus…Amitabh's first stage which lived on in him, always…the way *Ammi* and *Baba* did…the way Mrinalini will…maybe Amitabh wanted to win. The way you wanted, Avik. The way only knowing defeat makes you want to try again…at something, at the same things…'

I tried saying something else. I couldn't.

◈

The return flight to Mumbai was thankfully delayed by an hour. I couldn't get the conversation with Sarlaji out of my mind, just like I couldn't stop reading and rereading *Cut*. I had marked out portions that I constantly returned to. Lines that only Kulasheshtra could write. Rousing passages that took my breath away, wondering, at some level, if I was taking on more than I could chew. If I was being overambitious, thinking I could direct the last play scripted by a man who taught so many of us about theatre, about seeing life, a certain way. If I could finally forgive Kulasheshtra…for making me the man, I was now.

◈

Reading what he had to say about Sarlaji made me think of Reema, how cold she had been when I called her the minute I stepped out of Sarlaji's home, telling her about my new project. I asked her how she was feeling, when she was due, but she had evaded answering.

'Best of luck, AD, I hope you can now make peace with your father, your past,' was her only comment, before she hung up, abruptly.

I hadn't ever openly discussed my parents with Reema. It had been so long since I had seen Ma, in any case, or gone home to Kolkata. I remember promising Reema I would show her my city after we got married in a simple, court ceremony attended only by some of our closest industry friends and team members. I didn't want the media to know I was getting hooked. Maybe, somewhere, I didn't want to hurt Maya.

I stared at my cell-phone for a few seconds. Wondering if I should call Reema again. Tell her everything I was feeling. But the fact that Maya was being considered for my very first play was bound to rile her further. Should I tell her it had been Sarlaji's idea, from the start? A condition she had made abundantly clear before handing me over the manuscript of Kulashreshta's final work. Thoughts formed and melted.

Were Reema and I also essaying a part?

Had the space we had promised to give each other in our personal and professional lives, during our courtship period, swallowed us, in turn? Had we allowed ourselves to remain invisible because it's what our definition of modern-day companionship, was? Or, what it an excuse?

An alibi?

A white lie?

I took a deep breath, opening the script again.

My favourite lines from *Cut* stared me in the eye. Like Kulasheshtra knew my mind…

'Slowly we turned to ash, just the way we started.
Till there was nothing left, nothing except us.
And a few scars.
Maybe it was fated then.
I said to myself.
As I saw you burn.
First.
Every single inch of us.
Wasted whore.
Chasing something like love.
Always running.... breathless.
Dust to dust.
Always thirsty.
Drinking blood.
Drinking the salt of my tears.'

MAYA SHIRALE

'Your clinic in Jaslok Hospital was way better, doc...I mean despite the crowds there. This pretentious swanky high-rise business...*mujhe ghutan hoti hai yahan.* Bandra, Pali Hills...my foot!' I removed my glares, flopping down on a comfortable black leather recliner as I spoke to my shrink.

'Is that why you stopped coming for your sessions, Maya? It's been a long time since we've sat face to face, this way,' Dr. Pastakia, one of the most sought-after psychiatrists in Bollywood, questioned. His columns were everywhere these days, as were his appearances on national television. His secretary had insisted he had several other star appointments today. I always messaged him on a private number, especially, before a new release. After sending him and his wife premiere passes, each time.

Dr. Pastakia wasn't my friend. He was my fan.

'Can I be honest?' I leaned in, closer.

'That's what you pay me for.'

'When Avi happened, I didn't *need* a shrink,' I kicked off my neon green Nike trainers, wiping my face with a face towel, adding: 'He was a great listener, always sorted, despite being younger than me, a struggler himself, really, when we hooked up. He made all my problems disappear. Made me laugh. Threatened to thwack me, hard, when I threw tantrums; came home piss-drunk just to teach me a lesson, if I didn't answer his calls over a period of time, breaking down in my arms, within seconds. He was, in a sense, like family, doc.'

'So, you're here to discuss Avik Dasgupta?' Dr. Pastakia made a note in his hardbound leather diary. 'Hasn't he left you, though, Maya? It's been close to a year now? My wife Farah, who is glued to the gossip tabloids, mentioned that he had married someone else.' He paused, fixing his rimless glasses over his aquiline nose. Waiting for me to react. I bit the bait.

'Avi walked out on me in the end, doc, like all the other men in my life...the *filmi* magazines revelled in the scandal, making it about me, as usual...they hate me, anyway...my guts...so, they went on about how Avik Dasgupta had used me and moved on to greener pastures. How he was right to never look back. Maya Shirale, the bitch, the bimbette, the has-been...'

'But, Maya, all of this is over. I hope you aren't back on those ecstasy pills...mixing drugs and alcohol, again? No suicidal thoughts, I hope...?' Dr. Pastakia probed, narrowing his eyes.

'Avi was like an attention seeking kid, doc. He threw tantrums at the drop of a hat. Wanted me with him, twenty-four seven. He was opinionated, like all Bong guys. Buzzing with ideas, conversation, making me respond to each little thing he said. I was literally expected to know his mind, second guess. Avi was so damn different than men his age, in the industry, in particular. Like he couldn't care less. Had zero sense of style. I would even pick out his clothes and match his shoes, can you imagine? Me! Maya Shirale! He liked the fact that I dominated him...deciding his outfits for the events we had to attend. I taught him to coordinate his look. I advised him to opt for bright colours. Saying black made him appear much too glum. I got him a stylist. Got his hair fashionably cut, his beard trimmed. Avi…he, he'd begun to lose a lot of weight, dull hues tended to make him look even more worn out…like he was having sleepless nights, or something…' I lit a cigarette.

'*Was* Avik having sleepless nights? And were you?' he looked at me, pointedly.

'Avi wore me out. He'd fuck me for *hours.* He loved the doggy thing, especially. In bed, he wanted to be the boss… like he wanted to show me…his *mardangi*…like he owned my body…like he could not bear to have me out of his sight, for a single second…' I sighed in a dramatic way, placing my right hand on my cleavage.

'What went so grossly wrong, then?' Dr. Pastakia ignored my histrionics.

'He, he was there, again, doc, standing before me... silently, rain-soaked…as he had that night, his first night, with me, in Mumbai. Looking distraught. His clothes dishevelled He was trying to say something. But, but he just couldn't. His eyes were filled to the brim. He hadn't shaved…"I'm sorry… sorry for what happened to us," I whimpered. Reaching out. He moved away. I, I am saying it, now. Admitting that I was the one to blame. I was weak. Weaker. I shouldn't have…'

'Shouldn't have what, Maya?' Dr. Pastakia, cut me short, dragging his chair closer to mine.

'I betrayed Amitabh, doc, it was probably deliberate, looking back, now. Oh God…oh God…how can I ever forgive myself? For what my actions did to Amitabh, all those years ago? Oh God…what have I done? I would've told Avi everything, too, one day, trust me,' I broke down.

My body was wracked with sobs: 'It's just that I feel so dead inside, especially after Amitabh died. That's why I stepped out of that Nadiadwala big budget project. I just couldn't do it, the same gig, mouth the same old lines, sing, dance, strut my body on screen, do sleazy item songs, starve myself, have one surgery after another, hold on to my youth, play second fiddle to some womanizing, Botoxed, 50-plus leading man who would manipulate the script, as usual.

'You know when I joined films, I broke Amitabh's heart in two ways: first by signing my first film *Ishq* and second, by signing it with RK Chopra, the reigning movie mogul… it was the late 80s; it's why we fought like cats and dogs. Screaming at each other. Hurting each other, on purpose… Oh Amitabh…' the tears flowed silently, unstoppably.

'"RK! You were with RK all this while…you lied to me" Amitabh gasped, narrowing his eyes.

'"Yes, yes, I said yes to RK Chopra, Goddammit! I need the money…we, we need the damn money, Amitabh! How do you think we've been surviving a city as exorbitantly expensive as Mumbai, all this while, huh? Who has been bearing the brunt of this relationship, you think? Why are most producers suddenly so wary to even cast me as an extra? Why don't their assistants ever answer my call? You…it's all *your* fault! You're God to most of these folks…people worship Amitabh Kulasheshtra, everywhere. They think he can do no wrong. And so what does that make me, huh? A mistake. An indiscretion. An error of judgment…like your wife has publicly declared…I am not dead, Amitabh. You hear me? And, and I'm not Maya, either…s*he's* the dead one. A dead daughter you could never bury, both Aiyee and you, even as I paid the price for a loss that wasn't mine. Leaving Pune, theatre…a city I was born in…a life I had…just so that you both could live happily…after…'

'"RK can never do justice to your talent…he's just taking advantage of the fact that you are an out-of-work struggler…" Amitabh had clenched his jaws, cutting me short.

'"What talent? *Hai kya mere pass…jo aur kissi abhinetri ke pass nahin hai*? Why I should wait for your magnum opus to finally materialize? Talent, talent, talent…is that all you got? One play…you gave me one great role, Amitabh. That's all! How long can I survive on the glory of one memorable performance? How long?" I screamed, choking. "Someday, you *will* know what you are worth, and, how you have failed yourself, more than anyone, Maya…" Amitabh bent down to kiss my palms. "Don't touch me, don't you dare…" I pulled away. Amitabh looked up, his face dark. "Has RK slept with you, Maya?" he questioned, pointing his finger at my eyes. "It all boils down to that, doesn't it? Just like that newspaper interview. Even for the great Amitabh Kulasheshtra… ultimately you reduce me to what every man has…like, like my father…" my lips quivered with impotent rage. "Answer the question, Maya," Amitabh grabbed my shoulders. I shoved him away, violently. "If you have the guts, go ask your Sarlu that same question…RK told me all about them, also. Said you guys go back a long way, and that, that Aiyee was the first woman he, he ever…" I couldn't complete the rest. "You…how dare you?" Amitabh had slapped me hard.'

'Slow down, Maya, you're not making sense. Is it Avik Dasgupta we are talking about, or Amitabh?'

I ignored my shrink's question; as if transported back in time:

'Amitabh – who hated cinema, mind you,' I wiped my eyes, wrapping my arms around myself, 'promised that he was writing a film script for me! He was desperate to hold on to me, you see. Said he'd produce it himself, if the need arose. Put in all his money. His last *futi kauri*. He hugged me hard, making me swear I wouldn't ever act in commercial movies that he believed were no platform for my talent. He even visited some financiers, I heard later. I wanted to believe Amitabh, but, but, I was restless, doc. I knew he was penniless, refusing to touch the joint account he shared with his wife. Somewhere, I began to suspect his lofty intentions, after a point, especially after Aiyee discovered my letter to him. Finding it under his pillow, after Amitabh followed me all the way to Mumbai from Pune. For months, we lived together in a dingy, one-room chawl, in Kalyan. Aiyee made up the allegations…creating a whole new story, accusing me of breaking her home, branding me a home-wrecker in *Samna*, the Marathi newspaper…Amitabh too was stunned with the cooked-up story, knowing fully well that nothing had transpired between us, until he came searching for me, to this city, many months later. But, Sarla Kulasheshtra's confession naturally got the gossip circles activated. Till then, no one had really known for sure if Amitabh Kulasheshtra had actually moved to Mumbai…but everything changed after that one breaking story…as it was translated into almost every leading national daily and film magazine. That led to us…I mean…it was also the times, doc, there was no money…at home…no parts in films…no future…'

'I can't believe how you've never brought all this up before, Maya, I thought this was about Avik. *His* marriage…' Dr. Pastakia pressed his hand over mine lightly, his face creased.

'I thought so too, doc, until,…until last night. Avik called me, again. I didn't take his call…' I couldn't complete the rest of the sentence.

Dr. Pastakia tried saying something.

'He has got hold of Amitabh Kulasheshtra's last play…a play on his life with Sarla…and…and he wants me to enact the role! *Me!* Me as Sarla? I mean, what do I make of it, doc? Me as Aiyee?'

◈

Dr. Pastakia listened in stunned silence. Templing his fingers as he analysed my problem: 'I see a distinct pattern, Maya…' he shut his notebook, getting up from his chair. 'It seems to me that you are to blame for pushing them both away. Something you have done with possibly every person in your life. Punishing them for loving you, in some measure. Because you feel you are unworthy; because you can't bring yourself to forgive yourself; because you're guilt-ridden about your past, the way you ran away from Kulasheshtra's home, uncannily similar to how you left your own, one night, scribbling a letter for your mother, who you never saw after that day, right?

'Maybe, you playing the role of Sarla *will* be cathartic; you will see that the two of you are not that different, after all, Maya. That a woman like Sarla, whom you idolized, and a woman like you, whom you hate, are after all victims of a self-punishing gaze, of endless guilt and slow-moving regrets. Maybe that's what Amitabh wanted to tell you.'

I took a lengthy drag of my cigarette, closing my eyes.

'Your relationship with Mrs. Sarla Kulasheshtra…that newspaper piece in *Samna*…it seems to me that you held yourself accountable for what happened, *after* that night in their Pune home, the one she supposedly fabricated…you probably felt you had actually let her down by being the "other woman" in the marriage…something she may have only suspected the time she discovered you in Kulasheshtra's room…'

I exhaled, meeting his eyes.

'You have never really opened up about your mother, and her, in the past, Maya…and, so, I cannot help but surmise that maybe the late Amitabh Kulasheshtra, and Maya Shirale were nothing but mirror reflections…two people running away from love…who felt they were incapable of being loved…running headlong into each other…'

I slipped my trainers back on, and fumbled inside my handbag.

'Is that what is really haunting you, Maya?' Dr. Pastakia wiped his face, adding slowly, 'Are these recent hallucinations about Amitabh and these disturbing flashbacks from your past…the real cause of your disorientation…your desperation to talk to me…or is there more, Maya?'

'I don't know…' I murmured.

'What if you are actually searching for someone else, Maya? What if you always were? The real reason for that last fight? Why did you never try reconnecting with Kulasheshtra, either, post that? Or Avik Dasgupta, for that matter, after he stormed out of your apartment? If that is what scared you the most when he died…why couldn't you go on acting, anymore? What if Amitabh Kulasheshtra *was* coming back to Mumbai, as was speculated at the time of his death? What if Aiyee was right? What if you had just not broken a woman's home…but her heart? What if Avik Dasgupta and your fall-out with him is a mere symptom?'

◈

Dr. Pastakia's words echoed in my ears as Alam drove me home. What if my resistance to change and my innate non-conformism, were, in fact, a result of my own, deep-seated fears; my self-loathing?

Did Avi know all along that I could never love him back with the same desperate fierceness that he had loved me? Was that why he never called me or bothered to find out if I was repentant for the way things panned out? I never knew if Avi regretted trying to raise his hand on me during our last argument.

I placed my head on the backseat of the car, studying the shape of Alam's broad shoulders. One afternoon, a month after he had walked out of my apartment, Alam rang, saying Avi had sent his assistant Shirish to collect his things from my house. I told Alam to help him empty out all the cupboards. Together, they arranged Avi's belongings into three large suitcases. When Shirish left, I asked Alam to call Avi and tell him that now nothing of his remained.

Avi never answered. Later, he sent Alam a text. 'Cool,' was all it said.

And so I felt nothing when I decided to sell my Peddar Road penthouse, despite having painstakingly decorated the flat together with Avi, each corner bearing my personal touch, and moved into a more modest residence in Lokhandwala.

Frankly, all I wanted was to escape the last memory of us.

◈

Amitabh's sudden death, our subsequent breakup, my dependence on drinking and drugs, the violent mood swings they caused, had led to many burnt bridges, causing directors to be wary of working with me; the court case with the Nadiadwala's and Lux – from whose big budget film and much sought-after ad campaign, respectively, I had pulled out, at approximately the same time and that were both, finally settled out of Court, had caused me staggering financial losses. However, unlike in the past, this time I wasn't interested in plunging headlong into mainstream cinema, taking up just about any role to build back my bank balance; of course, it wasn't like plum roles were falling into my lap in any case, either. At thirty-eight my career as a 'heroine' was practically over.

I wasn't really lying to Dr. Pastakia; nothing felt the same after June 10, 2002, somehow. Not just script-reading sessions, I don't remember, how many movie projects that I had agreed to be a part of and expressed interest in, I now obstinately backed out of. Even as the movie deals dried up, I refused to dance at the high-profile weddings of the children of industrialists and politicians, held at exotic foreign locations, or to be a part of overseas stageshows and brand-endorsements – avenues most commonly used by yesteryears actresses, who either get married and leave the industry, or, take a sabbatical to become a mother, or, are simply wiped away, thanks to their back-to-back flops.

My adversaries laughed at my failure behind my back. I had never been a part of any camp in the past. It was payback time. Speculation was rife on why and how I had become a recluse, after 2002. Movie critics blamed my recklessness and trademark don't-care-a-damn attitude. Tabloid editors speculated on my current relationship status. There were rumours I was marrying a Sheikh in Abu Dhabi. That he had made me change my religion…my name…paparazzi traced down a woman in a *hijab*, alleging it was me they had spotted in a mall in Sharjah.

My trusted astrologers, the famous Jumani brothers, pointed out that my *Mangal* and *Shani dasha* were seriously messed up. Leading men sniggered about my fall from grace at premieres and *mahurats*. Some I had slept with; others, who weren't able to get into bed with me, tried their luck, now. 'Movie offers *nahin, toh kam se kam, apna* sex drive *ko toh healthy rakkha karo…*' one of them audaciously texted, once, going on to crib about how his divorce had cost him a bomb.

I never returned calls or answered mails, till my mailbox was spilling over, forcing Alam to make the same excuses for me, time after time. A part of me knew that this was sheer professional hara-kiri, that a woman, above the age of 35, no matter what her past box-office track record had been, could not afford such aloofness in our trade, that placed the highest premium on a heroine's age and networking skills. I was aware there were a dime-a-dozen, younger, prettier, more talented actresses, ready to fill my shoes, have no qualms about sleeping around for a break, willingly play second fiddle to a famous hero, say yes to starving herself to death just to bag the coveted position of a heroine…to be the next Maya Shirale…

◈

And so, just like that, I had watched, almost in third person, as the last couple of years of my life slipped out of my fingers. My erratic lifestyle, my unlimited extravagance, my hunger for diamonds, single malt, the occasional cocaine, and, imported cars finally got the better of me, as everyone whom I had rejected or not bothered giving a second glance, had predicted, at some point, or the other. I had anyway used most of my addictions to fill one kind of abyss, subconsciously knowing that they would consume me, eventually, like a lethal slow poison.

My bank accounts were depleted one by one. I was forced to let go of most of my cars and real estate investments. I pawned most of my jewellery next – my fate sinking to no better than the lowliest of Bollywood starlets. I had lived my life on the edge, since the time I had started out, but, now, I was close to being pushed off the brink.

Till, one day, two weeks before I had met Dr. Pastrakia, I received an unexpected call from a TV dance show.

◈

'Your career is not yet over,' Rosy had snatched the phone away from my hands, scrutinizing the number that flashed on the screen.

'Career *nahi*, Rosy, *jawani...*' I unzipped a short, lace dress.

'Anubhuti Productions has bought the rights to this show...*aap ko pata bhi hai kuch, aaj kal?* she hissed, handing me a wet tissue a few minutes later, muttering angrily to herself, 'AD sahib owns the company now. All these men are the same, madam. *Raat gayi, baat gayi...*'

In my absence, and mostly behind my back, Rosy, my hairdresser and make-up person, had called Avi, in the initial months of our separation, especially during spells when I remained untraceable. Occasionally, Avi's cell-phone was answered by someone else, claiming he was either in a meeting or on location.

'Go home, Rosy...your daughter is waiting for you...' I had cut her short, continuing in a cold voice before she could add another word, 'I know this is your pent-up anger against Avi talking. But they are paying me a whopping fifty lakhs upfront, understand? Two years...*do season ka* contract *hai.* It's not an offer I can afford to ignore...'

'You shouldn't have agreed so easil...Maya Shirale *ka ghamand hi usska pet palti hai,*' Rosy made a face, handing me over a change of clothes.

I lit a cigarette.

'Madam, I am more savvy than you in these matters... *wohich AD, unhone hi aap ko aur zalil karne ke liye itni badi rakam* offer *kiya hoga*...he wants to humiliate you...' she bit her lip, looking away in anger.

I remember staring at her reflection in the floor-length mirror, replaying the conversation I had just concluded.

The way I had gushed on the phone, as if overcome with gratitude. As if, I was hungry, all over again...'*Haan, mein hi hun*, Maya Shirale. You have dialled the right number. Thank you for giving me the opportunity to judge *Dhak Dhak India*, India's biggest dance reality show on Sony Television.'

◈

'Dance is my lifeline, like television,' I had said in the fake, bright, super-excited way expected of TV show panellists when my name was announced and I strutted on to the revolving stage of a Goregaon studio, surrounded with psychedelic laser lights and flabby extras, holding cheery pompoms, sporting outlandish costumes from my past hit films...supposedly my lookalikes.

I waved at them, widening my eyes, feeling the stiffness of my lashes. Fighting the suffocation of a heavily embellished, satin gown with a silk lining, with a sweeping feathery trail.

As the camera zoomed in on my cleavage, my thoughts travelled back to how I had superciliously rejected offers to host shows on television in the past, laughing when top channel heads narrated stories of superstars such as Mr. Bachchan reinventing their financial fortunes via this medium: 'I am not a yummy mummy yet...like that Madhuri Desai who returned with her engineer husband after bidding *tata* bye bye to showbiz...to then star in ads for water purifiers...Maya Shirale *ke* passport *aur taqdeer pay, abhi* expiry date *ka thappa nahin laga hai...*' used to be my pet line.

I took a deep breath.

In my heart, I had known Rosy was right. That she had been right, all along.

'Television to me is about selling big dreams on the small screen. It's why, why I am here. The reason we brought this show to India, to make the aspirations of a billion people a reality. Presenting before you, Indian television's most awaited reality dance show, *Dhak Dhak India*,' a voice had thundered from behind me as I swerved, nervously.

'*Dhak dhak karta hai mera dil*,' the two-bit anchor crooned, making moaning sounds.

'Miss Maya Shirale, ladies and gentlemen. What an absolute honour to have you back, with us. *The* Maya Shirale, for the first time, on primetime television, on none other than *Dhak Dhak India*. And seen here, after two years, close friend, and acclaimed director, Mr. Avik Dasgupta...ladies and gentlemen...'

I stared speechless as Avik joined me on stage where the panel of judges was being introduced!

'*Khub jamegi yeh shyam, jab mil baithenge itne saare purane yaar, dost, itne bade bade fankar...bahut rang layegi...Dhak Dhak India*...ladies and gentlemen...' the co-anchor, a popular face on television, quipped, her high-pitched voice echoing ominously as the studio audience laughed on cue.

'*Shukriya*, thanks Mr. Dasgupta and Sony Entertainment Television...I mean...Avi....' I tried looking composed, conscious of the camera panning into my face.

◈

I had stormed off the set, as soon as the promo recording had concluded.

Avik had followed me to my vanity van.

I had not seen him in a year.

'I'm sorry, Maya. I didn't want to be a part of the shoot today. I'd even told my guys to keep it from you, that it was my production company that had bought the India rights of this show. It was *my* fault, Maya, and you have every right to be pissed off seeing me, all of a sudden, that too, on camera.

I know you hate surprises,' AD had grabbed my right arm, banging the door shut, when I held it open, requesting him to leave.

'*Anubhuti* Productions was a dead fucking giveaway,' I remarked sarcastically, asking one of the production team assistants who was waiting with next week's shooting schedule, to leave us, alone, locking the door.

'Look, the truth was, I mean is, Peddar Road *ka ghar nilam ho gaya hai*, and, that bloody settlement with the Nadiadwala Brothers...the last few years...I haven't done anything... nothing interests me...I, I needed the advance money to stay afloat. All these people, my staff, the few I actually still have left...Alam, Rosy...their whole lives depend on how much I make at the end of the month,' I shot Avi a sideways glance.

'Maya...' Avi tried to cut in.

'Don't, Avi, I don't want any man to patronize me, least of all you. And, do me a favour, will you? Don't blame yourself for us meeting this way...I am not used to this weird distance between us...it was what probably made me go blank, initially...during the formal introductions...being referred to as close friend,' I added, somewhat tongue-tied, still.

'Maya, trust me on this, I couldn't be happier that you are putting yourself out there, again. The camera has missed you, and how,' Avi said passionately, standing behind me.

'I know what you are going to say, okay. You're a big guy, now, in this business. And, I am happy...it's what you've wanted all along, right? The acceptance, the fame, the money, your brand of commercial cinema that was noir and dark at the same time, that was populist and cerebral at the same time, and now your foray into television, with the hope of changing the rules, once again. Anubhuti Productions!' I widened my eyes, adding impatiently as I shrugged his hands off me, "Buzz!" Isn't that what you used to say your career lacked, back when we met? I still remember that word. It was your thing. I'm glad life rewarded you with everything you ever aspired for. Makes you one of the lucky ones, I suppose. *Ab toh tum producer sahib bhi ban gaaye ho*...Maya, Maya Shirale *tumhare isharon pein nachne wali hai...khush*? *Dil abhi bhara nahin, kya*?'

'Still have that badass humour. At least, something's stay the same,' Avi broke into a wry smile.

'Still think of me, kiddo, sometimes?' I clicked my tongue.

'Every day, every, single fucking day...' Avi breathed hard.

'Avi, relax, you don't have to be politically correct, off camera, anyway. I have dinner plans,' I unclipped my hair extensions.

'Cut the crap, Maya,' Avi ordered, pulling a file from the satchel he was carrying, 'take this, and, read it, okay. I leave tonight for L.A...my flight leaves in a couple of hours from now.'

'*Kya hai yeh*, Avi? Script? A new film you're directing? A TV serial, huh, this time?' I sniggered, throwing the file on his chest.

Avi pressed his hand over mine.

'I'm getting back to the stage. To do what I've always wanted, back to source...I am all set to direct my first play. Theatre has always been my thing, Maya...the reason behind me trying so hard to gain admission into the coveted National Centre of Drama...it's probably, why I'm even here, today, this city, Mumbai...even us, in some way,' his eyes glinted fiercely, his face flushed.

'What we shared is behind us, officially,' I cut him short, gesturing to the platinum wedding band on his left ring finger. 'Besides, what's with this sudden passion to return to theatre?'

'This *is* about us, Maya...' Avi took a deep breath.

'Avik Dasgupta, if this play is a means to come to terms with your residual guilt…of, of sleeping with an older heroine, using her fame and contacts, royally, as some alleged you did…what we both had, once, the way you just walked out of my life, never bothering to call or text, even when the Press was throwing muck at me…of getting back, getting even with me?' I coughed.

'There is nothing left to settle,' Avi touched my shoulder.

'Left to save, then, maybe? Your bruised ego? Your male pride? You know how much I have kicked myself about hurting you…you think it was easy for me to let you go, after the way you chose to finish our relationship? You think you can always walk away being the nice guy…Avi…' I choked.

'I was saving no one, Maya. I can't. It's what I realized after leaving you. We can't save each other, Maya…finding love doesn't save anyone,' Avi settled a stray strand covering my left eye.

'Avi…don't…please…not now…' I shuddered, weakened by his touch.

Rosy was outside, banging on the locked door.

'Maya, Maya, look at me, once,' Avi pulled up my chin, staring urgently into my eyes, 'Maya, promise me you will read this script. It's Amitabh Kulasheshtra's last script; the one he was writing all those years holed up in Pune; his curtain call.'

RK CHOPRA

I was sitting near a large window, sipping slowly on a glass of single malt, alone. It was my last bottle picked up from my last overseas trip. Before the raids. Before my offices were sealed. I watched through the hotel window as aeroplanes took off and landed. A part of me had longed to fly down to Pune every day since Amitabh had died two years ago. But the case dragged on and on and I was constantly scuttling residences, and being advised to lie low, till we had bought some more time. I wanted nothing more than to drive straight to Banno's residence…to ask if she had read the manuscript that I had had specially hand-delivered. Risking joining hands with Chotta Shamim, Bhai's sworn enemy, to lay my hands on the whopping funds I knew Amol Rawat would never refuse…to procure it just for her. I wanted to know if Banno had known it was really from me. If she resented the intrusion or saw it as a gesture worth appreciating – whether to her it was an act of cowardice or courage.

How would she react if she knew that I had sweet-talked Rawat, literally winning him over, dazzling him with black money accrued from illegitimate sources to get the cloth bag retrieved? Convinced him that Amitabh's last material posession should be returned to his grieving window, at the earliest – how that would be the best way to her being silenced, forever, in a sense. Making up something about rumours I had supposedly heard about the Malegaon case being reopened. Citing the example of Prakash Lele's daughter and how she had been bought out, in the end.

◈

Rawat had looked stunned when I told him the amount I was ready to shelve out.

'*Bahut khas dosti thi, kya*? Was he a special friend?' he had asked, picking his teeth.

I stuffed a tikka kebab inside my mouth.

'*Kuch aisa hi samajh lo...*' I replied, winking at my lawyers.

Mahesh and Jayant had been livid how a discussion that was supposed to be about my pending cases, had suddenly veered towards Amitabh Kulasheshtra.

Rawat had a large mole on his nose. He wore a *popat topi* and white, open sandals.

'*Yeh Sarlaji kya karti hain, aaj kal, din bhar*? *Buddha toh gaya...*' he shot me a cursory glance, as he pushed back his chair.

'*Kal...mein khud aunga lene...yaad hai na*?' I got up at the same time, my hands folded in a gratuitous Namaste.

One of Rawat's men pushed me back in my chair.

'*Nahin...*' Rawat swerved.

Then before my lawyers could react, he retorted, 'My driver will have it hand delivered to your address. *Khush*?'

I waved again.

It was how the meeting had culminated.

'You blew your chance, RK! What was all this about, all of a sudden? We were supposed to get your case scuttled and instead you settle for an old cloth bag?' Mahesh frowned, unable to mask his irritation at his client as I sat beside him, in his swanky new Merc.

I closed my eyes.

'*Koi aur mantri mil jayega...koi aur* party...besides, Rawat likes me...I can always tell such things...' I muttered.

Mahesh started the engine, shrugging his shoulders, like he had trouble believing me.

From the back seat, Jayant too eyed me suspiciously.

◈

The cell-phone now lying next to me beeped loudly.

'RK?'

'AD? Is that you?'

'Yes, it's Avik Dasgupta...'

'*Bol puttar...kaise...meri yaad aayi tujhe...*' I pressed my lips closer to the speaker.

'You knew Sarla Kulasheshtra, right?'

'What has knowing Sarla got to do with anything, *puttar*? I am a finished man. My production house is bust. My houses all mortgaged by the *behnchod* bank. My son Monty, *Ma ka*...never mind...I am living in Andheri these days, in a downmarket service apartment, was forced to leave Hyatt, the *haramkhor daru* burnt a hole in my pocket, anyway, I, I am desperately trying to restart my career in some way, AD, dabble in television, maybe...' I laughed nervously.

'Did you love her, RK?'

'*What?*'

'Will you be interested in associating yourself with a play?' My mind was racing. I never imagined in my wildest dreams that Banno would actually reach out to AD with Amitabh's script. But the moment I thought about it, I had to hand it to her. Her instinct was spot-on as always. AD was the perfect director to entrust this venture to. If anyone was the new generation Amitabh, it had to be Avik Dasgupta.

'Play? AD? Play *bola tune, puttar*?' I hammed, raising my voice by several notches.

'You heard me. I want to know if you'll be interested in being part of a new play, RK?'

'*Yaara*, I'm bloody broke myself…*meri toh gaand…aur gurdan…dono ke upar hi Bhai ne mehengi rakam lagiye huwi hai*,' I tried acting over familiar.

'This is not about the money, RK,' AD cut me short.

'*Phir kya fayeda, puttar*? If there is no money…' I wondered if AD knew anything about Rawat and my underhand dealings. If he was aware that it was I who had actually salvaged Amitabh Kulasheshtra's last written word. Conning not just the cops, but one of the most notorious ganglords of this city.

Had Banno made AD call me?

On her behalf?

Was this also her idea?

Just then, there was some disturbance on the line.

'What if I said, the play I'm talking about happens to be penned by none other than Amitabh Kulasheshtra?' AD resumed after a pause of a few seconds.

'Bhai Jaan? I mean, Amitabh…' I feigned shock, trying to fight the image of Banno in my arms, at dusk, her lips pressed over mine.

'*Cut*. It's called *Cut*.'

'*Cut?* I repeated, feeling the dead weight of Rawat's slanted smile, the way he snidely brought up Banno.

'In or out, RK?' AD sounded dead serious.

'Banno? I mean, Sarla, did, did *she* ask you to contact me?' I could no longer camouflage my feelings.

'That's irrelevant,' he cut me short.

'No, no, AD, you don't understand. I...I have been trying hard to...I mean...I called Banno...as in, Sarla, recently, again on her land line...you see, I want to talk to her...I need to talk to her, AD...I couldn't watch her the way I saw her on television when they broke the news of his death...the way she appeared...so pale...completely insignificant, insipid...I failed Banno, AD...not once, but twice...' I couldn't bring myself to complete the last sentence.

'Twice?'

'Yes, twice, *puttar*...there is so much I want to say, to be able to...' I tried rephrasing myself.

'I don't believe in second chances, RK,' AD said abruptly.

'Amitabh didn't, either...you sound a lot like him, strangely,' I added, softly.

'As in?'

'*Ek ajeeb si bechaini thi Bhai Jaan mein*...as if he was searching for something, constantly...like he was always running away...as if the stage was his only refuge...his sanity, his salvation, in a way,' I spoke slowly, walking towards the unfinished glass of whiskey.

'You mentioned being put up at Andheri, that's not too far from my office...I will come and see you personally to discuss this further. All I can say now is that I want this project started, as soon as possible, since Maya, too...Maya too may...' AD went on, matter-of-factly.

'Maya?'

'Maya Shirale,' he clarified.

'What has she got to do with *Cut?*' I frowned.

'Everything.'

'*Mein samjha nahin*?'

'Maya plays the lead role,' AD replied, tersely.

'Does Banno...Sarla...know about this? Have you talked about casting this magnum opus?'

'It's her idea; in fact, she insists on it. On only Maya Shirale essaying her role.'

'So, it was Sarla, then, huh?...Why did you suddenly pick up the phone, *puttar*? I mean...I am a veritable untouchable in this industry now...*mera toh* number *hi aadhe se zyada logon ne block kar ke rakkha hai...chutiye sab saaale...*' I paused, rubbing my eyes.

There was a long silence. '*Puttar*, you, you there?' I cleared my throat. '*Dekh*, days are bad and my stars are royally messed up, and I don't want the production of this play to suffer thanks to my ill-repute. This was after all Bhai Jaan's last chance...'

'It's my last chance, too, RK; and yours as well.' AD said before hanging up.

MAYA SHIRALE

Avi was late.

I was waiting at the coffee shop at Taj Lands End, as pre-decided. My hands trembled as I clutched the script he had handed me a few weeks ago. I hadn't slept a wink last night, and the night before, nor for many nights now. I checked my phone nervously. Alongside its main narrative about the the complex relationship shared between Aiyee and Amitabh, *Cut* etched the story of our forbidden love, details of the short relationship that Amitabh and I had been involved in, how it started, the year our paths first crossed in his Pune home, what happened after he followed me to Mumbai, how shattered he still was after the death of his only daughter…

Cut could easily be considered autobiographical.

Except, it was not. *Cut* painted a sweeping, almost cinematic canvas of Amitabh Kulasheshtra's tumultuous life, and career as seen by Sarla Kulasheshtra. The screenplay commenced on the night Amitabh returned from Mumbai. After our last fight, it had been Aiyee who greeted him, at the gate. Pointing him to the outhouse. It was where he had lived till the morning of his mysterious disappearance. His body being discovered on a train to Mumbai, hours later. Aiyee had identified the corpse.

Cut brought alive Sarla Kulasheshtra, a woman the world hardly ever saw except during rare public appearances, where she remained aloof, walking silently by his side. Aiyee never interacted much with the media or his troupe members. Never attending any of his plays, either. She remained her husband's only constant, a consort, a comrade, and, yet, no one had ever heard her voice.

Her thoughts. Her dreams. Her failures.

Except Amitabh.

Cut, a short play in three acts, drew its inspiration from the Kabuki tradition of Japan, an ancient theatrical form, characterized by the stylization of its drama and the elaborate make-up worn by its performers. Its first scene involved a lengthy monologue – a widow refusing to give up wearing colour and erase the vermillion from her forehead – who had supposedly despised her husband, in the time he was alive – it was she who now pieced together his last years. The screenplay, a retrospective of sorts, a heady mix of flashback and fast forward…the present and the past colliding…

I asked myself again and again why Avi chose me? How he could ever expect me to essay the role of Sarla Kulasheshtra?

How I could ever do justice to a woman, such as her? Who allowed me to steal her most treasured possession, before making me pay the price?

Had Aiyee always known Amitabh and I would never make it as man and woman?

Was Dr. Pastakia right in his assessment about me? And, Amitabh?

Were we the same, in the end?

I slowly opened the script. Reading to myself. Running my fingers over the word 'wife'. Many times…

Nowhere was Sarla Kulasheshtra's name spelt out.

'Wife…' I whispered under my breath, feeling the way I had, the afternoon Aiyee took me in.

It was what she had called herself.

It was her title.

It was her territory.

I loosened the silk scarf around my neck, looking around me, listlessly. At the opposite table, a young woman, possibly a newbie model or an aspiring actress, showed her portfolio to a man old enough to be her father. His pock-marked face was unusually familiar. I couldn't quite recall his name, though.

Our glances intersected briefly.

I looked away. It was here, in Taj Lands End, that I had met RK Chopra for the first time, when Amitabh and I were living together in Mumbai. Like now, it was about to pour, that evening. The sea unusually tumultuous...

◈

I had lied to Amitabh. Told him I had to pay the electricity bill. When the truth was the connection had been cut a week ago. There was hardly anything to eat. Amitabh had purchased some bread and a few eggs. He hated eggs. I told him I would return in an hour or so.

I had begged the landlord for some time to pay last month's pending rent. My stomach churning when he mentioned noticing a strange man in the house, and how that meant extra water usage...something always in short supply in Mumbai.

I had never discussed all this with Amitabh. I couldn't.

Like the young woman in front of me, I too had kept stealing glances at my wristwatch that time when RK had deliberately kept me waiting, wrapping up a lengthy meeting with his screenplay writers, before he had beckoned to me, clicking his tongue, insisting on me accompanying him up to his suite.

◈

I had been avoiding RK's overtures to reach me, ever since I had moved to Mumbai, literally begging me, at times, to come down to his office for a look-test. He had promised that I wouldn't be put through any harrowing audition.

'So, Miss Mrinalini Shirale, tell me about your *buddha ashiq*? What is his highness upto these days? Heard he's knocking on the doors of some financiers…eating humble pie…street plays, over!' he had poured himself a glass of single malt, before wrapping his hairy arms around my shoulders. I had left my dupatta at home. I sat down quickly with my legs crossed. RK had quite the reputation. All the heroines he was famously known to have discovered, he had first slept with. Staring at me, lust-ridden, playing with a thick, twisted gold chain that dangled around his stubby neck, RK had dialled Room Service and asked me what I wanted to eat.

'Who told you Amitabh and I are together, RK? That, that, my real name…is Mrinalini, and not Maya? Been spying on me? On us?' I took a tough stand.

'Well, well, well,' RK had chuckled, scratching his chest, 'The cat is out of the bag, *janeman*. Amitabh and you are no longer classified information. Apparently, his wife Sarla Kulasheshtra has finally broken her vow of silence and spilt the beans on your clandestine affair, openly admitting, that it was she who first discovered Kulasheshtra and you together.' He tapped the newspaper lying folded beside him. 'So, it is not some inane gossip magazine; this info comes straight from the horse's mouth. None other than Mrs. Sarla Kulasheshtra who claims that their married life was peaceful until the point you suddenly wandered in, betrayed her trust, and destroyed her *ghar ghirhasti*.'

I had grabbed the newspaper and read the article in shocked silence.

For a while, RK had said nothing. Then refilling his glass, he sidled closer to me on the leather couch, gently rubbing my thigh: 'Sarla, I know her…she will never forgive you for snatching her husband away from her, Maya; from theatre, from their safe home in Pune…everything he built. Everyone he loved. It's all over for Kulasheshtra, this time! *Saala do takke ka* director. Can't even keep a woman like her satisfied. Sarla – a noble woman, a dutiful daughter, a good wife – who sacrificed her own happiness, her dreams of acting in films…and, you know something else, Maya? I was the only man Sarla ever loved, Yes, me. The one and only RK Chopra who controls half of Bollywood…Sarla and I used to be lovers…'

'Aiyee? And You? Lovers?' I was taken aback, running my fingers over a picture of Amitabh and her, on the front page.

'*Meri baat man lo, jaan,*' RK had pointed at the headlines, adding, snidely: 'Nobody will offer you a film after Sarla Kulasheshtra's shocking confession…the way she's described discovering Amitabh, half-naked with you, after the last day's performance of *Maya* in Pune, his head sandwiched between your breasts. *Samna* is the biggest Marathi daily in the region. It's bound to be tomorrow's biggest headline on TV and be played up doubly by the film magazines.'

I tried saying something, when RK had suddenly grabbed my wrist: 'Do you have any idea what this article makes you, Maya? How this news will be blown out of proportion? Also, let's face it; the media has always nursed a love-hate affair with Kulasheshtra. This is everything they need to crucify him, again; this scoop will sell like hot cakes. I mean, haven't some papers already carried pictures of Kulasheshtra, in an auto, a while ago, speculating he was possibly involved with a struggling actress, rumoured to be living-in with her in a chawl in Kalyan.'

RK impatiently unbuttoned his polyester shirt. '*Janeman, jaane tamanna,*' he burped loudly and pulled my chin up, roughly. 'Can't you see where all this is finally headed? *Tumhara* career *thhap*, finished; even before it has officially started. Listen to me…Maya…*meri taraf dekho*…accept my proposition to star in my son's debut feature, *Ishq*…I'll pay you as much as you want...'

The girl facing me now pushed back her chair. Like I too had risen up in a huff.

'I'm not scared for him, Maya,' RK had blocked my way, 'there's no love lost between Amitabh and I. In fact, this serves him right. We all get what we deserve. Which is why Maya, Maya Shirale, you musn't allow this golden opportunity to get away. Let the world see your talent. Kulasheshtra *ke pyaar mein phasna asaan hai…nikalna namumkin…*'

I remember thinking of Amitabh just then, standing at the lone window where he watched me go, whenever I left home, alone. The one that overlooked a squalid housing colony at the far end of a dimly lit bylane, dotted with open, filthy drains. Where scrawny, bare-bodied boys played cricket on balmy summer evenings and autorickshaws parked in a haphazard line. Where stray dogs guarded the entrance, baring their fangs at passersby. Where on most days, there was no drinking water.

Had he read this article in *Samna*?

Did Amitabh hate Aiyee?

Could he ever hate Aiyee?

'I hope you're not aspiring to become the next Mrs. Kulasheshtra, now?' RK had laughed, clutching his ugly paunch.

◈

'You've changed...' I murmured, studying Avi when he arrived finally, flopping down on the wicker sofa beside me and ordering an Espresso for himself and a green tea for me. Nodding at the waiter who beamed seeing us together in the same corner we had occupied in the past, facing an azure sea.

AD wore a black shirt and dark denims. His breath as always reeked of nicotine. He asked for a lighter and an ashtray. Then before I could finish talking, he held up his hands, holding his cigarette between his fingers: 'I know I have kept *the* great Maya Shirale waiting, and not the other way round. I am *so* sorry. I was caught up. But, please, let's not get into an argument on this. Let's get straight to the point of why we are here.'

He took a lengthy drag.

'You've changed a lot since the time we stopped seeing each other, Avi. I wanted to say that to you, last time, as well as now. A lot has changed in here too, in this hotel, in this city, this industry. Maybe, I *should* have listened to Rosy; avoided the damn shoot for the promo of *Dhak Dhak India*. Running into you was never going to be easy...' I lightly touched Avi's tight fist.

'Was running away from me easier, Maya?'

'Avi,' I dropped my voice, leaning in close: 'I had no idea your wife has left you. I know you were there when I texted. Your office told me about your sudden Pune trip.'

Avi pulled back, at once. 'Reema has gone to visit her folks who live in Pune, and, I was there on work, Maya. Stop drawing useless parallels. Besides, how does the status of my marriage affect you?'

'So, so you're saying that the grapevine about you...and, and...Reema Karnik are baseless rumours?'

Avi finished his cigarette. 'Actually, it's Mrs. Avik Dasgupta,' he brought the cup closer to his mouth.

'Is that what you call her, Avi? Is that how you see her?'

'Please, Maya, I don't wish to dissect my personal life. That's all. What matters is we got married, when we did, and it's been a little over a year, so it's still an adjustment period for both of us, I guess. Besides, every couple squabbles…'

'Are you happy, Avi?'

'Maya, I thought you wanted to meet and discuss my offer on the play.'

'I can't do it, Avi; I cannot accept your offer on *Cut*,' I cleared my throat, looking away at the silhouette of the waves. 'I just can't be her…it's too hard. I've really struggled with this script and this decision…but I'm afraid I won't be able to do justice to the play…' I confessed slowly, meeting his hard stare.

'Afraid, of just what, Maya? What scares you the most, huh?'

'That it is Amitabh Kulasheshtra's story. That it is the man we never knew. The poet. The patriarch. The patriot. The passenger on a train to Mumbai…I don't know why, but I feel he's actually alive, still here, every time I read the scenes, like he's trying desperately to say something…like Amitabh is not dead,' my lips quivered.

The waiter cleared the cups.

'What is he trying to say, Maya? What is Amitabh Kulasheshtra trying to tell you?' Avi restarted the conversation, staring back in my direction.

'This play; the script you gave me, it feels like Amitabh is attempting to lay bare his own life for the first time. The man he was, not the messiah he was worshipped as; who he loved compared to what he lost, the scars and the secrets… Like this was the last thing he wanted to say…the whole truth, this time…'

'Maya, your instincts as an actor are impeccable, *Cut* is in fact, Kulasheshtra's last work…is in reality a play about a woman he wronged…his exile years when he grappled with his own memory and the myth of the man he was once…fighting charges of being labelled a murderer for the Malegaon episode and, at the same time, being accused of being an anti-national. Kulasheshtra's autumn years, Maya, a different Amitabh than the one we all knew, introspective, conflicted, anguished, abandoned…' Avi ran his fingers over the script, pulling it out from my hands.

'You know what they all said about him, Avi? That he had begun to lose his mind…that he suffered from Alzheimer's…that he had forgotten even his name on the train…the way he died…oh, Avi!' I covered my face.

Avik walked over to my side of the table, and stood behind me.

I said: 'Aiyee…that's whom Amitabh wrote this for…I know it's for her. *Cut* is the story of a man as seen through the eyes of his wife, Avi, not me – his so-called mistress; the silent caregiver, who happened to be his one constant companion; the manner in which they were a whole, again; the cracks in their marriage…and, and, how the light finally got in…' I exhaled.

'Maya…will you please reconsider your decision?'

'How *did* you get this play, Avi? I thought you hated him; that he was the reason you never took up theatre? Did you meet him behind my back? When he was really as sick as the media claims? Dying?' I questioned urgently.

'I never met Amitabh Kulasheshtra, after NCD. This manuscript was lost on the train where he breathed his last…lost in the scuffle, perhaps. Then someone turned it in at the police station where it lay unclaimed for two years. I want you to play the role of Sarla Kulasheshtra, Maya. That's all there is to it…it is my decision as the director of this play.'

'Avi, how *can* I essay the role of his wife? This is the trajectory…the story of Amitabh and Sarla. I was the alleged other woman, Avi…why don't you get this? I am always going to be regarded as an outsider, no matter how Amitabh saw it or you do, now…I mean, let's face it, Marie…what transpired between Bourdaine and Amitabh, was purely speculation, at some level…also it happened in Paris…not here, in India, in Mumbai…I was accused of wrecking his personal life, Avi…for staining his reputation as a stalwart…' I was breathless.

'Kulasheshtra never gave a shit about his reputation, Maya. I am pretty sure; it's what he too would have wanted, had he not met his end. Just the way I am certain, like you, that he *was* headed to Mumbai.'

'Amitabh never discussed death, Avi, you know. Maybe, it was too ordinary, too predictable for someone like him. A man who was unafraid to take the risks he ended up taking…I wish he had met me, Avi…I wish I could have told him…everything…' my words trailed.

'What, Maya? What do you wish you had said to Amitabh Kulasheshtra?'

Avi's voice echoed eerily in the coffee-shop.

There was a storm predicted that day.

SARLA KULASHRESHTA

My students came for dance classes six days a week so I looked forward to Sundays. Relishing the time I had to myself.

It had been a fortnight since Avi had left Pune. We had remained in touch. Avi assured me that he was going to try and get Maya onboard, the way he was also determined to get some of the old members from Amitabh's troupe, those who had dispersed over time, to be associated with the play. Avi kept assuring me that he'd do full justice to *Cut*, that he would produce it himself, if he didn't manage enough sponsors. 'I won't let him down, you have my word, Sarlaji...' Avi always insisted, before disconnecting.

I had just got off a call with him, hanging up in a hurry, as someone rang my bell insistently. The part-timer who had replaced Meena-tai, who was usually here at this time of the day, had taken a leave of absence. I didn't want to answer the door so I took my time, settling the folds of my cotton sari with my left hand, at the same time. My hair was wet. Open.

I pulled open the door and stared at the man outside, not believing my eyes. So long. What had taken him so long to muster the courage to meet me?

◈

I placed a glass of *sherbet* on the table. Then settling back in the wicker chair, I asked pointedly: 'Why are you here, Rakesh?'

Rakesh looked stumped. He had put on a lot of weight. His face was sweaty from the mugginess outside. He wore a shiny red polyester shirt, his front buttons open, two thick gold chains dangled around his stout neck. His ears were pierced with diamond studs. His complexion, a shade or two darker than I remembered. He kept wiping his face. Stone rings of different colours adorned his thick fingers. An expensive Rolex wristwatch caught my attention. He wore a brown tweed beret.

Rakesh had everything he had once wanted.

'I had to see you, Banno; I couldn't keep away any more. I tried calling you as well. I rang on the landline, so many times. I even contemplated writing a letter…as in, I wasn't sure if you used email…possessed a computer…laptop, I mean…' he bit his lip, tapping the table nervously.

I stared at the deepset lines around his eyes. A sudden tenderness rose in me. 'And I often thought of writing to you…in the early years, especially.'

'You *did*?' Rakesh sounded surprised, his face lighting up.

'Yes, but I wasn't sure if you would have the courage or the patience to hear me out…I wasn't even sure if it was right to reach out…'

'Right?' Rakesh looked up.

'You're married Rakesh, and so was I. But, just as you travelled to Pune because you felt it was the right thing to do…the way you almost forced your way inside…sitting in awkward silence for all this time, making small talk…in the same way I…'

'I have been holding back all these years, Banno. But then AD visited me. After he met you for the second time in Pune. He insisted he wanted me to be involved with Bhai Jaan's *Cut*. He wants me to help him recreate the era...especially, the time we spent together under the shadow of Dada Saheb. I told him I was broke, because I thought he was looking at me as a producer...But what I really wanted to know was if you had sent him to me...made him call me? If I was right...in... in assuming...?' his voice caught in his throat.

'Avik met you?'

'I said I needed some time to make up my mind, but, the truth was I wanted to come and meet you first; ask in person, if this is what *you* want; if this is what Bhai...I mean...' Rakesh searched my face.

'Amitabh...you can say his name now...he's dead, Rakesh,' I remarked brusquely.

'Banno, I'm sorry. I don't want you to misunderstand my involvement with all this. The reason I bribed none other than Amol Rawat to lay my hands on the manuscript...is because I wanted to do something for you to remember me by; something more...to prove to you that I meant what I said all those years ago...God knows I've let you down in the past...'

My heart broke to see Rakesh like this. He looked at me earnestly: 'You know Banno, the real reason I cast Maya in *Ishq*...was to get back at Amitabh...and you...this all-encompassing rage...Banno, it has consumed me since the day you agreed to Dada Saheb's marriage proposal...it was too raw, too potent, the pain I felt...the void...the sense of betrayal and failure I have nursed all these years, despite making it so big in Bollywood...living the high life...yet, every night, Banno, I wished Amitabh dead...oh Banno, how long will we have to live this way? Fighting shadows...' he covered his face with both hands.

I walked across to the window. Pushing open one of the wooden panes, I took a deep breath, 'I did it for my father, Rakesh. I married Amitabh because I felt that was the only way I could compensate Dada Saheb, for…for the ultimate sin of being a girl. He wanted a son, desperately, you know: "If only I had a boy," he'd always lament. It hurt me. Dada Saheb's words. The way he pronounced the word "son". I resented Dada Saheb in those moments…the fact that he longed for someone else. I never told Dada Saheb that he hurt me, though. The times he did. The way he did. I never talked much about my disappointments, either. About how unhappy I was.

'In the days leading up to my marriage, my father and I had slipped into a rehearsed silence, except, one full moon night when he sat beside me on my bed.

"Are you happy, now?" my lips trembled. I was holding a stainless steel blade that glistened in the glow of the moon. It was after he had announced my marriage. After you had stormed off…'

Rakesh looked up, his eyes smarting. 'You were ready to *kill* yourself?'

'I was particularly despondent that day. Because I remembered what you had said: "*You will never be happy,* Banno, *till the day Amitabh Kulasheshtra is alive…mark my words, this decision is going to cost you…both*!" Your words rang in my ears. This decision happened because of the way you had not looked back, when I followed you out, Rakesh,' I wiped my eyes. 'Anyway, Dada Saheb remained silent, for a while. Then he gently removed the blade from my grasp and said: "I was married once before, for a couple of years. I loved my first wife passionately, but she was in love with another man, Sarla. Ours was an arranged alliance. It's… it's why she died, committing suicide by drinking a bottle of acid. I never wanted to remarry; I had stopped believing in love or marriage and despised children, until I met your mother, an aspiring actress, who gave up the stage after you were born, after a very complicated pregnancy. That's when I understood the importance of devotion. Above love."'

RK came closer to me.

'Dada Saheb compared me to his dead wife. He called heartbreak "slow poison". "You want too much, like her, your eyes imminently alive, like hers, so, so different from mine. You share that same angst, my child, an ache that just doesn't go away; your intensity would have scorched Rakesh over time." Dada Saheb felt he understood your thirst for quick fame…your ambition to be famous; he was an astute observer of people…he was absolutely certain that we had no future. "I could not watch you destroy your life with the wrong man, nursing a bunch of fractured dreams. That's the reason I chose Amitabh…he, he is, good for you. Trust your father. He is like my son. He will never leave you, Sarla…he will never betray your heart." I had brought the blade closer to my wrist. Wanting to kill myself in front of Dada Saheb's eyes. Wanting him to suffer. To pay.'

RK froze in his tracks. 'Banno…no…' he gasped, placing his arms around me.

'"And what if he dies like your first wife, prematurely? Or chooses to go away, leaving me behind?" I had blurted bitterly, the blade slowly slipping from my hand. Dada Saheb's warm breath covered the nape of my neck. He was sure Amitabh would never desert me, that he would always come back to the home we would go on to build together, as husband and wife. "Amitabh will learn to love you," he told me.'

RK held me tight: 'You can't ever learn how to love someone, Banno, loving someone is not the same as cultivating a habit or memorizing a dialogue,' he had just started speaking, when I turned to face him, touching his chest:

'Dada Saheb stayed with me, that entire night. "You will make a beautiful bride and you *will* be loved. Amitabh *will* learn, such is the law of marriage, things come around in the end…as they must, as they were destined to…"' he had whispered, as I sobbed in his arms. I asked: "Did you ever love my mother? Me? Did you ever fall out of love with your first wife? Did you choose the stage to hide your own scars?" I shuddered. Dada Saheb didn't answer. Maybe, he was dead inside. Like I was to become.'

RK lifted my chin up, slowly, searching for words to comfort me: 'Banno…was my mother's pet name, you know…she died during the Partition riots…' he placed his cheek to mine.

For a long while, we remained like that.

'Sometimes, I wished he would die, too, Rakesh... that's the truth…and you must know this,' I pulled away, agitatedly.

Rakesh moved away and took off his beret. 'Truth?' he sounding startled.

'I was happy when the news came,' I looked away.

'How can it be possible?' Rakesh asked.

'My indifference towards my husband?'

'No,' he clarified, coming closer, touching my shoulders, for a fleeting second.

'Then?' I moved back, a few steps, 'I thought you wished to know more about us, like the rest…everyone seems to want to know what we shared…how Kulasheshtra was, as a husband…a man of flesh and blood…how it was, living with him, in the same house, especially, after my *Samna* interview…after Amitabh suddenly returned from Mumbai… one night…'

'I find that ironical…' Rakesh frowned.

'Amitabh's death? The way it happened in a stuffy train compartment?'

'No, Banno, what Amitabh's death represented…the stark truth about this country. Our political conscience. Fame. The price we all must pay... for the person we were thought to be... larger than life...' Rakesh murmured, staring at the garden outside.

'Saint…' our wrists brushed each other's, briefly.

Rakesh followed me back to the couch, after a while.

'I, I didn't mean for this to get awkward in any way, Banno... us, meeting, this way, again. Dissecting Amitabh's death, bringing up the past...'

We sat beside each other on the same sofa.

'Actually, I've done it almost every day since Amitabh went away,' I confessed, turning to face him.

'To Mumbai, first, you mean? To Maya?'

'Our Maya was dead, Rakesh. She died in Amitabh's arms. We could do nothing to save her…she suffered from a rare congenital heart problem…it's what the doctors said.'

'And, is that why you hated Bhai Jaan so deeply, Banno? Because he wasn't there for you when you needed him the most…when your child was ailing…because he wasn't ever a good husband in the ways wives are conditioned to expect and…how he never loved you back, as a woman?' Rakesh's lips quivered.

'It's okay, I told myself,' I rested my head on his shoulders.

'When?' Rakesh stiffened, at once.

'When the call first came. I felt we were equals, in a sense.'

'Because?'

'Because, Amitabh was to never have the thing he loved the most,' a tear rolled out of my eye.

'Maya? His Maya? Maya Shirale?'

'They told me Amitabh couldn't even recall his own name when he was being asked for his identity on that train... he, he had lost his memory... most of it, by then...all the recollections of who he was or where he may have been headed...' I moved closer.

Rakesh gently removed a strand of hair from my eyes.

'Memory, Rakesh. That intangible construct between man and a woman, people like us. Brought together by circumstance ... but fated to love someone else... memory is all Amitabh had. It's all I lived with, too. The times...all the years we spent under one roof...the fights, the fall-outs, the success, the silences, the awards, the aloneness... the lies... the lovers...the bed we slept on, in different directions – his legs facing me. I'd touch them lightly, some days. Never waking Amitabh...not making too much noise, either. It was my place, I suppose. It's the way my marriage was designed…fated, perhaps, from the start,' I pressed my face into Rakesh's shoulder.

'You know, Banno, I never looked at you both that way… as man and a woman…maybe, I was in denial too…' Rakesh paused abruptly, covering my hands with his. 'And, if I may ask, is that why you took it upon yourself to have this play staged? Amitabh Kulasheshtra's last wish...his swan song...?'

'I am no victim, Rakesh. I owe this to myself, equally. Or, maybe, I am not afraid to own the power I have always possessed…anymore,' I lifted my head.

Rakesh raised an eyebrow.

'I don't understand. How can a play based on a man like your husband – an icon, a legend – be about you, Banno?'

'Just the way I slept for all those years, lying opposite Amitabh. Never looking into his eyes, directly, making my station in the shadows, and, yet knowing his every move... the times he'd get up to visit the toilet, around midnight. Or when he'd stir. In the throes of a nightmare... screaming her name,' I answered, stiffly, rising up.

Rakesh rose up, wiping his face.

'Will you come when the play opens, Banno? AD wants the first show to be staged here, in, Pune…' he searched my eyes.

'It depends on how I feel on the day. I am not getting any younger,' I shrugged my shoulders, almost dismissing his request.

'I…I need you, Sarlu…' Rakesh grasped my hands and placed them near his chest.

'Sarlu?'

'I apologize, I must have got carried away,' Rakesh looked down, embarrassed.

'No one has called me by that name since Amitabh went away,' I said slowly.

'Everyone will be happy if you can come…I mean…' Rakesh leaned in, pressing his fingers over mine.

'It's exactly what Amitabh said to me, every time a play of his opened, he'd say it in exactly the same way…never using the word "wait"…'

'Would it have made a difference, if he had said he would wait for you? Would you attend any of his plays, then?' Rakesh questioned, a slight tremor in his voice.

'I don't know, maybe, it *was* my place...' I mused.

'That can change, Banno! You are the reason behind *Cut*,' Rakesh slipped his fingers inside mine.

'Behind, yes, but, never in front, Rakesh. It was the way Amitabh would have also wanted. That was his place and he selfishly guarded that spot. Anyway, Rakesh, it's pretty late, and, I suspect it may rain…and…I must rest a while,' I remarked, gently cupping his face.

The phone rang just then.

◈

I answered the phone and then turned to RK: 'That was Avik. Maya has agreed. She will play me in *Cut*,' I turned to convey the good news to Rakesh.

He nodded and pressed his hands over mine, 'I'm happy for you, Banno. This is the moment you have dreamt of…'

I was about to say something, when Rakesh looked into my eyes, 'It's time for you to take your place on the stage, this time, Banno. For Bhai Jaan. For Dada Saheb… For yourself…I will think of you…imagine you the way we had first met…although I cannot attend the opening of *Cut*. My trial is coming up, actually it happens to be on the very same day…'

I frowned.

'I will be implicated, this time, in all probability…I've been running from the law, forever, I feel, sometimes. For as long as I can remember…bribes, black money, Dubai dons, drugs, mistresses, casting couch…I have seen it all…finally, I have exhausted all my alibis…my lawyers say I should be prepared for the worst…'

I took a deep breath.

'Are you scared?' I asked, softly, after a few seconds.

Rakesh shrugged his shoulders.

'I have tried my best with *Cut*. Pulled all strings to get this manuscript to you…to help AD find sponsors, Banno…I had to…it was my…' he took a deep breath.

'Is that why you didn't want your name anywhere? Did you get involved just to be close to me?' I questioned him directly.

He stared at me in silence, for a while.

'I did it for Bhai Jaan, Banno…though, you know as well as I do, that I would do anything to meet you once…be close, this way…' Rakesh sighed, his breath falling on my face,

'I have always blamed myself, somewhere, that because of me...you hated Amitabh...because of the way I left, wanting to punish you, by never looking back...maybe, if I had not been there in your life...you would have loved him more spontaneously. The way you do now.'

Rakesh looked away. 'Last night, my lawyer, Mahesh Singh called. Apparently, Monty has come to know about me reaching out to Chhota Shamim...that I am double-crossing Bhai...and, and the law. He's been in touch with the top cops. Maybe, he can't trust me, either. It's an open and shut case, frankly. The *swaad* of being betrayed by one's blood...to finally pay up, Banno. The police are probably waiting for me, back in Mumbai, as we speak. *Kissi ka koi bharosa nahin*... it's why I had to come, to Pune. Why I vowed to get the manuscript out of Rawat's hands. Why I did what I have. What I intend to confess before the Courts...'

Rakesh caressed the lines around my eyes.

'*Mein shayad kabhi* hero *nahin bann paya*, Banno. *Tumhara hero...*' he whispered, adding slowly, as his fingers ran over my damp eyelashes, '*mein* Amitabh Kulasheshtra *nahin bann paya. Shayad hum dono mein farq bhi itna hi tha. Hamara dil. Hamara imaan. Aur tum*, Banno. *Farq bhi. Aur fasla bhi...*'

I walked Rakesh to the front door, unlocking it, taking my time: '*Har mohabbat ka, ek mausam hota hai...*' Rakesh turned around, then, as our glances intersected, one last time, he smiled wistfully and quoted a dialogue from one of his first films, '*aur...wohi usski taqdeer...*'

He tipped his beret. Copying Dev Anand's inimitable style.

Then he was gone.

AVIK DASGUPTA

It had been a year since I had begun working on *Cut*. In this time I had been working tirelessly, researching Amitabh's life, meeting people, assembling an ensemble cast, working with RK to find financiers, to get the right venue, prefereably in spaces sacrosanct to Kulasheshtra, to block dates and hire the finest technicians. I vowed to do theatre on the scale I had visualized all those years ago, when I had shared my dreams for the first time at the final selection stage at the National Center of Drama; dreams that had been trampled upon, dreams that I sacrificed, sans a fight, dreams that made me the man I was today.

In retrospect, I knew Sarlaji was right. I wouldn't have had the power and influence to have done things my way if I hadn't returned to theatre from film. Kulasheshtra's harsh rejection of me, I now knew, had a deeper purpose. The darkness of the stage, that in many ways, seemed like a slow, surreal surrender, after the shallow, screeching spotlights of Bollywood. Like coming back to the arms of an old lover.

Both of us – the world of theatre and I – we had changed. Nothing was the same.

And that, I knew, was the point.

I was a nobody again. Ready to push myself to the brink, one more time. To pay not just a rich tribute to a man who had been my mentor, who had changed the idiom of theatre in India, but, to the true artist who recognized my mettle. Who saw me as no one had before. Whose walking away defied and defined my destiny. With *Cut*... that wasn't mine to begin with at least... I felt more attached than to any of my films or the television company I now ran. I wasn't just a director or a producer.

I was a simple storyteller. A vast medium.

There were going to be no retakes, here.

It's why having Maya on board also felt so right, why the project was more meaningful. There was still something about seeing her every day, to have her in my life again, to know she had my back. That like when I had debuted with *Anubhuti*, Maya was always around. My fiercest critic, as much as my deepest friend. It was while gathering material on Amitabh's life that she mentioned Razia Siddiqui; she told me about Razia having being commissioned to work on a book on Kulasheshtra based on interviews with members of his troupe; others like him, whose lives had been lost to the shadows of time.

◈

I contacted Razia, who was now based in Delhi, telling her all about *Cut* and the way the manuscript had reached me, making her promise she wouldn't breathe a word in the media, until rehearsals began, especially about Sarla Kulasheshtra's involvement in the project. In turn, she told me about all the people she had spoken to, and even shared the unedited interviews with Marie Bourdaine. I explained how Sarlaji was passionately involved with this play, but was an extremely private person. Razia gave me her word.

I needed her help in getting in touch with Sultan Ahmed, one of India's foremost lighting technicians who had practically rewritten the rules of stage design with his innovative lighting methods, such as the *dalda-ka-dabba* effect, where, in one of Kulasheshtra's plays on farmer suicides, in a sequence where a man tries to kill himself by jumping off a train, a car headlight was directly beamed on to the audience and a *dalda* can with cut out windows, housing a bulb was rotated at great speed to create an illusion of a fast paced train.

◈

In all my notes and facts collated on Kulasheshtra, Sultan Ahmed's name was a constant, though the two had allegedly fallen out when Kulasheshtra had suddenly moved to Mumbai in pursuit of Maya. Razia called me a fortnight later, saying that his divorced daughter Zeenat who looked after him had agreed to meet us, 'Not as a journalist…as a friend, perhaps,' she added.

'Zeenat has been standoffish; I think she wants money…' Razia warned, while we waited in a dilapidated courtyard. I surveyed the surroundings from the corner of my eyes. It was apparent that Ahmed had fallen on hard times and for all he did towards developing a contemporary understanding of stage lighting in India, I wondered if he too, like his comrade Kulasheshtra, was now a forgotten entity. The line, 'respect the darkness' posessed a new, double edged meaning. My mind clouded over with a lingering sadness.

A middle-aged woman in an ill-fitted salwar-kameez stood facing us now, her hennaed hair hung loose, covering her shrunken chest. '*Abba* usually likes to read his final *namaaz* outside, before he sleeps…' but before she could finish, a voice from inside called out: 'Zeenat…*beti*…tell them to come inside,' taking us all by surprise, adding, as we turned, 'This way, *barkhurdar*…come closer to me… here... hold my hand…'

I walked over, my heart pounding.

'It was Sheshtra who taught me treat the light, like a blind man learns to recognize it…how to smell the darkness, from afar, sensing its direction. He always said light is the most vital part of a dramatic experience, making me close my eyes for hours, endlessly. Learning to listen, training my mind to be soaked in a meditative silence, to contemplate emotions, like laughter and pain, the behaviour and misbehaviour of rays, with reference to its surroundings, make pictures, the way a child paints on a blank sheet of paper. Guided not so much by what is right, but what feels right, at that point in time…'

I couldn't believe I was actually listening to *the* Sultan Ahmed. Clad in a faded vest and a striped, cotton *lungi*, he gripped my wrist, firmly.

I helped him sit down on a low charpoy.

'I know why you are here, Zeenat has told me about the play,' he resumed, adjusting his glasses, 'I will join this production…if you let me do things my way on stage. I hate interference. The way I hate lighting up bodies. Sheshtra said to us that the body is an aspect of light, self-lit, and therefore it was more important to light the space. Can you trust my vision the way I tell you to? Despite my blindness? All the technological advancements that must have happened by now. I am ready to learn about them, improvise, collaborate with a team of new age technicians you will naturally hire… '

'Sir, it will be an absolute privilege,' I was overcome with emotion.

'You know, when Sheshtra returned from Mumbai and tried to regather his old team, I pushed him away, seething with pent-up rage. "Do you know how hard this is…how everything just came tumbling down after you left?" He replied: "I couldn't breathe, Sultan. Without her, it was dark. Every corner of my life, pointless…it was like she had awakened the man in me…the man who wanted to love back, for the first time. A man who wasn't running anymore…a man who was desperate to be saved, for a change," he confessed, breathing hard.

'"So, what the hell are you doing back in Pune, again? What the hell do you now want? Haven't we all paid the price for your…your…" I checked myself.

'Sheshtra bowed his head. Then looking up after a few seconds, he answered in a low voice, "I had to come back, Sultan. I had to let her go…I was ruining her with my obsession…she, she is so talented, so young, so, so beautiful…and yet, she couldn't see any of it…she was so scared of failing me…it's why I had to walk out, this time… tell myself that she will soar on her own, one day…that she will be found…Maya.."

'I wasn't convinced. "And what about you, huh? Haven't you lost enough, already? Your marriage, your reputation, your damn credibility…?"

'Sheshtra, I remember, stood outside. "Illusion. Maya is my illusion, Sultan. But, Mrinalini Shirale was a woman of flesh and blood…and, I don't want her to stay trapped inside, forever…suffer the way she was, living with me in Mumbai, taking on the onus of keeping us afloat…I saw that angst in her eyes, Sultan…I was turning her into a monster…a wreck…I couldn't kill her aspirations with my own hands…"

'"And what happens to your career? Your body of work? Everything you stood for? That we represented as a theatre company…our ideals…the things we believed in…?"

Sheshtra wiped his face. "There will be always something to fight for, Sultan, something else."

'By the close of next year, the Babri Masjid was demolished. Sheshtra wrote a new play again. Blaming the Rashtriya Dal for the raging communal violence. He was right to sense that the country he so loved was about to be changed. That the revolution would be falsely carried out, in the name of religion. That men would murder men. That children would be rendered homeless. That fathers would abandon their families. Women would be brutally gangraped. That abject poverty, gross social injustice and widespread illiteracy had manufactured widespread communalism that would be used by opportunistic political parties.

'"You could get killed, this time, the situation is extremely volatile…and there is a ban on this play…you will be blamed for further inciting communal feelings"…I warned him.

'"You're scared, aren't you? You find it hard to trust me, Sultan?" Sheshtra cut me short.

'"Yes. I have a daughter, I have a family who look to me for their sustenance…besides, I've found work with a prestigious Government project, they want me to create the outdoor lighting practices for Kauri…the pay is favourable, too, and it's a first of sorts, they insist, a Muslim light designer in an ancient Indian temple, it could just as well be the beginning of a new life, more respectable," I coughed, my throat dry.

'"Respectable…" Sheshtra repeated the word, like it was a lie.'

◈

From the outskirts of Pune, Razia and I drove further into the heart of Maharashtra. To Satara – home to another theatre stalwart, Govind Dewal, a stellar dialogue writer associated with not just Amitabh Kulasheshtra, but Dada Saheb. A man who had been witness to the blossoming of Kulasheshtra, from protégé to genius. Now, in his 90s, wheelchair-bound, Dewal had been interviewed on almost all TV channels, in the aftermath of Kulasheshtra's death. I had couriered him the manuscript of *Cut*, with detailed direction notes, set design sketches and some minor changes I had made to the lines.

After exchanging routine pleasantries, Dewal brought out a copy of *Cut* himself. The pages, photo-copied.

'Dasgupta...this is good. I like the way you have visualized the scenes...' he spoke with difficulty.

I had taken permission to record the interaction.

'What do you think he would have said, Govindji?' I pulled up a stool.

'That's hard to say; Amitabh was an unpredictable sort of fellow,' Dewal shrugged his shoulders, adding, after a while. 'Also, the last time I actually saw him was when he left Joglekar...it's the way I remember him always...young, arrogant...so very sure of where he was going. Sometimes, I ask myself, what if he hadn't met Sarla? If Joglekar had a son of his own or if he had trusted any of us as intimately as he had Amitabh...if we could have saved him...'

'Saved, as in?' I interrupted.

'Dada Saheb used to be anxious about Amitabh ultimately craving his own theatre company...knowing his political activism, his innate interest in national politics...in poverty, in prostitution, in anything that involved the minorities...it was amply clear that he wasn't just happy to hang around in the troupe anymore; Dada Saheb knew that, all along...how Amitabh was beginning to want to outshine him...'

'Were they competing with each other at some point, then?' Razia interrupted, this time.

'Amitabh worshipped Joglekar, so leaving must have broken his heart too. But, I think he was also weighed down by Sarla...He felt he didn't deserve her, in some way. I mean, they were friends, but everyone knew that her heart belonged only to that Punjabi rogue...Rakesh. Amitabh never said anything to Joglekar, despite knowing about Sarla's secret affair. But, it was obvious he was consumed with guilt for marrying a woman against her desires. For betraying Sarla at a very deep level. I think his ultimate breaking away wasn't just about a thirst for individual fame or power... it was simple, his logic. He wanted to prove his mettle to Joglekar, and, eventually, win Sarla's heart. Knowing both were equally stubborn and hard to please.'

'Is that the way Dada Saheb saw the betrayal?' I probed, frowning hard.

'Joglekar was a man who had a great understanding of human psychology. He let Amitabh go, knowing it was time. He did it as much for his best student to bloom, as much as for Sarla to begin to love Amitabh...that struggle together would bring them closer, inevitably...was his strongest belief.'

'The story of Amitabh Kulasheshtra as told by Sarla Kulasheshtra...a woman who never left his side, and yet, someone whom he deserted,' Razia walked up to us, staring at the script lying on Dewal's lap.

'Or, maybe, that *was* the strength of their relationship. That they let each find their way in the world, fall, make mistakes, pursue their individual dreams, fight their own demons, carve their own creative places, struggle with the resultant aloneness...and, then come back to source. It's what made them equals,' Dewal wheezed.

'Is *Cut* about infidelity then, Govindji? Was Kulasheshtra guilty, in his last years...repentant? Is that why he makes his wife the *sutradhaar*? To reinstate her respect, maybe?' I spoke fast.

'You say it like love is a sin, Dasgupta?'

'No, what I meant is, isn't a man supposed to just be in love with one woman? And was Kulasheshtra torn, because he wasn't...because he couldn't...' I searched Dewal's wrinkled face.

'Are you referring to Maya Shirale here? Are you worried that the casting might be seen as too deliberate, too contrived…are you saying Kulasheshtra wrote the script for Sarla, but wanted to reach out to Maya, actually?'

There was a minute or two of suspended silence.

'Why *did* Amitabh Kulasheshtra love Maya Shirale the way he did, frantically, at first? Why did someone of his stature leave everything behind, literally chasing after her, to Mumbai? I mean, with Marie Bourdaine, with whom Kulasheshtra was also rumoured to have had a fleeting affair, he didn't move lock, stock and barrel to Paris? Why then, did he suddenly turn his back on his work and family, Sarlaji, especially? How could he live that way? How did they make love? How did Kulasheshtra and Maya manage to stay content, even as strong rumours raged about his philandering, with the media on his trail to know why he was in Mumbai, living in a dingy chawl with a woman half his age?'

'I have pondered all these questions while reading *Cut*, Dasgupta, especially, what made Sarla hate Amitabh so deeply, for as long as she did? And yet, care so dutifully at the same time? Representing him in Court; never missing a single trial? Working tirelessly, teaching dance every day of her life, to ensure that there was enough money for his medicines… tests…I mean…even the way she approached you, with his last, unfinished script? Insisted on Maya Shirale playing her, as you wrote to me in your letter that arrived along with the manuscript of *Cut?* If there was some connection, with the world wanting to forget Kulasheshtra, as quickly as it did, and so heartlessly? Was it a case of divine retribution, a heartless punishment for a man who stormed out of his marriage, so carelessly…a commonplace cheater? Was that why Amitabh died the way he did…. with so little…just an empty wallet…a cloth bag…a pair of spectacles. Beaten by an angry mob. Was it a cruel twist of fate? Or was *Cut* Amitabh Kulasheshtra's answer…the last time he wanted to remember…anything…everything…?'

Dewal stared at his hands.

MAYA SHIRALE

Rehearsals were on in full swing. AD was meticulous about practising the lines. A demanding perfectionist, he planned each scene of *Cut* meticulously, and while improvisation was natural on stage, he knew exactly what he wanted. It was hard memorizing the lines, words penned by Amitabh…that brought time back, in more ways than one… just like being back on stage proved more daunting that I had ever imagined.

There would be no second chances, I told myself, in front of the green-room mirror. A part of me still wondered if I was at all eligible to play a character, so different from myself. If this was what Amitabh would have wanted? Was I ready to surrender to a medium that had taken away so much from me…from us?

As actors, we're supposed to remember things, almost in arithmetic precision, to step out of our physical selves by training our mind to remain suspended in third person, I kept reminding myself. My pulse raced as I slowly walked up on stage, in full make-up, an hour later, a wig of white hair weighing down on me.

Avi stood on the side, with a hard-bound script in his right hand. The set behind us was a plywood replica of Amitabh's Pune home. My stomach churned as my thoughts travelled to the last time I had been here. The quaint garden. The discoloured front gate, the winding staircase. The outhouse, where the scene was set. I took a deep breath, trying to visualize Amitabh sick, lying in bed. I swallowed hard.

Avi nodded. It was time.

◈

I couldn't speak. I threw down the script and fled from the stage. Unable to control my emotions.

The green-room door was slightly ajar. Avi pushed it open with his forearm, barging inside unannounced. I was still trembling. Avi stood towering over me. His chest heaved. I was about to offer an explanation, when he screamed:

'You just can't walk out that way, Maya. This isn't a film set! What's the problem, huh? Why couldn't you complete your lines, despite us having read the scene so many times?'

'It's hard, Avi…'

'What is hard, Maya? You are a seasoned actor…'

'But this isn't acting, Avi. I don't know why you just can't get it; this is Amitabh's last play, goddammit…and playing the character of his wife…Aiyee…retelling his entire life…bringing up so much…even us…through her eyes…it's just…'

Avi kneeled down and looked deep into my eyes, saying, 'Maybe, it's the only way you can let go of him, Maya…and maybe, it's why he wrote this play…'

'How, how did you get this play, Avi? How did it fall into your hands?' I struggled to speak.

'I told you…someone found it on the train and had it in his custody before he sold me the rights…'

'Does Aiyee *know* about this? That you are directing this play? That her husband's last work was about her, in a way...that she is the main protagonist...' I stared up in his direction, adjusting my wig, feeling my cheeks burn up.

'I intend to invite her when we stage *Cut*,' Avi replied casually.

'I think you are taking a huge risk with this casting, Avi. I mean, seeing me, after all these years...what will she say? We haven't met, as you are aware...since the night I left Pune. And after that damaging *Samna* interview appeared...I think it's abundantly clear she will never wish to see my face again...' I wiped my eyes, rising up from the chair and walking towards Avi.

'I think, it's quite the coup. Being able to do this, Maya... I've brought back so many of Kulasheshtra's old cast members...the legendary technicians he worked with... Imagine someone of the stature of Sultan Ahmed agreeing to come onboard!' Avi took a lengthy drag of his cigarette changing the topic.

'You're letting go of Amitabh, too, then...' I murmured, touching his back.

'No, Maya, you are wrong there,' Avi swerved.

'How? What do you mean?' I was taken aback.

'I'm letting him in,' Avi stubbed his cigarette under his shoe.

◈

The next day, the same thing happened during rehearsal. Only this time, I added a line, inviting Avi's ire as he screamed at me in front of the whole cast. I chose not to react, walking off the stage in silence. Avi was no less than a tyrant. Guarding *Cut* with his life. It was hard to convince him to see anyone else's point of view...He stormed into my green-room five minutes later:

'What's with you, huh? Either you cannot finish a full scene, or this...' his nostrils flared: 'These lines are sacrosanct…you cannot do this, Maya…there is no way I will allow you this liberty,' he had thundered, pointing his finger in my face.

'You said to me earlier that I had the licence to see Sarla's character through my own eyes…when I was unsure about playing her on stage,' I retorted. 'And, I felt it lacked something, Avi…like someone was strangling Sarla. I wasn't desperate to prove a point or be one up on you. I know how sacred Amitabh's writing is and I know just how clinical you are about authenticity. But, I just felt the anger in Sarla was slightly diffused, that's all. You know what I mean, right? Avi, this is a woman who is speaking about her husband leaving her for another woman…without a legit explanation… having to explain his betrayal to the world…a man as well-known as Amitabh…'

'Go on…' he clicked his tongue.

'Stop patronizing me, okay?' I flopped down on the couch facing a lone window.

'Fine, sorry,' Avi, calmer now, sat down beside me.

'No, Avi, sorry won't be enough…in fact, that's precisely where the mistake lies. As a director, you are viewing Sarla Kulasheshtra with an impassive impunity…but, have you ever thought what Aiyee would have actually felt…after that night, when Amitabh returned to Pune…to their home… how she never asked him why he returned…how she had no choice? How she was never given a choice? What did she do, when he went away…all the times, he left her, alone? When he was in Paris? When he was in Mumbai fighting for the mill-workers? When he was in Delhi staging street plays, in front of Parliament? In Malegaon? When he was on that train, even? When he was with me?'

'Can you just come to the point, for once, Maya…' he cut me short, restlessly.

'Why can't you allow her this outrage, Avi? Imagine this character, as Sarla, just Sarla, not as Amitabh's restrained and dignified wife. Not as Sarlu.'

Avi listened in rapt attention, and then lit up. Blowing a ring of smoke, he said, 'Okay, so now that we are on the subject of wives... what the hell were you thinking telling Reema that she needed to come back to me? Give our relationship another chance? Who are you to interfere in my marriage?'

I adjusted my wig. Thoughts crowded my mind.

Was I getting overly attached to this play? Why had I botched up my lines? Why was I so desperate to do justice to the screenplay, even tampering with Amitabh's script to have my say?

Was it because I didn't want Avi to fail?

Was I trying to save him?

The way Amitabh tried to save me?

By loving me enough to see who I really was?

As an artist? And as a woman?

'Maya, let me put this on record, *calling up my wife is not your job.* You need to focus only on *Cut.* We open in two months. There's already so much of media publicity for this play…the word is out that this is Kulasheshtra's last work,' he snapped.

'That is not why you are here though, right?' I slowly removed my wig.

'Maya, look, I understand I may have overreacted this afternoon – or maybe, it was the way I wanted the scene to play out in my head. The exact manner in which I hoped each thing would fall into place, eventually…'

'Avi, we have to stop creating a scene each time we disagree on method, on, anything, going forward,' I interrupted.

'I know, Maya. I get that it's weird for us to be working together, this way; just as I know how challenging it is to essay this character…how demanding each day of rehearsal has been…to see yourself as a woman you have run away from…. your whole life, practically. I too am so damn stressed about the production. What if *Cut* bombs?' I'll have lost everything, Maya, but what unsettles me the most is the thought that I will take down all the people involved… those who sank their money in this venture with me… the formidable cast…the backstage team…the sound, set design and light technicians…Sarlaji…and, and most of all, Kulasheshtra.'

'Please don't be so hard on yourself…' I reached out to touch him.

Avi backed away. 'No! Don't do this, Maya! Not now. Quit trying to protect me. My marriage! My issues with Kulasheshtra, his memories, the guilt I felt when I never tried again for NCD, for moving to films, for dating you…for the way he died…How we failed him as a society, as a people. I mean, Reema going away was my fault, Maya. Not yours,' he said, when he was done.

'Reema is hurting, just as much. She's not a bad person,' I resumed in a soft voice, reaching out, again. 'Besides, she is pregnant, and you are going to become a father soon, Avi. Look at what this means, this new phase: You coming back to theatre, your biggest dream ...and starting a family…it's all meant to end well, Avi…'

'It's not that simple…' Avi threw up his hands in exasperation.

'Nothing is, Avi. But, you have a responsibility towards the kid. Talk to Reema, see what she needs,' I said, trying to calm him down.

'And, and what if she asks me what we are doing here, now? Look Maya, you know jack about my marriage…so stay out of it,' Avi got up from the couch with a start.

'Reena has called me a couple of times on her own. I've asked her to come and watch the play when it opens. I said she must attend the first show in Pune,' I rose up, glancing back, to add, 'She said she'd think about it. I told her everything, Avi...things she needs to know as a woman in love with you, carrying your child...things I should have told you when we were together...secrets and lies that ruined us, in the end.'

'I said I don't want to talk about it, okay?' Avi screamed, his eyes inflamed.

'What do you want to talk about then?'

'Getting the scene right,' Avi grabbed my shoulders, violently. 'Let's get back to rehearsal.'

I grimaced.

'*Cut* means more to me than anything, Maya. More than anyone,' he said.

AVIK DASGUPTA

Two months later, *Cut* opened to a packed auditorium in Pune. There were throngs of people waiting outside for tickets. My phone hadn't stopped buzzing. I stood backstage, alone, for a few minutes. In my hand, I held the original manuscript Sarlaji had handed me, here, in the same city. The crew manning the sets made last-minute adjustments. A thick black curtain separated me from the audience. I flopped down on a wooden stool, kept in the wings. The exhaustion and excitement of the last few months had worn me. I wiped my face and opened the file. To a passage that was my favourite. Looking at the stage shrouded in shadows.

Shirish and Razia stood behind me. I looked back, facing them, after a few seconds, wondering if something was amiss.

'Looks like a full house AD, there are people still waiting outside, well done,' Razia flashed a victory sign.

'Is Sarlaji here?' I searched Shirish's eyes.

'Nope. Not yet,' he answered, his brow creased.

'Has someone from the production team tried reaching her?'

'The call is not going through, I tried from my cell, and from my camera person's, too,' Razia pitched in promptly.

'What is it saying?' I cut her short.

'Nothing,' Shirish shrugged his shoulders, impatiently.

'What does that mean?'

'As in…the call is just not getting through. Shall I make someone try and call again?' Shirish volunteered, hoping to calm me down.

'You just said the call's not connecting. Make up your mind. Do we have a lot of Press, tonight?' I paced up and down.

'Yes. Some really big guns have also specially requested for passes, Vishnu Jain, NDTV CEO, with his wife and Girija Prasad, Editor-in-chief, *AajTak* have especially flown down for the first show as have a whole lot of national media heads and celebs from Bollywood and the arts fraternity. In fact, I believe some of our rival channels were desperate to cover the sound check etc., this morning… kept calling someone or the other from your team. Who would have thought the opening week would turn out, this stupendously? The kind of crowd this play is getting is nothing short of historic. *Cut is* literally on everyone's lips…the next two shows in Pune are fully booked. Social media too has exploded with news of the play, every detail being eagerly anticipated. The *Bookmyplay* head called, he's asking if there are extra shows being added in Mumbai, the next stop…. before the six-city tour begins. This kind of euphoria has never been witnessed before, for a play…I mean it's bigger than a godamn film premiere…' Razia replied emphatically.

'Did she leave any alternate number?'

'We've called everyone, AD. Everyone's saying the same thing…' Shirish walked alongside me.

'Which is?'

'*Woh apni marzi ki malik hai,* she has always been stubborn and listens to know one... but…*siwaye…*' he bit his lips.

'*Siwaye*?'

'*Siwaye apni dil ki*...they used the word *dil.* All of them...everyone we called. Everyone close to her...to Sarla Kulasheshtra.'

Razia shot me a sideways glance.

'What do you mean?'

'Avi...I think what Shirish is trying to say is simply this,' she touched my chest, lightly, 'What you have achieved is a bloody casting coup. Amitabh Kulasheshtra's wife, being played onstage by Maya Shirale, in his last play, being directed by Avik Dasgupta, ace Bollywood director, also Maya's one-time *aashiq,* who hated Kulasheshtra with a vengeance...who turned away from the stage, thanks to him. Who broke up with Maya Shirale exactly a year after Amitabh Kulasheshtra died on his way to Mumbai. Everyone knows the chequered history all of you shared...the media, like the audience, are completely bloodthirsty, possibly hoping to piece together a part of their lives, through this production, and, maybe, wondering, if it's all an act of fiction or purely autobiographical...*Cut* as you know, is being touted as a magnum opus...*the* theatrical offering of the year...the dramatic stage debut of Avik Dasgupta... Sultan Ahmed...Govind Deval...the original team members of Kulasheshtra...and...' Razia threw her hands in mid-air, panting slightly.

'And *what?* This is not just about Maya, Razia...though I am aware what her comeback on stage probably means for the media and her fans...I mean, after Kulasheshtra's death, especially...' I raised my voice.

'You are getting me wrong. I wasn't talking about her at all, AD. The whole world knows why you chose Maya for this part...the fact, that you guys were a couple, apart, you've always idolized Maya Shirale, since, ever since the day you first saw her light up a screen. You were a youngster, back then, and you fell for her watching a hit number of hers, on television? That *Dhak Dhak* song, all this stuff...most papers have been carrying the same trivia, ever since you all started rehearsing for *Cut*. The insinuations going back to when she was chosen to judge the dance reality show, *Dhak Dhak India*, that your newly-launched, television company co-produced. Post the casting for this play...naturally those rumours have been fanned...but...' she suddenly paused, glancing down.

'But what?'

'But these two women meeting, in person...' Razia pursed her lips.

'And, you think that pushed Sarlaji to stay away?' I searched both their faces.

'Maybe, it just made it a tougher decision, AD. One that she didn't want to take now...given the excess baggage *Cut* already carries...' Razia remarked, pointedly.

'Excess baggage?' I was taken aback by her choice of words.

'It's almost six twenty...' Shirish checked his wristwatch, and announced, looking anxious.

'Nearly time for the final seating request,' I muttered, distractedly, checking the time again.

Shirish received a call just then. Hanging up, he faced us, and excitedly said: 'Good news! The production team head just saw Sarlaji enter the auditorium. I think there's no reason to delay matters further. Should I get the announcement going, in that case, AD?' Shirish held up his left hand, and pointed at his watch.

'It's showtime, yes...' I whispered, feeling a weight lift off my chest.

'Stage, in fifteen,' Shirish gestured urgently, speaking into his walkie-talkie.

◈

The curtains parted slowly. There was thunderous applause. I placed my hands before my eyes, pulling the cordless microphone closer to my lips. The hall was chock-a-block, the back of the auditorium jam-packed with television cameras. Everyone's eyes were on me…

Ladies and gentlemen, I am Avik Dasgupta.
As many of you maybe aware, this is my first play.
I couldn't make it to the National Centre of Drama.
I just tried getting in once.
I cared a shit for the longest time.
It's the only thing I really did.
Cared about things that hardly mattered to me.
This is however not my story, none of it.
This is everything I could never be.
This is stuff I learned to stop wanting, a long time ago.
This is real.
This is robust.
This is raw.
Parts, of it.
The parts he wrote.
The parts I imagined.
The parts she narrated.
Only, tonight, I'm going to shut up and let you decide.
Who you want to be?
Missionary or mercenary?
Platonic or passionate?
Failure or famous?
Dead or alive?
Or, barely breathing?
Cut.
The story of a man who wanted to change the world.

A King.
And a woman who never loved him.
His Queen.
In an ancient empire that was rapidly changing.
A bloody war.
Until a girl with eyes the colour of rain, appeared.
The Enemy.
Standing before us.
We. The people.
Today, you will have to conclude.
Who wins and who loses?

I looked down into the sea of faces. The seat reserved in the first row for Sarlaji was empty. Had she left? Changed her mind about watching *Cut*? Was Razia correct in her assumption? Was Maya Shirale playing Sarla Kulasheshtra, the real raison d'être? Both for the audience? And us?

MAYA SHIRALE

Avi had allocated a separate green-room for me. I sat in front of the large mirror now, its circumference dotted with tiny light bulbs, as Usmaan Bhai, veteran hair and make-up expert whom Avi had brought back on stage after years, once a core member of Amitabh's team, expertly transformed my face. I watched my reflection in fascination as, under his adept hands, my face gradually transformed into Aiyee's.

I had always known that I had to resemble her, physically. That's what Avi had insisted on, for me to get totally into character. But, now, watching the dark lines around my mouth, I was hit anew by a fresh attack of nerves. Woud just looking like Sarla Kulasheshtra be enough? Did I even have the moral standing to be allowed to play her?

'Am I a good enough actor, Usmaan Bhai? *Kya...kya woh khush hote*...if, if he was here, now? If Amitabh was alive?' I drank a sip of warm water, mentally rehearsing my lines.

Usmaan Bhai was a man of few words. He looked at me with a kindly smile: 'I think of him, too, Madam. And I do wonder. But, this morning, as I was reading my namaaz, I happened to look up at the skyline, here, in Pune, and I felt as if Amitabh Kulasheshtra was looking down on us. I felt, then, that *he's* the one directing each thing happening on this stage; happening to us, now, from above. It was his will that has brought you here today. *His* will that AD is the person coordinating it. Even back then, as today, he knew what he wanted. And why. The stage was his salvation, Madam. He was invincible. And the stage is invincible because of him…'

Just then there was a knock on the door. Usman Bhai looked at me and I indicated to him to answer the door.

Aiyee stood outside.

◈

Many times, in the past, I'd imagined what it would be like to stand in front of Mrs. Sarla Kulasheshtra. What would she say to me? Would she simply walk past me, indignantly? Insult me, publicly? Refuse to acknowledge me even? Hold a grudge? Abuse me? Treat me with the scornful disdain reserved for a husband's mistress…?

Aiyee walked into the room with slow, measured steps, greeting Usmaan Bhai politely, before making her way inside. Before occupying the faded green-room couch, her hands neatly folded in her lap. She was attired in a traditional, Maharashtrian weave in olive and ochre. Her neatly-pinned pallu was a carbon copy of my costume. Her hair was in a tight bun, the way I was wearing mine. Her hands were without bangles. I ran my fingers slowly over my dry lips, over the wrinkles that Usman Bhai had so brilliantly created.

Aiyee looked at me, in silence. As did I.

Her eyes had aged; she looked tired, but at peace,

I removed the spectacles I was wearing. I tried speaking to her, hoping to come up with a suitable greeting to begin with, especially after all this time. But, I just couldn't. Feeling completely tongue-tied, I knelt on the cold, hard floor and buried my face in her lap.

Aiyee caressed my head for a while and then gently raised my chin. Wiping my eyes, using her softened pallu, she said, 'Shiish…You are ruining Usman's brilliant work! He's done such a great job! The only difference is I stopped wearing a mangal-sutra a long time ago…it's probably the only difference between us…Maya Shirale and Sarla Kulasheshtra…on stage, tonight.' She ran her finger over my collarbone and along the length of the thin black-and-gold beaded mangal-sutra necklace that hung around my neck.

I swallowed hard.

'You are just the way he would have wanted me to be, Maya…and, and I was right about knowing Amitabh's mind…this play, *Cut*, would be nothing without you,' she brought her face closer to mine: 'That's why I came here. I needed to thank you for saying yes to this part. I know what must have gone through your mind when you read the script the first time…Avi…he, he told me all about your self-doubts…why you initially turned down the role…I guess I would have felt the same…'

'Avi…?' my lips quivered, 'You have been in contact with Avi? You both have met before? Avik Dasgupta?'

Aiyee was briefly lost in her own thoughts, before slowly looking up to talk to me: 'I gave him the manuscript of *Cut*. I wanted Avik Dasgupta to direct the play, and I only laid down one, strict, precondition; that no one but you was to essay the leading role…I made Avi promise, however, that he would not share details of my involvement with you before tonight. I didn't want you to feel any more pressured than I knew you were…or, maybe, I just wanted us to meet, like the way we first did on that the afternoon you stood at the gates of our Pune home…Maybe, I missed being alone with you, Maya.'

I felt myself tear up again.

'I never wanted things to turn out this way, Aiyee. You must believe me,' my shoulders trembled.

She nodded. 'Maya, I remember how it is to be young and impetuous in love. I also know why you left Pune that night; not so much because of Amitabh...but, what you felt for me, what you felt you probably owed me, after what I had done for you...what you were correct to sense, I was also set to lose...' She took a deep breath: 'The way I lashed out against you in the *Samna* interview...I owe you an apology, Maya... it was just that I needed to accuse someone to make sense of my own feelings...the humiliation I felt when rumours about Amitabh living in with you in Mumbai made their way to me...I would always ask the person or persons carrying this news, if they had seen you with him. If they were *sure* it was you, Maya...Mrinalini Shirale...the girl who I took in, who lived in my home...Their silences, the way they refused to say anything else...it, it added to the pain...making me want to hurt you in the way only a woman can hurt another woman...instead of understanding you...and, maybe even Amitabh...in a way he had always wanted me to, perhaps...'

'Is that the truth? Your truth?' I searched Aiyee's eyes.

For a while, she remained silent, studying my face. Then she resumed:

'We happened to love the same man...make love to the same body, Maya... confront the same mind...the same quirks, the same fantasies, the same fears, the same fallacies...the same principles...the same lies... the same losses... the same dreams, the same dilemmas. The same demons. We are the same. You and I. Separated only by this thing... called time.'

'You're in love with Amitabh, aren't you, Aiyee? And you've only just come to terms with it now...what you feel... the things you could never quite put a finger on, earlier,' I questioned, softly, staring back into her tired eyes.

'We don't fall out of love, Maya. We only stop pretending...' she murmured, meeting mine.

'You were his wife, Aiyee,' I stood up. 'A bond I could never share with Amitabh. Something I realize all the more after reading *Cut.* Maybe, we ran out of memories, after a point. Perhaps, that's why Amitabh never came back to me, in Mumbai, and, I too, didn't reach out; rebelling against his rules and transforming into a mainstream Bollywood actress. Though, looking back, Aiyee, it was all for him. I've never really stopped proving myself to Amitabh, in a way, waiting for his acceptance. You know something, Aiyee? Despite everything that was said and speculated about us, all the rumours and the reality of us living together in Kalyan, he was my teacher. My mentor. Mrinalini Shirale…she, she died with Amitabh Kulasheshtra. I died on that train from Pune to Mumbai. Whereas, you, Aiyee, Amitabh, set you free with his death. Free to find yourself. Find yourself in him, all over again.'

'And where does that leave you, Maya?' Aiyee walked over to where I stood, facing the green-room mirror, once more. Our facial features almost identical.

'I don't know, Aiyee, but for once, I'm at peace with the uncertainty,' I took a deep breath, speaking to her through the hazy glass, 'All I know is that every time I mouth my lines...I can tell he's watching. I feel him, in the darkness, the shadows like the darkened edges of his eyes. Luring me eternally, melting my insides. I could never love him, fully, Aiyee, during the time we stayed together in Mumbai, all those years ago. Something was amiss, even in me; as if there can be anything more important than loving someone…'

'You are being too hard on yourself, Maya. Amitabh *was* a difficult man to understand. I never could fathom him when we were married; for all the years, we spent under the same roof. I held him responsible for too much. My father. Losing Rakesh. My daughter. But, now, in his absence, and, minus the enormity of the daily struggles I went through trying to sustain his genius and substitute our collective losses, I think I'm finally allowing myself to see him…to…to feel the way I did when he first came to live with us. When he stood watching us from a distance, in Satara, as we rehearsed for Dada Saheb's adaptation of *Sita Swayamvar*. Just like then, Amitabh awoke a plethora of feelings in me…things I could never understand in totality or at once…emotions not as simplistic or as holistic as love, or, love at first sight…the journey felt so new to me, Maya… these were altogether new sensations, in a sense…curiosity about a new person, protectiveness, almost a maternal urge, in some way, compassion for his poverty, the struggles he had seen, the squalor of his background…the pain at the way he lost his mother…how he was never really loved by one, or remained attached to anything, beyond a point… and, and then…slowly, after he lived with us, when he just wouldn't leave…when I realized, the way my father knew, that Amitabh had nowhere to go to…and that walking out of Ganesh Circus was as much to prove a point to his blind father who was a clown, as much as it was to avenge Ammi's death…the way the world had failed his family…the angst Amitabh carried with him…till his dying day…the reason he directed and wrote the plays he did…why he always fought for those who lacked a voice…why he could never love a woman...the way he hated his father for never standing up for his mother…I began to admire Amitabh's smouldering courage…the way he didn't care for my father's larger-than-life persona, leaving his troupe even after he was married to his only daughter and had been handed his legacy on a veritable plate…the manner in which he answered back, the first afternoon he stood in front of him, sans self-doubt. A part of me wished I was Amitabh. That I had his heart. More than once…'

Aiyee coughed, placing her hand over her heart as she continued:

'Last year, on September 16, we were headed to the courts. We had lost our daughter, Maya, on the same date. Our cab stopped in front of a traffic signal. A small girl, her torso bare, wearing only frayed pajamas, was performing difficult headstands and somersaults on the pavement. After her act, she banged on my rolled-up window, her lips pressed to the glass.

'"Don't pay them a penny, Mataji…all these children who beg like this are actually a part of a much bigger racket, *padhaiye kyun nahin karte…*" the cab-driver scorned, shooing her away.

'The girl showed him her middle finger, narrowing her eyes. "*Ghar mein beti nahin hai kya*?" she screamed.

'Suddenly, Amitabh got very agitated and wanted to get off the cab. He was suffering from Alzheimer's. The condition had worsened, and doctors feared that given the history of his head injuries sustained at Malegaon…that it was a matter of time, before he would develop dementia… anyway, he started following the child.

'"Amitabh!" I called out. "It's too costly to keep the cab waiting. And we have to reach the court on time. Today you will be called to the witness-box. Our lawyer says this is your last chance."

'But Amitabh had picked up a *dhol* and was sitting in the middle of the road and was banging it furiously, his face alive, radiant, as the little girl danced for him, sans inhibitions. Throwing up her dark, skinny hands into the air. Their eyes spoke a secret language.

'After the dance finished, Amitabh scooped her in his arms. "What's your name, *thōḍē rāṇī* (little queen)?" he asked, kissing her forehead.

'"My friends call me Meenu, but that's not my real name. Abba would always call me Mumtaz. My father named me."

'"See, I could tell you *were* a queen! *Mere naye natak mein kaam karegi*, Mumtaz-Mahal?" Amitabh affectionately cupped her cheeks, before I could respond.

'The girl giggled and kissed him on his forehead then. Over the line of stitches that stood out. After Malegaon.

'"*Nach ne dega*?" she retorted sassily.

'Somehow, little Mumtaz, reminded me of you, Maya. The way Amitabh kept correcting her, telling her how she should sing a particular high note, and holding her back when she tried performing a complicated head-stand. I had never thought of you, until that day, with anything but disdain...I had vowed that I would never discuss you with anyone... even Amitabh...never as much as take your name...and, and, then...just looking at both of them...it was like suddenly your relationship with Amitabh, why he needed you, became clearer to me, Maya. It was like I saw you, the way the audience will see you after they watch *Cut*...through his eyes.

'When we reached the court that day, we learned that Prakash Lele's daughter had also agreed to an out-of-court settlement. Our lawyer had offered us a monetary settlement as well, advising Amitabh to walk away, adding how he had picked the wrong fight. I said nothing. By the time, Amitabh was finally summoned to the witness-box, he was so disoriented that all he could speak of was Mumtaz, a streetside child-beggar. He rambled on, sans context, going on and on about the importance of standing up for a little homeless Muslim girl who had been abandoned after the 1992 riots. Who had watched her family being killed in front of her own eyes. Who had been molested as well in the shelter she was sent to by the cops and the courts. Who hadn't eaten for days, and who now performed tricks in the blazing sun. Her tresses matted.

'The lawyer representing Rawat had grinned salaciously all the while. "Open-and-shut case, huh? A man who is out of his mind, clearly as we can all see. Who cannot even think straight! Who is bedridden for the most part of the year… sloganeering, as he's known famously for…maybe, his next play is going to be called *Mumtaz*. Note, my lord…how he's always inciting the communal angle. How he is manipulating our minds…"

'The judge duly made a note.

'"As you can see, there are no witnesses. And yet, this man cannot seem to understand that his allegations are baseless…and that he was the one to blame…that Prakash Lele being killed was a simple accident…that he died thanks to the unruly stampede that ensued…" he went on, pointing his fingers at Amitabh's eyes.

'The court proceedings lasted less than an hour.

'Rawat's name was cleared of the charges. His two sidekicks were not. The judge would set another date, we were told. Another wait…

'On our way home, we stopped again by the same light. Amitabh jumped out of the car, screaming, "Mumtaz *mujhe maaf kar dena…Mein aaj phir se har gaya…*" That's when I remembered, "Mumtaz" was his mother's name too.'

Aiyee sighed deeply, closing her eyes, for a few minutes: 'After reading *Cut*, and *Blindside*, after meeting all the people he had influenced, after the outpouring of grief…the candle-lit vigils, the genuine expressions of regret and respect…I realized why.

'I'm going back to the courts tomorrow. It's what strengthened my resolve to stage *Cut*, come what may, my reason behind asking Avik to direct this play and to make it amply clear that only you could play Sarla Kulasheshtra.

This play, Amitabh's battle…this crusade…this country… its conscience…my husband's unfortunate death…the slander…the silence…the survival…this moment, now… that, that stage, waiting for you, outside…*Cut* is not just Amitabh Kulasheshtra's unfinished legacy, Maya. You must know that. Amitabh may have started a war with Malegaon. But, this battle, it's now mine. And, Avik's. And Usmaan Bhai's. And Govind Deval's. And Sultan Ahmed's. And yours. We owe Mumtaz a win. We owe it to ourselves, first.'

◈

One of the backstage assistants knocked on the door. It was time to go on. Wordlessly, Aiyee adjusted the pallu of my dull brown Narayanpeth sari, settling a few stray strands of hair behind my ears. Her fingertips icy.

We stood face to face. Just the way we had. Once.

'Maya, to take position on stage, *Act One, Scene One.* Sarla Kulasheshtra,' Avi's voice wheezed from a walkie-talkie.

I stretched out my hand in Aiyee's direction. She fought back her own tears, 'Amitabh shouldn't have to lose, Maya…'

I smiled back at her reassuringly, walking out.

'Amitabh didn't like to lose, Aiyee…' I whispered.

Before we parted.

The spotlight shone brightly, almost blinding me, at first.

Everything else was invisible.

Everything else was inconsequential.

I stood on the spot marked 'SK' on the stage.

I spoke my first line:

'Artists don't die. Artists must never die. Amitabh Kulasheshtra is not dead. Not in here.'

My heart skipped a beat. As it always did.

There was thunderous applause.

'Amitabh Kulasheshtra *amar rahein*,' someone screamed.

I opened my eyes. Soaking in the moment.

As Amitabh's words, in a deep voice-over, resounded on stage:

All your life you fought my wars,
Wore my victories as a crown of thorns,
All your life you swallowed my salt tears,
Camouflaged my bloodied cuts,
With a fleeting touch of your soft palms.
All your life you stood in my tall shadows.
Your eyes so sanguine; so still.
Your face never fully visible.
Who were you in secret?
In the light of the setting sun?
In your own skin?
When the curtains came down?
Who burns out, first, Sarla,
Leaving things unfinished?
Which of us is the hero?
Whose side is time on?

ACKNOWLEDGEMENTS

The idea behind *Cut* came to me on a long, bleary night in Mumbai, which is where I lived and worked as a journalist a decade ago. A tiny snippet in a leading national daily, almost inconspicuous by its placement among more gritty, hard-hitting, attention-grabbing headlines told of a forgotten Marathi theatre personality, a character actor, obscure to most, a recovering alcoholic, who had been found dead on a train to Mumbai. The nature of his accidental death juxtaposed with the irony of fleeting public memory left a lasting impact on me. *What was an artist's life worth? What was his darkness? What were his demons? His deities?*

Cut is, in more ways than one, and much more starkly than any of my other books, also my own trajectory. The voice of Amitabh Kulasheshtra that permeates this novel, is akin to the shadow of another artist, a poet, my biological father, Basudev Kundu, to whom *Cut* is dedicated; whose life was cut short by the all-encompassing darkness of schizophrenia when in his early thirties.

I have lived practically all my adult life grappling with a suffocating anger and hatred towards the man who so selfishly abandoned my mother, leaving her widowed in her late twenties, to struggle against the social stigma and familial shame, to raise her only daughter. The pain of not knowing my father, of being estranged from his family, of growing up sans even a single portrait of him in my maternal grandparents' home – where I grew up in Kolkata – of lying about his identity to escape being bullied in school where I was perhaps the most obese girl in the class, of discovering how he died a day before my tenth board exams, of blaming every failure and obstacle in my own life to his absence – to writing imaginary letters to him that were perhaps my first works of literature, being desperate to know if he loved me, and of desperately wanting to be loved.

Cut is a search as much as it is a swansong. A letting-go, as much as it is a letting-in. A prayer, as much as a protest.

Cut, my fifth book, changed me in more ways than one, and because it was the novel with the longest gestation period, so to speak – from the time I began writing it in 2015 to its present year of publication – the manuscript transformed itself many times, much in the way I, as a writer and as an artist, have – and in the way this country and its conscience has. I can safely say that this is a book that echoes what a lot of us free-thinkers are thinking and feeling in the present climate.

In *Cut* seeing the light of this world, I would like to thank my firebrand of an editor, Nandita Aggarwal, who had wanted to acquire this book when she worked at Hachette India – home to my first three books. And subsequently, volunteered to edit it when I chose to publish it with a different publisher. To my publishers at Bloomsbury India; literary agent, Kanishka Gupta; my wonderful and ever-supportive parents, Sushmita Kundu and Krishna Rao; my little sister who is growing up way too fast, Sreelekha (Geru) – my bestest friend in the whole, wide world; Janine Martin who is my voice of sanity; my Lamaji in Delhi and Kolkata; members of my Buddhist practice, and my core circle of close friends spread over the cities of Kolkata, Delhi, Mumbai and Bangalore - you shall always be my tribe.

Finally, to my readers, you keep me going. It is for you that I tell my stories, time after time. For you, that I have the courage to keep creating. Thank you for the loyal patronage, the mails and letters of appreciation. I could come this far, because of you.

Sreemoyee Piu Kundu is an acclaimed journalist and columnist on gender and sexuality. She wrote *Faraway Music*, her first novel, in 2013, followed by her bestselling feminist erotica, *Sita's Curse*, which explored female desire through the eyes of a Gujarati housewife. *You've Got the Wrong Girl*, her third work of fiction, a light-hearted rom-com, broke new ground in Indian 'lad-lit'. In 2017, she wrote her first non-fiction work, the widely-appreciated and critically-acclaimed *Status Single*, a narrative drawing from the lives of 3000 urban Indian single women, about the daily struggle of being single in a country where the highest validation for women remains marriage and motherhood. Sreemoyee is the recipient of the NDTV L'Oréal Women of Worth award for Excellence in Literature. She has been signed up for her memoirs, *Bad Blood*, by Bloomsbury and has just completed an inter-generational family saga set in Kolkata, *All Our Other Lies*.

Sreemoyee is single and lives between New Delhi and Kolkata.